# SAVAGE DE

## *Desire, Oklahoma: The Founding Fathers 3*

## Leah Brooke
writing as
## Lana Dare

**MENAGE EVERLASTING**

**Siren Publishing, Inc.**
**www.SirenPublishing.com**

**A SIREN PUBLISHING BOOK**
IMPRINT: Ménage Everlasting

SAVAGE DESIRE
Copyright © 2015 by Lana Dare

ISBN: 978-1-63259-652-9

First Printing: July 2015

Cover design by Les Byerley
All art and logo copyright © 2015 by Siren Publishing, Inc.

Printed in the U.S.A.

**PUBLISHER**
Siren Publishing, Inc.
www.SirenPublishing.com

# SAVAGE DESIRE

### *Desire, Oklahoma: The Founding Fathers 3*

**LANA DARE**
**Copyright © 2015**

# Chapter One

She had to get out of here.

There had to be a life better than the one she lived now. It was out there, and she just had to find it.

She'd been planning her escape for years, but the small amount of coins she'd managed to scrape together over the years wouldn't even be enough to leave town.

The smell of tobacco, whiskey, and sweat hung in the air on the second floor of the saloon Sarah had lived in her entire life.

It was a bordello, and her mother worked there. She'd given birth to Sarah in the same bed that she currently used to entertain men who had the money to spend for a night of pleasure.

Sarah feared that she'd have no choice but to work there, too, and it scared the hell out of her.

She considered herself lucky that it hadn't happened yet, but she knew that soon she'd have to earn her keep on her back instead of by doing the laundry and keeping the place clean. She mended, and made new dresses. She aired their rooms and changed their sheets every day.

She did everything she could to make herself useful without drawing any attention to herself. She'd been lucky so far, and did her best to look as young and unattractive as possible, but she knew her luck couldn't last forever.

She'd seen the way the men looked at her, and had even heard them ask Rose, the woman who ran the bordello, if Sarah was available.

Sarah also knew that only her claim to be younger and her struggle to look as ugly and inconspicuous as possible had kept Rose from noticing that she'd filled out years earlier, and had already become a woman.

She used Rose's disinterest to her advantage, lying about her age and knowing that no one, not even her mother, remembered exactly how old she was.

Dropping the laundry she'd already gathered, she paused outside her mother's room, taking a deep breath before turning the knob and pushing the worn wooden door open.

Seeing what she'd expected to see—her mother alone and sound asleep in bed, she entered the room, wrinkling her nose at the smell of whiskey and smoke. Closing the door behind her with a sigh, she made her way silently to the side of her mother's bed.

Everyone called her mother Lily, and Sarah had been taught to call her that, too, by a mother who didn't want to be called anything else.

Not until about a year ago did she accidentally learn that her mother's real name was Edna.

When she'd learned the truth, she'd cried for days, the realization of just how much distance stood between her and her mother making her feel even lonelier.

Despite the hot, dry summer in Waco, she felt cold inside and wondered if she'd ever feel warm again.

Looking down at her mother, she tried to imagine what it would have been like to be part of a family. To be around people who actually wanted her for something other than doing chores for them.

To feel loved—something that would never happen here.

She'd been saving every bit of money she could get her hands on for years, knowing that if she didn't leave, she'd end up used and old before her time—just like her mother.

She took in sewing when she had the chance, but she didn't have nearly enough money to even think about planning her escape.

Turning to look in the mirror her mother loved so much, she eyed her reflection critically.

She was short, which helped her look younger, and she did everything she could to make herself appear unattractive.

She'd turned twenty-one three weeks ago, but her mother hadn't remembered her birthday in years.

Sarah hadn't even thought of reminding her.

Still studying her reflection in the cracked mirror, she untied the shawl she kept around her shoulders. No matter what the weather was outside, she always wore a shawl to hide the low cut of the worn dress that had once belonged to one of the other girls.

Sarah had taken off the beads and lace in an effort to make the dress as plain as possible, but not even the handkerchief she'd sewn into the plunging neckline hid the upper curve of her breasts.

Although she washed every day, she didn't wash her hair often. Greasy and straggly, it made her appear unkempt and unattractive, and had a dirty smell to it that she would have loved to get rid of.

But she didn't dare.

It gleamed with blonde highlights when clean, and fell in soft waves around her shoulders, so she either had to keep it dirty or wear a shawl over it—another thing she hated about her life.

Depressed, she averted her gaze, looking down at the things her mother kept on the dresser—the small amount of things that gave her mother happiness.

Lifting her gaze to the mirror, she studied her mother's reflection.

Her mother looked tired. Older than her years and worn out.

Satisfied that she still slept deeply, Sarah picked up the bottle of perfume her mother treasured and lifted the stopper. Closing her eyes, she breathed in the floral scent, wishing she could dab just a little behind her ears the way she'd seen her mother do countless times.

Her mother groaned in her sleep, startling Sarah into shoving the glass stopper back into the bottle and hurriedly setting it down again, knowing her mother would be furious if she caught her touching her things.

She waited until her mother settled again, uneasy at the jittery feeling inside her that compelled her to linger in her mother's room longer than she normally did.

Keeping one eye on her mother's still form, she reached out to run her fingertips lightly over the silver brush and comb that had been prominently displayed on her mother's dresser for as long as Sarah remembered.

Her fingers hovered over the pot of rouge that her mother used to bring color to a face that seemed to lose more color every day.

Pulling her hand back, Sarah studied her reflection in the mirror.

Her own cheeks lacked the color they'd once had, and she had an emptiness in her eyes that made her so uneasy that she turned away.

She didn't want to think about spending the rest of her life with the loneliness that plagued her.

She had to get out of here.

She wanted to be somewhere, and with someone who made her feel as if she belonged.

Anxious to get away from the sickening smells and out into the fresh air, she gathered her mother's dirty clothes and went out into the hall to place them in the basket with the others before she turned to once again look at the bed.

A memory flitted through her mind, one that had a cold knot forming in her stomach.

She'd been young, probably around three or four. Straightening, she tightened her hands on the handles of the basket, her gaze settling on the armoire standing against the far wall.

She'd been watching her mother dress in what she'd thought at the time to be the most beautiful dress she'd ever seen. It had been red, sparkly, and had feathers on the front and the sleeves.

Her mother had worn a hat that matched it, her hair piled high under it.

Sarah remembered being entranced by the dance of light on her mother's earrings which, like the sparkles on her dress and hat, seemed to catch every bit of light from the smelly oil lamps, making her mother appear almost magical.

Entranced, she'd sat on the bed, watching her mother get ready for the evening, startled at the loud knock at the door.

Rose had opened the door without warning, her presence scaring Sarah into hiding beneath the covers. "Hurry up. You've got someone coming up. Now." The door had closed, leaving Sarah and her mother alone again.

A heavy tread on the stairs had her mother scrambling, and before Sarah knew it, her mother had tucked her into the armoire, hissing for her to be quiet.

Sarah had been forced to stay in the hot, dark armoire and listen to her mother with a strange man.

Her mother had made sounds—frightening sounds to a little girl.

Remembering her mother's order to be quiet, she'd pressed her hands over her mouth to muffle her sobs, very afraid that the man was hurting her mother.

Since that night, she'd been afraid of men, and did everything in her power to avoid them.

They all seemed so mean, and had glints in their eyes that scared her.

Now, with a last look at her mother, she sighed and left the room, closing the door quietly behind her.

She had only one room left—Rose's room. She dreaded going in there, and always saved it for last.

As the madam, Rose always had the best clothes and the most important clientele. She was hard and cold enough to handle even the meanest men, and she prided herself on bedding the bosses.

She didn't seem to care if the man she took to her bed was the boss of an outlaw gang, one of the self-important oilmen, or a railroad tycoon.

She loved men of power, and bragged about how she could use her body to bring them to their knees.

Years of seeing things she'd rather not see and hearing things she'd rather not hear left Sarah knowing what they meant—and it disgusted her.

Pausing outside Rose's door, Sarah pulled her shawl around herself—despite the fact that the early morning chill had long ago given way to a warm, humid late morning.

Hunching her shoulders, she knocked lightly at Rose's door, her hand trembling. She'd waited as long as she could before entering, but the man that Rose had brought up the previous night had a habit of sleeping for most of the day.

Willy Krenshaw—one of the meanest outlaws around.

"What?"

Sarah swallowed heavily, Rose's angry tone clear even through the thick wooden door. "Miss Rose? I just want to collect the laundry."

She hated that her voice shook, the knowledge that such a hateful woman could put her on the street on a whim making her nervous every time she got near her.

The door swung open and Rose appeared, her hair disheveled and her eyes barely open. "Fine, just hurry up and be quiet about it. I ain't alone and Willy won't appreciate bein' woke up."

Nodding, Sarah kept her head down and slipped through the opening, pausing to let her eyes adjust to the room darkened by the heavy curtains hanging at every window.

The curtains also kept out even the smallest breath of fresh air.

Holding her breath as much as she could against the stench of whiskey, body odor, and sex, she rushed to gather the dress and stockings hanging over the back of the chair before crouching to gather Rose's undergarments from the floor. She didn't even glance at the bed, but out of the corner of her eye, she saw Rose fling off her robe and crawl back beneath the covers.

A scrap of pale material puddled on the floor, partially hidden by the ridiculously elaborate silk bedspread, caught her attention. With a sigh, she gathered it and the other clothing against her chest, almost gagging on the combination of perfume, smoke, and sweat emanating from it as she reached for the clothes she'd almost missed.

Finding more than she'd expected, she struggled to get them all in her arms, and hurriedly straightened.

A hard pull at her hair shocked her into crying out, the pain to her scalp bringing tears to her eyes. Instinctively reaching back to ease the pain, she found herself yanked to her feet.

"Well, what do we have here?"

Struggling to hold on to the dirty clothes, Sarah found herself standing face to face with a man.

Willy Krenshaw—a very naked Willy Krenshaw.

Terrified, she fought to get away, sobbing when the hand in her hair tightened. "Please!"

"Don't worry none about her, Willy. She's just gettin' the laundry." With a groan, Rose slid from the bed again, walked naked to the window, and pulled the curtain aside.

Blinking against the bright sunlight, she raised a hand to shade her eyes, apparently completely unconcerned by her nakedness. "Go on, girl. Get outta here."

Willy stepped closer, his gaze raking over Sarah. "Not so fast."

Sarah's heart pounded furiously at the dangerous glint in his eyes, a look she'd learned to recognize and fear.

He wanted to fuck her.

Shaking, she gulped back a sob and stared into eyes glittering with evil. "Leave me alone."

To her horror, he threw his head back and laughed, a laugh that sent chills up and down her spine.

"Feisty little thing, ain't she?" The hand tightened in her hair, pulling her head back so hard that it knocked her off balance.

Bending her knees to stay on her feet, she gripped his arm tighter. "Let go of me. I'm not one of the working girls. I'm not for sale."

Glaring at her, Rose approached on her other side. "She works for me, Willy. Let her go. She's got chores to do."

Willy smiled, revealing rotten and missing teeth, his bad breath gagging Sarah. "She works for you, huh? I ain't seen this one yet. Where you been hidin' her?"

Rose stepped closer, running her hand down Willy's chest. "I haven't been hidin' her. She's busy. She does the cleanin' up around here, and the laundry. She's Lily's girl and way too young for the likes of you."

His eyes narrowed, his gaze sliding down Sarah's body and up again to linger on her features. "She ain't broke in yet?"

Rose seemed to come wide awake with a start, her eyes hard and cold on Sarah's. "No. She ain't ready."

He yanked the shawl aside, his eyes widening when they lingered on the upper curve of her breasts. "Oh, she's ready."

Rose gasped, clearly furious. "How old are you, girl?"

Not about to confess her real age, Sarah blinked back tears as the hands in her hair tightened. "Fifteen."

Willy chuckled and released her, his eyes narrowed and sharp with evil. "I don't care how old she is. She's got a body made for sex. Have her ready for me tonight. Get her gussied up in one of those fancy dresses." His gaze went to her breasts again. "Not that she's gonna be wearin' it long."

To Sarah's relief, he turned his attention back to Rose. "She's got me all riled up again. On your knees, whore."

As soon as Willy released her, Sarah bent to gather the clothing she'd dropped and her shawl, holding the pile against her chest. Never taking her eyes from him, she backed toward the door, prepared to make a run for it if necessary.

But, thankfully, he no longer seemed interested in her.

Breathing heavily, she backed away, blinking back tears she hadn't been aware of shedding.

She'd never been so scared.

Her breath came out in harsh, ragged gasps, and dizzy with fear, she clenched the clothes in her arms tightly, never taking her eyes from the dangerous outlaw.

When Rose dropped to her knees in front of him, Sarah spun and rushed out of the room, her heart pounding nearly out of her chest. Slamming the door behind her, she turned to race to her room instead of the back porch where the other laundry waited.

She had to get out of here—and it was clear she couldn't wait any longer.

Still holding the pile of clothes against her chest, she ran for the stairway, grateful that everyone still slept as she rushed to her room, closing and locking the door behind her. Leaning back against it, she dropped the dirty laundry and fought to catch her breath.

She had to think. She had no money, but she had to leave town.

Somehow.

She had to find a way to escape before tonight.

After Willy took her, she'd be sold to any man who had the money, and become a whore—just like her mother.

She had no time to waste. Everyone except the cook would sleep for most of the day, so she had to move quickly.

She would have to walk, and dreaded being alone in the wilderness after dark, but she didn't have enough money to take the stage out of town.

She didn't even have enough to buy a meal.

Thinking about the small amount of money she'd managed to squirrel away, she rushed to the corner of the room and dropped to her knees to tear at the loose floorboard. Her heart pounded furiously, her head spinning at the turn her life had taken in the last few minutes.

Taking out the small handkerchief she'd hidden under the floor, she stilled at the unmistakable sound of the stage coming down the street.

Hoping the noise would cover her escape, she tucked the handkerchief with the few coins she'd managed to save into the top of her dress, and pushed the floorboard back into place.

She tossed her meager belongings, including the only other dress she owned, onto the bed, and tied everything up in the thin blanket, her hands shaking so hard that it took three tries before she got the knot secured.

She looked around the room, blinking back tears at the realization that, from this moment on, she was on her own.

She'd love the chance to say good-bye to her mother, but knew she couldn't spare the time.

Her mother wouldn't risk angering Rose, and would rush to tell her that Sarah had gone.

They'd find out soon enough, but Sarah wanted to put as much distance between her and Waco as she could before they did.

She was truly alone.

Pushing that thought out of her mind, she took several deep breaths, closing her eyes and lifting her head toward the ceiling.

*You can do this. You have to.*

She didn't even want to think about the alternative.

With a hand on the doorknob, she paused, turning back to look at the pile of dirty clothing she'd tossed to the floor.

If she could find another scarf or shawl, she could cover her dirty hair and hopefully draw less attention to herself. She didn't want to be noticed.

No one would even miss her—except for Willy, and he'd only be angry because she got away from him.

Just the thought of having his hands on her, and the thought of him seeing her naked had her struggling against a wave of terror again.

Breathing heavily, she dropped to her knees and tossed dirty laundry in every direction, desperation making her clumsy.

Red dress. Stockings. Underthings.

No shawl.

"Hellfire." She threw everything aside, stilling when she heard a dull thud.

Picking up one piece of clothing at a time, she tossed them aside, her heart pounding furiously when she uncovered a man's vest.

Willy's vest.

Lifting it, she frowned at its weight.

Opening the vest, she fingered the small leather pouch pinned to the inside.

Then she saw another. And another.

Her heart pounded as she turned the vest inside out and saw that three small leather pouches had been pinned inside.

Barely breathing, she unpinned the smallest one, surprised at the weight of it in her palm.

With hands that shook, she untied the strip of leather holding the pouch closed, her breath catching at the flash of light.

*Gold.*

She counted the gold coins, her heart pounding faster. Twelve of them in the small pouch, and there were two more pouches.

More than enough to buy her freedom.

*Thank you, God!*

It took her several minutes to unpin the pouches from the vest, and pin the two larger ones to the inside of her skirt. Shaking the entire time, she jolted at every sound, knowing that it was only a matter of time before Willy realized that his money was gone.

He might not come after her, but he'd definitely come after his money.

Straightening, she tucked the pouch she'd opened into the top of her dress, knowing that the cloth she'd used to bind her breasts would keep it in place.

She had to move fast.

Gathering her meager possessions, she raced as quickly and silently as she could down to the kitchen, taking several small loaves of bread and pieces of fruit and hurriedly tying them into a napkin. Trying to control her breathing, she rushed out the back door and around the saloon to the sidewalk.

She'd grown up in Waco, and knew too many people. She didn't want anyone to recognize her as she made her way across the street to buy a ticket for the stage. Just as she got to the other side of the street, the sound of the train whistle pierced the air.

If she took the train, she could get away faster, and go farther than she would have been able to go on the stage.

Willy Krenshaw wouldn't be able to catch her so easily.

There would be more people. She could lose herself in the crowd, and hopefully, no one would remember her.

Changing direction, she kept her head down and headed toward the train station, acutely aware of the pouches pinned inside her skirt hitting her legs with every hurried stride. Only a block away, she found herself in the middle of a crowd of passengers from the train, just as a loud commotion broke out in the center of town.

Keeping the shawl in place with a hand fisted in the material below her chin, she sneaked a look over her shoulder, her stomach clenching when she saw Willy outside the saloon.

He looked mad as hell, whipping his head from side to side, obviously searching the street for someone.

Her.

She had to get out of here.

Ducking lower, she kept walking briskly, but not fast enough to gather unwanted attention, not slowing until she got to the train depot.

Slipping behind the small wooden building, she fought for composure. If she cried or acted guilty, people would notice and remember her.

She had to blend in.

If she could just get away, she could have a life—a real life.

Taking a deep breath, she straightened, her gaze drawn to a poster nailed to the side of the depot.

*Brides wanted. Circle T Ranch. Desire, Oklahoma. Safety guaranteed.*

*Safety guaranteed.*

She'd never even considered something like that, but at least she would have a man to keep her safe.

She would have a place to go—a place to hide. A husband. A family of her own.

Women alone seemed to end up in trouble. Even Rose, who ran her own business, had to do disgusting things with strange men in order to survive, and she had no man to turn to.

Sarah couldn't forget the look of fear on the other woman's face when Willy had made her get on her knees to please him. She'd seen her mother drink in order to face taking strange men into her bedroom.

Sarah wanted no part of a life like that.

The sound of Willy calling her name sent a jolt of terror through her, one that made it nearly impossible to think.

*Safety guaranteed.*

She couldn't even imagine what it would feel like to feel safe, and she was too shaken to even think of anywhere else to go.

Without hesitation, she went to the counter on legs that shook. "A ticket to Desire, Oklahoma, please."

The man behind the counter looked up. "Train don't go to Desire. Closest station is Tulsa. You can get a ride from there."

"Fine. Thank you." She bought the ticket, grateful that the man behind the counter didn't seem at all surprised that she paid for it with a gold coin. Maybe she could just stay in Tulsa and get a job there.

Pleased that she'd figured out another option, she hid a smile and accepted the ticket.

Although it seemed to take forever, it took only a few minutes to board the train and take a seat on the opposite side, placing herself as far from the bustle of Waco as she could.

Trying not to gape at her surroundings, which seemed so extravagant to her, she held her bundle of belongings close, prepared to run if she had to.

Trying not to gape, she lifted her head just enough to blend in with the others, taking in the ornate curtains on the windows and sliding her hand surreptitiously over the soft, velvet covered seats.

She'd never seen anything so lavish.

No one sat in the seat next to her, and she could only imagine it was because of her worn clothes and hair that smelled of tobacco, whiskey, and sweat.

She just hoped it wouldn't cause people to remember her.

Sweating, shaking, and praying, she waited—each second seeming to take forever. Her breath caught at the gravity of what she'd done, but she couldn't look back.

Finally, after what seemed like an eternity, the train lurched, the movement so unexpected that she had to hold on.

Watching the street as they passed, she saw Willy riding his horse through town with two of his men, and he looked mad as hell.

He whipped his head around several times, and although she couldn't hear what he said, it was clear he was yelling.

Blinking back tears, she turned to look out the window on her side of the train, her heart pounding furiously as the train pulled out of the station.

She'd escaped.

She was on her way to another life.

She was on her way to a new town—to a husband.

To a man she didn't even know.

It terrified her, but not as much as returning to Waco.

She'd made her decision, and there was no going back.

Staring out the window, she settled more comfortably in her seat and imagined the man she would marry—a nice, gentle man.

Like Mr. Andrews, who always smiled at her and fussed over his wife, who'd taught her to sew.

Like Mr. Smith, who worked in the livery and always had a piece of fruit or a cookie for her.

Like Mr. Johnson, who owned the General Store and slipped her candy when no one was looking.

She knew nothing about love, and didn't plan to find it.

She needed safety, and a place to hide.

She didn't dare dream for anything else.

# Chapter Two

Phoenix Royal hid a smile, amused that two of Tulsa's bad asses and the town's worst troublemakers quieted when they saw his oldest brothers, Hawke and Blade.

Giving his two stone-faced brothers a wide berth, they strode past them and headed down the street toward the livery.

He and his brothers had reputations for not backing down from a fight—any kind of fight—but a glare from his older brothers seemed to strike terror in men who liked to terrorize others.

Phoenix, as always, thought it funny as hell. He'd always been proud of them, and because they'd been left alone at an early age, the three of them had always been close.

His brothers were unlike any other men he'd ever met, and made others nervous, much to Phoenix's unending amusement.

Both Hawke and Blade wore clothing made of buckskin, as if they didn't want anyone to forget that they were half-Indian. Blade wore his hair in a long braid down his back, while Hawke wore his loose, giving him a wild, savage look that made even the toughest men take notice.

Phoenix wore his hair shorter and bought his clothes in town. He didn't look for trouble, but didn't go out of his way to avoid it. Unlike Hawke, he and Blade spent as much time as they could enjoying the amusements they found in town, including the bordello across the street.

Looking in that direction, he grinned, smiling at the two giggling women standing on the small porch in front of the saloon. He and Blade had bedded both of them several times, and he wished he had the time to enjoy them right now. Knowing he'd never be able to convince Hawke to spend the night in town, he nodded in their direction and turned back to his work.

Lifting another bag of flour onto the buckboard, he waited until the men still eyeing Hawke warily were several yards away before he spoke, careful to keep his voice low. "Everyone in town seems to be scared of you."

Hawke grunted in response and turned to go back into the general store for another load of supplies.

Blade smiled and followed his brother. "Maybe they're just afraid we're gonna scalp 'em."

The train whistle sounded as the train pulled into the station at the edge of town, so Phoenix didn't even try to answer. Following his brothers, he glanced around, nodding at the greetings from several townspeople. They called to Blade as well, but very few dared to address Hawke.

He reached the store just as Hawke exited, and stepped aside so his brother could pass with his armload of supplies. "It wouldn't hurt you to go have a drink while you're here in town."

"Don't drink."

Phoenix shook his head, knowing his brother never touched alcohol because Hawke never wanted to be out of control. Phoenix thought it would be good for his brother to relax once in a while, but *relax* wasn't a word in his brother's vocabulary. "I know the saloon girls would love to get to know you. They ask about you every time I go. It would be good for you to have some fun."

Hawke grunted again, not even slowing. "You have enough fun for both of us. The saloon girls seem to be waiting for you."

"And for you."

"If you decide to pay them a visit, you'll have to make your way home by yourself. I'm leaving as soon as I check the train station."

Accepting the bags of sugar from Blade, Phoenix headed back to the buckboard. "We could all spend the night, and head back after breakfast in the morning."

Hawke grunted again and headed back inside the store, his expression hard with disapproval.

Shaking his head, Phoenix loaded the bags onto the buckboard and sighed in frustration. He hated that his brother never seemed to enjoy anything. He worked and slept. Day after day.

Hawke seemed to get harder and colder with every year that passed, and it worried Phoenix.

His older brother got especially cold when the subject of women arose.

Clenching his jaw, Phoenix started back inside with the intention of trying to talk Hawke into visiting the bordello with him.

As far as Phoenix knew, Hawke hadn't been with a woman in years—not since the woman he'd courted back east had informed him in no uncertain terms that she'd never tie herself to a half-breed—and Phoenix worried that he'd keep getting worse.

As he started into the shop, Blade came through the door with bags of flour over his shoulders.

"You're wasting your breath." Blade's lips thinned, his eyes glittering with anger. "Hawke isn't about to mingle with the townspeople, Phoenix. He barely speaks to the men on the ranch, and he actually likes them. There's no way he's going to put himself in the position to be humiliated by a woman again."

Wincing, Phoenix gestured toward the women across the street. "They always ask about him. There's something about his cold attitude that's a challenge to them or something. They all want to be the one to make him smile, and to soften him up a little."

Blade's lips twitched, but his expression remained hard. "That's not ever gonna happen."

"Bullshit. We've just gotta find the right woman for him. He needs to take a wife—to have someone warm and soft to come home to."

Blade lowered his shoulder, dropping the bag of sugar onto the buckboard and sighing as he straightened. "Don't hold your breath. Our older brother is too stubborn to lower his guard again."

With a curse, Phoenix scrubbed a hand over his face. "That chip on his shoulder is gonna get him in trouble one day."

Blade's lips twitched. "I've never seen trouble that Hawke can't handle."

Gripping his brother's shoulder, Phoenix turned him toward the saloon. "Look at them. Don't tell me you wouldn't want to get between Annie's thighs again. Look at the way she's looking at you. Hell, she's even waving you over. She must like those games you play with her."

After lowering the bags to the buckboard, Blade shrugged. "She likes 'em. She wiggles that ass at me until I turn her over my knee." Blade's eyes narrowed, a small smile playing at his lips. "Tempting, but not as tempting as it used to be."

Stunned, Phoenix tore his gaze away from the women and faced his brother. "What the hell are you talking about? Look at them. Thick about those creamy breasts and soft thighs." Phoenix's cock stirred at the thought of sinking his cock into Betsy's soft pussy.

Shaking his head, Blade pulled away from his brother to return to the buckboard. "No, thanks. It's getting boring. I want something a little different now." Shaking his head, he frowned. "I want someone of my own. Someone who'd be mine to take care of."

"You're both turning into old men. I still want some fun." Frustrated, Phoenix turned and went back into the store to grab another sack of flour. Eyeing Hawke as his oldest brother strode past him, he bent to hoist it over his shoulder and headed back outside. He passed Blade, surprised to see Hawke standing outside, leaning against the buckboard.

After stacking the sack on top of the others, Phoenix eyed his brother. "Something wrong? There are still a lot of supplies to load."

"I know." Hawke's gaze slid to meet Phoenix's. "I know you like coming to town, but don't forget what we are. Don't get too attached to these people, and don't trust any of them."

"What's wrong with them?"

"They can turn on you. The girls at the saloon cater to you because you pay them to. Don't ever think otherwise." A muscle worked in his jaw. "I don't want you to get the idea that you fit in here. You might dress like a white man, but that doesn't make you one of them."

Biting back anger, Phoenix crossed his arms over his chest, wishing he could get through to his brother. "I'm not trying to be one of them, but I'm sure as hell not going through life with a chip on my shoulder. Life is what you make of it and I'm sure as hell not going to spend it alone—the way you seem hell bent on doin'."

Hawke clenched his jaw, his eyes narrowing to slivers. "You've gotten worse ever since Eb and Jeremiah married Maggie—and since Wyatt and Hayes married Savannah, you've been impossible. Men sharing a wife. I know it sounds exciting to you, and it's a way of life we've never even heard of, but don't think it would work for us. Get it out of your head, Phoenix, or you're just going to end up miserable."

"Like you?" With his hands on his hips, Phoenix moved closer, careful to keep his voice low. "I'm not the only one who's changed. You want what they have, but you just won't admit it."

"You have no idea what I want."

Recognizing his brother's icy tone and the yearning and anger behind it, Phoenix swallowed his own anger and smiled. "In case you haven't noticed, there's not a lot of women around here. Sharing a wife just makes sense. What's wrong with wanting a woman in my bed every night? What the hell's wrong with wanting a family? Blade wants the same thing."

Hawke's gaze sharpened and narrowed. "There's nothing wrong with wanting either, but expecting it to happen is just askin' for trouble."

Straightening, Hawke turned back toward the store. "Go check out the train station while we finish loading the buckboard."

Phoenix sighed. "Do you really think anyone'll be there?"

Hawke shrugged. "We got orders to check, so we check."

They'd all waited for months for the women and the doctor Eb and Jeremiah had advertised for to make their way to Tulsa looking for Desire, but so far, none had shown up.

Phoenix stilled as something flickered in his brother's eyes, something that looked very much like regret.

Stepping down from the buckboard, he caught Hawke's arm as his brother started back toward the store. "You want a woman, too."

Hawke's sighed and jerked his arm away. "I have needs like any other man, Phoenix."

"Then why haven't you come with Blade and me to the saloon?"

"Too busy and using my money to furnish the house we just built." He nodded toward Blade as he approached. "Help Blade finish loading the supplies. I'll go to the train station."

"Damn it, Hawke!"

Blade shook his head and caught his arm before Phoenix could go after him. "Leave it, Phoenix. Give him a few minutes alone. Let's get the rest of this loaded. He's gonna be in a hell of a mood when no one shows up again."

Watching his brother stride down the street, Phoenix cursed. "What the hell's wrong with him lately? He's had a burr under his saddle for a long time, but in the last several months he's been worse. He avoids Maggie and Savannah as much as possible. Oh, hell. He was hell bent on building that cabin."

Blade flung a rope across the buckboard and started securing the supplies. "What does that tell you?"

Phoenix sighed, bracing his hands on the back of the buckboard. "That he wants a woman of his own as much as we do."

"Yeah. He does. Probably more."

Phoenix frowned, staring after Hawke before turning to Blade. "Why won't he admit it?"

"You know Hawke." Blade yanked the rope and knotted it, securing the stack of burlap bags. "He wants a wife, and it pisses him off. He's already made up his mind that he can't have one, so wanting a woman to care for infuriates him because he knows it's futile. He's getting a little more bitter every day, and seeing the women at the ranch and how happy the others are makes it even worse. That's why he's been avoiding them."

Squinting against the late-day sun, Phoenix gritted his teeth. "There's no reason we can't get one of those brides for ourselves. Why the hell is he so damned stubborn?"

Blade smiled at that. "I think he was born that way. Besides, it doesn't look like any women are showing up, so wantin' one is just a waste of energy. Go on and get the rest of the supplies. I want to get back to the ranch before it gets too late."

Phoenix glanced toward the train station as he started back into the store. "Who knows? Maybe Hawke'll come back with someone."

Shaking his head, Blade moved around the buckboard to tie the other side. "Doubtful, but if he does, you can be sure she won't be interested in bastard half-breeds."

# Chapter Three

Irritated at himself, Hawke strode down the street to the train station, anxious to finish the chore so he and his brothers could get back to the ranch.

Each week, someone came to town to stock up on supplies, and they always came on the day the train came in.

Each week, the men at the ranch waited anxiously to see if a potential bride appeared, and each week, they ended up disappointed.

As he walked up the stairs to the platform, he tried to convince himself that he didn't hope for a woman of his own, too.

Having a woman just wasn't in the cards for a man like him.

He'd wandered from place to place with his brothers his entire adult life, never fitting in anywhere. He'd finally found a home at the Circle T ranch. He'd made friends there, something he'd never thought possible, and felt as if he belonged for the first time in his life.

Eb and Jeremiah were easy to work for, and seemed to draw people in who didn't fit in anywhere else.

They'd become a family, one that Hawke had begun to trust.

He and his brothers had settled in at the ranch, and he'd been content—until the women started coming.

Soon, there would be children running around the ranch—sharp reminders of what he couldn't have.

What he wanted more with every breath he took.

Restless again, he'd begun to think about moving on.

Another town. Another job.

But he knew he could never escape from himself—or his need for a woman he could love.

Pushing his thoughts aside, he headed toward the counter, standing aside to wait for others to buy their tickets, while scanning the small depot for arriving passengers who might need a ride to the Circle T.

He hated crowds, and being in town smothered him. The activity and number of people all around him made him nervous as hell, and he couldn't wait to get the hell out of here.

He should have sent Phoenix, but his youngest brother seemed hell bent on goading him into the whorehouse, probably hoping that fucking a woman would somehow change his mood.

Phoenix didn't understand that it was the yearning for a wife that plagued him—a hunger for a sweet woman who would be strong enough to put up with him and his bad moods.

He wanted a woman of his own—a woman who would accept him for what he was.

He wanted a woman who would look at him the way Maggie and Savannah looked at their husbands—a woman he could protect and give all the love that had been building inside him for years.

It would never happen, but as hard as he tried, he couldn't fight the yearning inside him.

Fisting his hands at his sides, he called himself all kinds of a fool and concentrated on the throng of people, impatiently scanning the platform.

The fear on people's faces as they gave him a wide berth irritated him, but at the moment, also gave him a small amount of satisfaction. He was taller than most of the people around him, but their distance made it even easier to see through the crowd. He remained motionless, his arms crossed over his chest as he waited.

Phoenix loved the crowds and the energy of crowds, and Blade didn't seem to mind one way or the other.

He had a calm about him that nothing seemed to ruffle, an edge to him almost as sharp as Hawke's.

He didn't quite understand his brother's desire to explore the more edgier of sexual acts with women Hawke had always been content to give as much pleasure as he got and give the woman the affection and closeness that would give her the security he knew they craved.

Aware of the wary looks he received, Hawke clenched his jaw and continued to scan his surroundings. Inwardly sighing at the number of people in line, he leaned back against the wall, prepared to wait until the line disappeared before speaking to the man behind the counter. As soon as he confirmed that no one had come in on the train, he could get the hell out of town.

When the line moved again, he found his gaze drawn to a woman standing in it that he hadn't noticed before.

She didn't stand much above five feet tall, blending into the crowd with ease.

Watching her, he got the feeling that she wanted to remain unnoticed.

Intrigued and inexplicably drawn to her, he watched her, seeing by her body language the exact moment she realized it.

Stiffening, she somehow managed to make herself appear even smaller, hunching over the small bundle she held tightly in front of her.

She kept her head down, scuffling along as the line moved, making his hands itch to reach for her and tear the ugly, worn scarf away.

It was hot as hell outside, but she gripped the scarf tightly against her neck as if freezing.

He couldn't take his eyes from her, finding himself captivated by her defensive posture. Lifting his gaze, he searched for anyone who might have accompanied her, his hands clenching into fists at the thought of her being with a man who couldn't give her the confidence she appeared to desperately need.

Finally she reached the front of the line, and he stepped closer, irritated that she wouldn't look up at him.

And then she did, and the kick to his gut almost took him to his knees.

Her stunning blue eyes met his, the impact stealing his breath.

She was pale—too pale, her delicate features making her stunning blue eyes appear too large for her face.

The sadness and desperation in them tugged at his heart, his chest swelling with the knowledge that he could wipe the sadness from her eyes—if only she would let him close enough.

Cursing himself for his fanciful thoughts, he continued to watch her, unable to look away.

The flash of fear in her eyes angered him more than usual, but she seemed to be afraid of every man who got close to her—not just him.

"Excuse me. I'm going to Desire. To the Circle T Ranch. Can you tell me how to get there?"

Entranced by her soft voice, and distracted by the vision of her whispering to him in the dark, he didn't catch the meaning of her words at first.

When he did, his heart leapt, the longing to make her his own as sudden as it was unexpected. He took a deep breath and let it out slowly, his heart pounding nearly out of his chest. "I'm Hawke Royal. I'm from the Circle T."

He wanted her—badly.

He wanted to surround her with all the warmth he could give her, and wipe the sadness and loneliness from her eyes.

Her beautiful eyes went wide, and she looked as if she might bolt, until Lee, the man at the counter, smiled—a tender smile Hawke had never seen from the elderly man before. "He's tellin' the truth, ma'am. He's from the Circle T. He's trustworthy. The men on the Circle T are the most trustworthy men I've ever known. I'd trust him with my life."

He turned to Hawke, but Hawke barely glanced at him. "Hey, Hawke. When I saw you standing there, I knew you were looking for one of those brides the Tylers advertised for."

Hawke nodded, anxious to get her away from the crowd so he could have her undivided attention, biting back a grimace when she deftly avoided his touch. "Thanks, Lee." Taking her arm in a light grip, he bent low, instinctively lowering his tone the way he did when dealing with a frightened animal. "We're attracting a lot of attention."

Nodded, she went with him. "Is the Circle T close to Desire?"

"The Circle T *is* Desire. The men who own it are building a town, and women's safety is one of their main priorities."

"Are there many women there?"

Frowning when she stiffened again, he shrugged. "Only two so far. The owners share a wife—the reason they bought the place to begin with. They don't want their wife open to criticism. The sheriffs also share a wife."

Stopping abruptly, she stared up at him, the sadness in her beautiful eyes replaced by shock and intrigue. "They *share* a wife? Oh, God. Are you telling me that the women are outnumbered?

Hawke rushed to reassure her, her fear of men obvious. "Yes, they're outnumbered, but they're protected at all costs. Women aren't exactly growing on trees there. It only makes sense to share them. Believe me, the women are guarded and spoiled. Their safety is our first priority. They make it work and they all seem really happy." Fighting bitterness, he took her arm again and led her away from the crowd, biting back a groan at the quiver that went through her.

Her responsiveness to his light touch created an ache inside him that he could no longer ignore.

He forced a smile, wanting her more with each passing minute. "Did you come to be a bride?"

God help him.

He wanted to throw her over his shoulder and carry her to the minister, staking his claim before taking her to the ranch and letting one of the others have her.

If he didn't take her as his own, he'd have to avoid her as well, because he sure as hell couldn't stand seeing her with another man.

She didn't answer at first, her eyes darting from one person to another as if she expected someone to jump out and attack her at any moment, her fear heightening his senses. She shrugged her small shoulders. "I-uh, yes. I guess I did. Um, who am I supposed to marry?" Her cheeks turned an enticing shade of pink, but it was her eyes that enthralled him. They gleamed with curiosity despite her obvious shyness, tugging at his heart and making him wish for things that could never be. "Am I supposed to marry you?"

Hawke stilled, his heart pounding furiously at the trust displayed when she edged closer as a group of people passed, including the men who'd avoided him earlier.

Anger fisted his hands at his sides, the recognition that no woman would ever want to tie herself to a man like him hurting like never before. "You wouldn't want me for a husband. There are several men at the ranch looking for a bride. You can meet them and decide who you want to marry."

His words sounded colder than he'd intended, but the look of panic in her eyes created an odd sensation in his stomach.

Her smile had a nervousness to it that made his arms itch to hold her. "Why wouldn't I want a man like you?"

\* \* \* \*

Sarah found herself edging closer to him, uneasy at being in such a large crowd. Expecting Willy and his men to appear at any moment, she tried to hide herself, keeping Hawke between her and the bustle of people on the platform.

The men who'd just passed her looked at her the way Willy had, scaring her so badly that she edged closer to Hawke.

He had a way of talking to her—looking at her—that gave her a warm feeling inside, much like the feeling she'd gotten from Mr. Anderson, Mr. Smith, and Mr. Johnson.

Over the years, she'd learned to trust her instincts, and her instincts told her that she could trust Hawke.

He was a big man, so it proved easy to hide behind him, but he drew attention to himself like no man she'd ever met.

Wearing a gun belt with a gun and what looked like an axe dangling from it, he looked more than capable of taking care of himself. With a bow strapped to his back and some kind of oddly-shaped wooden stick over his shoulder next to it, he was an intimating sight.

His shoulders were wide, wider than she'd ever seen on a man. His hair, so black that it gleamed with blue highlights, hung down to the middle of his back, straight and so silky looking that her hands itched to touch it. He looked and smelled so clean and fresh, with no trace of whiskey or tobacco clinging to him.

He wore his hair loose, giving him a wild, untamed look that created an aura of danger around him that appeared to scare those who walked by him.

She knew that she probably should have been scared as well, but something—a loneliness that had lived inside her so many years and she recognized easily—shone in his eyes and made her feel safe with him.

He moved in a way that she'd never seen a man move before, a gracefulness in every step that didn't resemble the swagger of the cowboys and outlaws like Willy Krenshaw and his gang at all.

He moved with purpose, and with the kind of strength she never knew existed—the strength of a man who didn't have to show off or speak loudly to intimidate others.

A confidence that he could handle anything life threw in his path drew her in closer, making her yearn to lay her head on his shoulder and feel his strong arms come around her.

She could only imagine how safe she would feel in his arms.

She knew it was silly to feel that way about a stranger, but he had the kind of confidence a woman could depend on.

Fascinated, she found herself enthralled by him, his presence making her feel safe for the first time in her life.

He kept himself between her and the rest of the world in a way that made her feel protected.

For the first time in memory, she could breathe.

Straightening, she took a deep breath and smiled at the sense of freedom.

She felt so safe with him.

His eyes narrowed. "It's not possible. I won't ever get married."

Her face burned at his abrupt answer. Lowering her head, she looked up at him through her lashes, captivated that such an obviously dangerous man could have such gentleness in his eyes—a sorrow that tugged at her heart. "I'm sorry. That was rude of me."

Hawke folded his arms over his chest, his posture making him appear even larger and more intimidating, but his eyes held a concern and tenderness that seemed to rip away the protective shell she'd built around herself. "You have nothing to be sorry for. You keep looking around. Who are you looking for?"

Startled by the question, and even more surprised that he'd noticed, she lowered her eyes again, knowing that it was only a matter of time before Willy found out she'd bought a train ticket and where she'd gone.

Shocked when Hawke gripped her chin and lifted her face to his, she gulped. "No one." She'd had to tell lies her entire life in order to survive, but shuffled with unease at lying to Hawke. Hoping her face wasn't as red as it felt, she met his gaze squarely. "I don't know anyone in Tulsa."

Hawke's dark brows went up, his eyes lit with amusement. "Except me, and you haven't even told me your name."

"My name's Sarah."

"Sarah what?"

Her face burned. "My mother said it was Smith, but she said she wasn't really sure."

Cursing her own stupidity at leaving a trail for Willy to follow, Sarah chewed on her lower lip. "I think I made a mistake. Is there a hotel where I can stay until another train comes?"

Hawke stiffened, lowering his arms to his sides as another Indian, one who looked very much like him, approached. "What kind of mistake?"

Alarmed by the appearance of the other man, Sarah took several steps back. "It doesn't matter." Pulling her shawl closer, she started to turn away, alarmed when Hawke's hard hand gripped her arm and turned her back. It brought back the memory of Willy grabbing her in Rose's bedroom. "Please. Don't hurt me."

She tried to twist away, cursing herself for letting her guard down, and allowing herself to be drawn in by his tenderness.

The small pouches of gold coins hit her legs, a sharp reminder of what her impulsiveness might cost her.

She couldn't allow herself to trust anyone.

To her surprise, Hawke released her at once, his eyes glittering with anger. "I'm not going to hurt you. Who did? Is that who you keep looking for?" His gaze lifted, his eyes narrowed as he scanned the crowd as if relishing the thought of confronting whoever had hurt her.

Panic made her stomach clench, the enormity of what she'd done hitting her hard. She had no choice but to keep running. "No one. I'm sorry. I can't go to the Circle T."

Hawke shot a glare at the man who'd joined them. "Nice timing, Blade." His eyes gentled again as he turned back to her. "Sarah, this is my brother, Blade. You have no reason to fear him. Blade, Sarah's here to be a bride."

The other man smiled, a flash of white against his dark skin, the tenderness in his eyes so much like Hawke's that she smiled. "I wondered what was taking you so long."

Blade had to be the most beautiful man she'd ever seen.

Hawke frowned at his brother before turning back to her. "Sarah, when was the last time you had something to eat?"

Surprised by the question, Sarah studied Blade, startled by the hardening of his features, which made him appear almost as fierce as Hawke. "I'm just thirsty. I finished the water in my canteen hours ago. Do you know where I might refill it?"

Blade's jaw clenched, his eyes hardening as some unspoken message passed between him and Blade. "We've got canteens of water in the wagon. Why don't we get out of here?"

She was so thirsty that she would have done almost anything for a drink of water. "Thank you."

With Hawke on one side and Blade on the other, she made her way across the platform, the sense of security surrounding her bringing tears to her eyes.

She allowed them to lead her through the crowd, their big bodies on either side of her protecting her from being jostled as they led her down a wooden walkway toward the bustling town. She couldn't help but notice that people kept their distance, even the men who had a glint in their eyes that reminded her of Willy.

Troublemakers. She'd learned at a young age how to identify them.

She'd also learned how to avoid them.

Hawke and Blade seemed able to repel them, much to her amusement.

Blade paused. "I'm going to run into the hotel restaurant and get her something to eat."

Hawke nodded, gripping her arm while Blade turned and headed in the other direction. He led her toward a buckboard where another Indian leaned against the side, this one with shorter hair and dressed more like a cowboy.

Letting Hawke guide her around a puddle, she looked around, but kept a wary eye on the other Indian. "There's even more people here than in Waco."

"Waco? Is that where you're from?"

Inwardly cursing herself for letting that slip, Sarah slowed her steps as they approached the packed buckboard.

The other man straightened, his eyes going wide. "I'll be damned. I wondered what was taking you so long."

"Watch your language." Hawke turned to her, gripping her waist and lifting her onto the buckboard. "Sarah, this is my other brother, Phoenix. Now, tell me why coming here was a mistake." Reaching into the supplies, he produced a canteen. "Here. Drink this."

Guzzling the water, she almost choked when Hawke took her bundle from her. "No!"

Hawke paused, his eyes narrowing. "I'm just setting it aside. Your arms have to be tired. I won't steal your things. I promise."

Inwardly cursing at how silly she must seem to him, she nodded, wiping her mouth with her shawl.

Lowering her head again, she looked up at Phoenix through her lashes, surprised at his teasing grin. Warmed by his smile, she smiled back. "Hello."

"Hello. So, your name is Sarah?" He turned to Hawke. "So, who do you think she'll end up marrying?"

A muscle worked in Hawke's jaw. "I have no idea. Sarah, talk to me. Why was coming here a mistake?"

After drinking her fill, she recapped the canteen and sighed. "I won't be marrying anyone. I have to leave. I left a trail. I panicked and ran and left a damned trail."

Phoenix frowned, glancing at Hawke. "A trail someone's gonna follow?"

"Yeah." Sarah's mouth watered at Blade's approach, her stomach rumbling at the sight of the small basket he carried.

Blade set the basket in front of her, pulling the napkin covering it aside to reveal several pieces of fried chicken. "What's going on?"

Hawke shook his head, never taking his eyes from Sarah. "Who's going to come after you, Sarah? A man?"

Nodding, Sarah dug into the basket, her stomach rumbling again. "Thank you." Her eyes filled with tears as she lifted her head to meet Blade's. "It looks and smells delicious."

Blade shrugged, his blush so endearing that she smiled at him before taking a bite. "You're welcome." His eyes sharpened with interest. "There's a man coming after you?" He glanced at Hawke. "Your husband? Brother? Father?"

Wiping juice from her chin, Sarah shook her head. "No." She hadn't realized how hungry she was and couldn't seem to stop eating.

Crossing his arms over his chest, Hawke frowned. "Who is it, Sarah, and why is he coming after you?"

Not willing to answer him, she finished the chicken leg, set the basket aside and jumped from the buckboard. Turning to gather her bundle of meager belongings, she jerked away from Blade's hold. "No. Please. I have to go. I'm sorry."

She would have loved to have eaten more of the contents of the basket, but it had started to get dark, and she wanted to be safely ensconced in her hotel room before night fell.

Hawke took a step to the side, effectively blocking her. With him on one side, Blade on the other, and the buckboard against her back, she had nowhere to go. "Please!"

Phoenix shot a look at both of his brothers, his smile tender as he moved closer. "If you keep carrying on like we're hurting you, someone's going to think we are and are going to come after us. We're only trying to help you. Do you think we could really leave you alone, knowing that someone's after you? Why don't you come with us to the ranch? No one could find you there."

"Yes. He could. Oh, no." Closing her eyes, she groaned at the realization that she'd put others in danger. "I've really made a big mistake."

Opening her eyes again, she looked at Hawke. "I'm so sorry. I saw a poster in Waco, advertising for brides, and I asked the man who sold me my ticket how to get to the Circle T ranch in Desire. The man at the ticket counter here also knows where I was going. I'll have to leave on the next train, so he can tell Willy that I left."

Blade folded his arms over his chest, his expression hard. "Who the hell is Willy?"

Phoenix smiled. "Watch your language."

"Shut up. So, who is he?"

A shiver went up her spine. "Willy Krenshaw. A bad man. An outlaw, and I have something that belongs to him."

Hawke's frown deepened. "And where do you plan to go?"

Shrugging, Sarah looked around again, scared that Willy would appear at any moment. "I don't know yet. As far as I can get. Maybe California."

With his hands on his hips, Hawke scowled. "If he wants to find you bad enough, he'll follow you there. Do you have enough money to keep running?"

Thinking about the small pouches of gold coins, Sarah grimaced. "For a while. After that, maybe I can get a job somewhere—"

Blade, his posture identical to Hawke's, gripped her waist and lifted her back onto the buckboard. "So, you're going to keep running, alone, and hoping this Willy doesn't catch up to you. What's going to happen when you run out of money? Who's going to protect you while you're doing all this running?"

Phoenix shook his head. "A woman alone is just asking for trouble."

Sarah had seen enough of how women alone were treated, and how vulnerable they were to know he spoke the truth.

Being along left a woman defenseless, with no rights at all.

Hawke's position shifted slightly, his expression like stone. "You'll stay here. We'll be able to protect you, and you won't have to run anymore, but first I want to know why this man's after you." He nudged the basket closer to her, silently urging her to eat.

With a sigh, she reached into the basket for another piece of the delicious chicken. "It doesn't matter. I can't stay here anyway." She didn't know how much she should tell them, not wanting to put them in any more danger, but knowing that she had to make sure they watched out for trouble.

Blade's dark eyes narrowed, glittering darkly in the waning light. "Why can't you?"

Sarah set the chicken aside, her appetite gone. "I might as well tell you so that you know why I can't stay." After all, she'd never see them again anyway, and had to make sure they would watch out for trouble.

She glanced at each of them to find them patiently watching her. "I'm a bastard. My mother's a whore in a saloon, and she got pregnant with me. I don't even know who my father is, and neither does she."

She stared down at her hands, her face burning with shame. "I grew up in a saloon. In the bordello upstairs." She yanked the shawl from her dirty hair. "As I got older, I started disguising myself by not taking baths and trying to look as ugly as possible."

Phoenix's eyes flashed with anger. "So that the patrons didn't bother you?"

Nodding, Sarah blinked back tears. "My mother couldn't protect me from Rose, who would have given me to Willy tonight."

Blade uncapped the canteen and handed it to her, his lips thinned in anger. "Rose ran the business?"

Gratefully accepting the canteen, Sarah took a sip of water to swallow the lump in her throat. "Yes."

"And she wouldn't have protected you?"

Sarah wanted to laugh at that. "No. The only reason she didn't put me to work was because I kept lying about my age, and no one paid enough attention to me to know the truth. I've been planning to escape for a long time."

Conscious of the upper curve of her breasts now exposed, she drew the shawl around herself again. "But my time ran out."

Hawke took a step closer, as if trying to protect her, the fury in his eyes making her uneasy. "Tell us."

After taking another sip of water, Sarah sighed and told them about the incident with Willy, and about the gold coins. "He had to have stolen them somewhere. He's an outlaw, and dangerous."

Setting the canteen aside, she dropped her face in her hands, consumed by guilt. "I know what I did was wrong, but I panicked. Rose would have made sure that I was dressed and ready for him."

\* \* \* \*

Hawke's stomach clenched with a fury that he hadn't felt in a long time.

He wanted to hit something, and wanted nothing more than to beat Willy Krenshaw to a pulp.

It infuriated him that such a sweet little thing like Sarah had been left to her own devices, with no one to protect her.

He wanted to fight her demons, and stand between her and the rest of the world—a world that could be harsh and dangerous for a woman alone.

Glancing at each of his brothers, he could see that both Blade and Phoenix seemed as drawn to her as he was.

He already knew he would do everything in his power to make her his.

When she lifted her face and lowered her hands again, the tears swimming in her eyes ripped his heart to shreds. "He wanted me and Rose was going to give me to him. I had no say. He wanted to do things to me. I know taking his gold was wrong, but I was so scared. If I'd stayed, he would have—"

Her voice broke, a sob escaping, and then another.

Hawke stilled, looking at his brothers, grateful that she'd managed to escape before Willy hurt her.

His stomach clenched hard, and for the first time in years, he didn't know what to do.

He'd rather face a gun pointed at him than a woman's tears.

He'd be much more comfortable dealing with Willy, something he looked forward to very much.

Thankfully, Blade rushed forward, crooning softly to her in a low, whispered tone that seemed to settle her.

Sitting on the buckboard next to her, Blade gathered her in his arms. "Don't think about that. It didn't—and won't—happen." Rubbing her back, he began to rock her. "Running again is just stupid. You'd be running and looking over your shoulder. Either he would catch up to you, or you'd run out of that gold you took. Stay here. You'll be safe on the ranch, even if this Willy shows up."

Wiping her eyes on her shawl, Sarah sniffed. "You're very nice. Thank you for being so kind to me, but I don't have any illusions. No one is gonna want to marry a bastard—a daughter of a whore. No man wants a wife who was raised by working girls above a saloon."

For the first time in his life, Hawke spoke without thinking. "I'll marry you."

"I'll marry you."

"Marry me."

Both of his brothers spoke at the same time that he did, leaving all three of them looking at each other in shock.

Schooling his features, Hawke looked at a clearly stunned Sarah. "Stay put. I want to talk to my brothers." He wanted to make it clear to his brothers that he was more than willing to take on the responsibility of her, and didn't want them to think that they had to.

Hawke motioned for his brothers to follow him and moved several feet away, but close enough to keep a sharp eye on Sarah. "I'm going to marry her. I know that both of you feel sorry for her, but—"

Blade's jaw clenched. "Don't tell me what I feel, big brother. I'm marrying her. She's a sweet little thing, and she needs someone. She seems very resourceful. She's also brave. I want her for my wife."

"She's also beautiful." Phoenix couldn't seem to take his eyes from her. "Those eyes." Turning, he faced Hawke. "Since we all seem to want to marry her, why don't we do what the others did?"

Hawke frowned, his heart beating faster with an excitement that was almost unrecognizable. "You mean share her?"

Blade shrugged, smiling in Sarah's direction. "It seems to work for the others. I know we've never talked about it, but I like the idea of her having protection even if something happens to one of us."

Phoenix's eyes narrowed. "She looks like she's going to bolt. She probably thinks we're crazy. We'd better get back to her."

Hawke fought a tinge of jealousy at the idea of sharing Sarah with his brothers, but the thought of marrying her thrilled him. Approaching her, he forced a small smile to reassure her. "Sarah, I know this might sound strange to you, but we all want to marry you."

Shaking her head, she looked at each of them. "I know you said that the others back at the ranch share wives, but—"

Phoenix sat next to her on the buckboard. "The owners of the Circle T are both married to the same woman. So are the sheriffs. Eb and Jeremiah, the owners of the ranch, built it and founded the town for that reason. They were both in love with the same woman. Think about how much protection you'll have with three husbands."

Hawke frowned. "I already told her that."

Blade touched Phoenix's shoulder. "Sarah, before you make up your mind, you should know that Hawke, Phoenix, and I are bastards, too. And half-breeds. Our mother was white and our father a full-blooded Lenape Indian. They were never married."

Sarah hugged her bundle tighter to her chest, averting her gaze. "I suppose you'd want to exercise your husbandly rights."

Hawke shot a warning look at his brothers. "Not until you're ready. In fact, we'll take you back to the ranch and you can think about whether or not you want to marry us."

Her eyes went wide, so wide that Hawke found himself in danger of losing himself in them. "Where would I stay?"

"There's a house that Eb and Jeremiah had built for the brides he advertised for. It's a place for them to live until they're claimed by a prospective husband and they accept." Alarmed at the fear in her eyes, he moved closer. "Is something wrong?"

Her eyes went impossibly wider, her breath hitching as she jumped from the buckboard. "I've never lived by myself before. No. What if Willy—?"

Hawke moved quickly, stepping in front of her to cut off her escape. Desperate to reassure her, he shook his head. "You don't have to stay there if it scares you."

Phoenix rose. "Where can she stay?"

"With us." Crossing his arms over his chest, Blade smiled at her. "But not until you're our wife. I won't risk your reputation."

Sarah stilled, her eyes going wide again. "My reputation?" She giggled, and then started to laugh in earnest. "I'm the daughter of a whore, Blade."

Enraged, Hawke jerked her to his side. "Something that no one else needs to know. And before you say that you'd embarrass or disgrace us—don't. I won't have you treated with disrespect. You're going to have enough to endure being married to us."

Phoenix wrapped an arm around Sarah, pulling her against him. "It sounds like we're a perfect match. So, are you going to marry us? We'd be real good at protecting you, and I promise, every man at the ranch respects women. You'll be safer there than anywhere else in the world."

Sarah's eyes lit with excitement, her entire body trembling with it. "Are you sure? I mean—we'd really be married? A family?"

Hawke inclined his head, feeling as if he'd waited his entire life for her. "Yes. We will." Lifting his gaze to Phoenix, he nodded once. "Phoenix, you don't have to get married. Blade and I will take care of her. Since it appears we'll be spending the night in town, I'm sure you'll want to go to the saloon."

Phoenix frowned. "I no longer have any interest in the saloon, or anyone there. I'm marrying her, too. You ready to go get married, Sarah?"

Sarah took a deep breath and blew it out in a rush. "It seems that I have no other choice." She looked at Hawke. "I trust you. I feel safe with you."

Hawke sucked in a breath, his chest swelling. "Is that a yes?"

She beamed, her eyes glittering with excitement and making his cock swell. "Yes."

His heart felt as if it would burst, the surge of possessiveness almost knocking him off his feet. "Let's go find the preacher." Knowing that she would belong to him in just a matter of minutes had him hurrying down the street. "We'll stop and buy you a ring."

Her blush fascinated him. "I don't need a ring."

Hawke's steps never slowed. "I want you to have one. I don't want there to be any mistake that you're already taken."

# Chapter Four

Blade's chest swelled with pride.

She was his. *Theirs*. To keep.

He had a wife to care for—a wife to warm his bed and hold in the night.

He had a woman in his life now, a woman he could enjoy to the fullest—a woman he could possess in ways he could never possess another woman.

Still stunned at the sudden turn of events, Blade walked into the hotel room, scanning for danger before opening the door wide and stepping aside to admit his wife.

*His wife.*

Sweet and innocent, but with a curiosity in her eyes that made his cock ache, she smiled shyly at him, her cheeks flushed. "I've never seen such a beautiful room."

Blade smiled back to put her at ease, anger stirring in his belly that she would be so taken in at such a plain, ordinary room.

It gave him an insight into her life in Waco, one that made him even more determined to spoil her.

He wanted to surround her in comfort, and mentally envisioning the cabin they'd just completed, he decided that a few changes would have to be made.

He and his brothers slept on thin mattresses on the floor, but the thought of a huge bed where he could make love to her in comfort for hours made his cock stir.

The thought of having her back at the ranch and coming in after a long day to find her waiting for him filled him with a longing and sense of excitement he hadn't felt in a long time.

His hands actually shook as he lit the lamps in the room, the anticipation making his cock pound furiously.

They wouldn't take her tonight, but soon she would be in their cabin back home, and he could take his time with her.

He would have to be gentle, but he didn't have to rush the way he did with the girls in town. He could take her step by erotic step and lead her into the world of the dark pleasures he'd long ago become addicted to.

Careful to keep his distance, he dropped her bundle on the bed and clenched his fists at his sides to keep from reaching for her. "You'll be safe here."

Watching him warily, she moved to the window, pushing the curtain aside to look out into the night. "I feel bad for delaying you. You would have travelled at night to go back to the ranch if not for me, wouldn't you?"

Blade shrugged. "We sometimes spend the night in town, but we've travelled at night before, especially this time of year when it's too hot in the day. We'll get an early start in the morning, though. We'll stop at the general store and get some things for you before we go." He smiled at her look of shock. "It'll be nice having a few womanly things around the cabin."

He bit back a groan when she slid the scarf from her shoulders, his cock getting harder each time he caught a tantalizing glimpse of the fullness her ill-fitting dress barely contained.

They'd have to make sure she had dresses that fit her better, or she'd drive the other ranch hands crazy, and his jealousy would create fights between him and the other men. "Including some material for new dresses."

Sarah bit her lip, making him crazy to taste them again.

He and his brothers had kissed her after the ceremony, but it had only been a taste, a taste of sweetness and innocence that he wanted to drown himself in.

Lifting her gaze to his, Sarah nodded. "You'll want the gold now, won't you?"

Blade clenched his jaw. "I don't want your money. My brothers and I are responsible for providing for you."

Her eyes went wide. "But—"

"Keep it hidden until you get back to the ranch, and never mention it while you're here in town."

"You'll let me keep it?"

Blade understood the relief in her eyes. It was another measure of security for her to know that she had it and could escape if she felt threatened.

He wanted to give her all the security he could, and knew that this was one thing they could do to begin to earn her trust. "Yes. It's yours. Keep it tucked away. It makes you feel safer, doesn't it?"

She nodded again, her eyes brimming with tears. "I can't believe I'm married. I can't believe I have a last name now—a real last name. Royal. I'm Mrs. Royal. Sarah Royal."

Amused, Blade smiled, finding it hard to believe himself. "Yes, you are." The surge of possessiveness and pride surprised him, filling him with a sense of purpose and satisfaction he hadn't expected.

He watched her wander the room, noticing that she kept her hands folded in front of her, not reaching out to touch anything. He had a feeling that she'd never been allowed to back home, and was scared of breaking something. "A bath will be brought up for you in a few minutes." He wondered what she'd look like with her hair clean, and without smudges of dirt on her face. "Can you sew?"

"Yes. Mrs. Andrews taught me. I did all the sewing for the girls. My mother liked the dresses I made for her."

Blade nodded, mentally listing some of the things he'd need to buy. "Good. We'll buy some cloth so you can make yourself some dresses. We've got to do something about you showing so much. I find I'm a jealous man. "

Blushing deeper, she looked away, her shyness delighting him. Obviously nervous, she wrung her hands in front of her. "Am I really married to all three of you? The preacher looked real funny when we went there. Almost angry about marrying us."

Folding his arms over his chest, Blade wanted to dispel her of any doubts about their marriage. "He doesn't like that marriages like ours are legal in Desire. Under the law in the rest of the country, you're married to Hawke, but we're all your husbands. Make no mistake about that."

His voice had taken on an edge that had Sarah's eyes going wide again, and taking several steps back, she slid a glance at the door, obviously searching for Hawke.

She seemed to trust Hawke, and Blade promised himself that soon she would trust him, too.

He'd have to work on it, but he knew the results would be worth it.

Reminding himself that she'd grown up fearing men, he unfolded his arms and smiled, hoping to appear less intimidating. "The preacher's too afraid of Eb and Jeremiah, though, to do anything to anger them, so he performed the ceremony."

If possible, her eyes went even wider. "Hawke told me that they own the ranch. Are they mean?"

Thinking about the hardships and dangers they'd all faced at the ranch, Blade shrugged. "They can be when necessary." Holding her gaze, he moved closer, pleased when she didn't back away. He didn't want to admit that he was jealous of his brother, but he was, and wanted her to trust him the way she trusted Hawke. "We all can. Sometimes we have to be. Out here, danger can come from anywhere. You should know that as well as anyone."

The door opened, admitting Hawke, whose gaze went immediately to Sarah. "Your bath's here."

Blade stepped in front of Sarah as Hawke crossed the room, both of them positioning themselves between Sarah and the two men carrying a heavy tub through the doorway.

Sarah moved in behind Hawke, who smiled faintly, apparently pleased.

Once again promising himself that he'd do anything to earn her trust, Blade glanced at his brother to see Hawke's eyes flash with satisfaction. The unfamiliar show of emotion disappeared as quickly as it had appeared, but it made him feel good to see the change in his older brother.

Hawke had always been cold, especially since their mother died when they were children. The change in him since going to the train station was nothing short of remarkable.

Hawke had spoken more to Sarah in the short time they'd known her than he usually spoke in an entire week.

As they poured buckets of water into the tub, Blade swallowed heavily and willed his cock to behave, trying not to imagine his wife's naked body sinking into it.

He glanced at Hawke as the men left. "We're going to have to buy a tub. Maggie and Savannah begged until they got one."

"I don't need one. I'm sure there's a creek or stream on the Circle T that I can use." Sarah's soft voice held a sense of embarrassment, one that stroked his masculinity and made him want her even more.

Both he and Hawke turned to face her. Watching her pace again, Blade shrugged. "Both, and a pond, but you certainly can't take a bath in it."

The thought of another man coming across her naked infuriated him. Hiding his anger, he forced a smile. "Especially in the winter. There's a hot spring as well, but you can only go there with one of us. Didn't you have a tub in Waco?"

Eyeing the warm water, Sarah shrugged. "My mother did. She let me use it sometimes, but usually I just washed in the creek."

Hawke's jaw clenched in another rare show of emotion. "You'll have a tub, so you can have a bath whenever you want one."

Blade looked her over, taking in her matted hair, angry that she smelled of sweat, instead of sweet, like Maggie and Savannah. "Eb and Jeremiah's wife, Maggie, makes scented soaps that she sells here in town. We'll get some for you tomorrow."

Sarah got a panicked looked on her face, shaking her head furiously. "No. Please. Don't go to any trouble. I swear I'll smell better after I get clean."

Blade forced a smile, vowing to do his best to help give her the confidence she needed. "No trouble, and I'm not worrying that you won't smell better. I just know that the other women like them and thought you might, too. Take your bath."

Hawke went to the windows, making sure they were locked. "Then get some sleep."

As Blade turned away, she reached out to touch the sleeve of his buckskin shirt, dropping her hand before she actually touched him. "Where will you be?"

Trying not to think about his wedding night, Blade forced a small smile. "Hawke and I will sleep in the hall. Phoenix is sleeping on the buckboard."

"But—" Her face turned a fiery red.

Hawke turned, pulling the heavy curtains closed. "We've slept in worse. You're safe, and Phoenix will keep anyone from stealing the supplies."

She shifted restlessly, lowering her gaze. "You're my husbands. You have the right to …"

Blade could see she was scared and uncertain. Lifting her chin, he forced her to meet his gaze. "There's plenty of time for that. I have no intention of making love to a scared woman. Take your bath and get some sleep. We'll be right outside the door. We sleep light, so don't worry. Nobody will get past us. Don't lock the door. If you get scared, just call out. We'll hear you."

After a last long look at his wife, Blade went out to the hall with his brother, trying not to think about her getting undressed and into the tub.

Naked. Wet. Warm.

Settling against the wall on one side of the door while Hawke settled against the other, Blade once again willed his cock to behave. "It's going to be a long night."

Hawke nodded once, but didn't look particularly disturbed. Closing his eyes, he leaned his head back against the wall, a small smile of satisfaction curving his lips. "I have a feeling this will be the first of many."

# Chapter Five

Sitting in the seat of the buckboard, Sarah fingered the material on her lap and glanced at Phoenix. "This is really mine?" There were two more bolts of material braced behind her, along with an assortment of thread, needles, lace, and ribbons.

She couldn't wait to get started on her new dress, but felt odd about accepting gifts from virtual strangers.

She felt odd accepting anything from anyone.

She'd never really had anything of her own—nothing that couldn't be taken away from her without notice—including her home.

Except the handkerchief wrapped around the coins she'd hidden away.

She'd tried to use another gold coin from the pouch she'd kept in her bodice, but Hawke had glared at her in a way that had her hurriedly tucking it away again.

Holding the reins, Phoenix turned to smile at her, a flash of white against his dark skin. "It's really yours. You'll need some dresses. The next time we get back to town, we'll buy you more." Reaching out to touch her hand, he smiled again. "You sure are pretty." He slid his hand over her hair, his eyes narrowing. "Your hair's so light. So soft."

Her face burned at the compliment. "Thank you. I'm glad you like it. Is it far?"

Her stomach fluttered with excitement and nerves as they made their way to the ranch that would become her new home. She couldn't stop looking behind her for any sign of Willy, wondering if she'd ever be able to settle into her new life with the constant threat of being found.

Hawke and Blade rode their horses on either side of the buckboard, never getting too far away. Neither man had spoken since they left town, but she was aware of their sharp attention, and the stares they gave her every time she looked back.

Phoenix, on the other hand, seemed to like to talk and had been asking her questions almost the entire time. "Did you tell your mother that you were leaving?"

She had a feeling that he talked in an effort to make her more comfortable, but the sheer size of him made her nervous.

He stood about an inch or two shorter than Hawke and Blade, but he had a bigger build, his muscular frame making him as intimidating as his brothers. She couldn't stop looking at his hands, admiring the effortless way he handled the buckboard, while nervous at the apparent strength in them.

He could hurt her so easily, and he was only one of the men who now had the right to do whatever they wanted to do to her.

Being alone with them had made her realize just how vulnerable she'd be. She hadn't seen a single person or building since they left Tulsa, the open wilderness filled with dangers she'd never dare face on her own.

Dangers that her husbands seemed to handle with ease, but that she wouldn't stand a chance of surviving.

She would be helpless here, and would have to count on them for everything—just as she'd always had to count on Rose and her mother. Reminding herself that they couldn't be worse than Willy, she grimaced at the memory of Willy's stench and the evil in his eyes.

Phoenix frowned at her, his eyes dark with concern. "Sarah?"

Sitting up abruptly, she looked away, trying to remember what he'd asked her. "No." Finding her gaze drawn to his hands again, Sarah shook her head. "If I'd told her that I was leaving, she would have told Rose. I'd like to write to her to tell her that I'm safe, but if I tell her where I am, she'll tell Rose."

Shifting the reins to one hand, Phoenix reached out the other to cover hers. "And Rose will tell Willy."

Pulling her shawl more firmly around herself despite the warm, humid morning, Sarah nodded. "Yes. Rose will do whatever pleases him, and won't stand a chance if he starts hitting her." She glanced at Hawke and Blade before lifting her gaze to Phoenix's. "If he finds me, he's going to cause trouble. A lot of trouble. He's a dangerous man. I feel so guilty for bringing trouble with me to your ranch. Hawke, Blade, and you are going to be on guard and looking over your shoulders all the time."

Phoenix raised a brow. "The way you are now?" Patting her hand over the silver ring she'd been turning on her finger, he smiled. "Don't worry. My brothers and I have been looking over our shoulders our entire lives. We're used to it. We watch over ourselves, each other, and the women."

"If he hurts any of you or anyone else at the ranch, I'm never going to forgive myself." Shifting restlessly, she shivered despite the heat, so nervous that she trembled. "Do you think the other women will like me?"

Phoenix shrugged. "I don't see why not. We all try to get along at the ranch. We all depend on each other, so fightin' amongst ourselves makes life dangerous for all of us."

Not quite believing him, Sarah gripped the bolt of material tighter, her hands chilled now that he'd removed his. "What are they gonna think about me when they know I brought trouble to the ranch?"

Phoenix grinned. "You think you're the only one who ever brought trouble to the ranch?" Looking forward again, he shrugged. "You're our responsibility now. Just do what we tell you to do and everything'll be fine."

Shifting restlessly, and aware that Blade and Hawke listened to every word, Sarah glanced behind her again. "I guess when you went to town, you didn't plan on comin' home with a bride."

With a hand at her back, he urged her to look forward again. "No. We didn't, but life tends to make decisions for us that we hadn't expected." He turned to her again. "You should know that better than anybody. Don't worry. Willy's not going to get the drop on us. I have good hearing, but my brothers are nothing short of amazing. No one could ever sneak up on either one of them."

Grinning, he nudged her. "Not even me."

Blade chuckled, shaking his head and sharing a smile with Sarah. "But, that doesn't keep him from trying."

Her face burned at the intimacy in his smile, and she felt herself relaxing at the tenderness in his eyes. She pulled the bolt of material closer, marveling at its softness. "It's real comforting to have a man's protection. I didn't think any man would ever marry me."

Her face burned hotter at the admission, but she'd brought her problems to them and they'd been so generous, that she felt she owed them honesty.

Phoenix's features hardened. "We didn't really expect any woman to marry us, either, so I guess we're all in the same position."

"Why wouldn't you think a woman would marry you?" She lowered her gaze again, her face burning as she twisted the ring around her finger again, the weight of it filling her with a sense of warmth. "You're all so handsome. You're kind, and you're strong. Most men aren't kind, and their strength just makes them mean." A chill went through her at the memory of what Willy wanted to do to her. "It's hard to be so defenseless."

Phoenix gave her another reassuring smile. "You're not defenseless anymore. Hell, you even took Hawke on."

Fascinated by the blue highlights in his shorter ink-black hair, she studied his features. "Why do you wear clothes like other men, but both Hawke and Blade wear buckskins?" She glanced at Hawke, who rode on her side of the buckboard, her fingers itching to sink into his thick, almost waist-length hair that gleamed in the early morning sun.

Phoenix sighed, glancing at Hawke, bending his head to whisper in her ear. "They don't want anyone thinking they're pretending they're white. Hawke's got a chip on his shoulder about it."

Hawke turned his head, glaring at his brother before turning away again.

Surprised, she glanced at Blade. "With the sound of the buckboard, I'm surprised that he heard you."

Phoenix's lips twitched. "No much gets past either one of them, but Hawke sees and hears things that no one else does." Turning his attention back to the horses, he gave her a warning look. "Don't try to hide anything from him. It just makes him mad."

Sarah gasped at the sight of riders approaching, crying out Hawke's name as she turned to him. "Someone's coming! Oh, God! Are you gonna shoot them?"

Phoenix stilled, slowing slightly as he looked down at her hand gripping his arm. "Take it easy, honey. That's just Hart and Gideon Sanderson. They work at the ranch. No cause to shoot anybody."

Yanking her hand back, she pulled the material and her shawl closer, her heart pounding nearly out of her chest. "Oh."

His eyes narrowed, making him look even more like Hawke as he watched the other men approach. "We were due back at the ranch by now. Eb and Jeremiah must have sent out a search party."

Keeping an eye on the approaching men, Sarah noticed that both Hawke and Blade moved closer to the buckboard in a protective gesture she greatly appreciated. "Do you mean your boss would send someone out to make sure that nothing happened to you?"

Phoenix frowned, turning his head to glance at her. "Of course. I told you that we all watch out for each other."

* * * *

Phoenix shifted slightly, uncomfortable as hell. He'd been hard ever since he saw her that morning, and riding beside her and breathing in the clean, fresh scent of her only made it worse.

Her hair, no longer dirty and matted, gleamed like gold in the sunlight, making his fingers itch to sink into it.

He wanted to run his fingers through it as he held her close, and use his fingertips to spread the silky looking waves over his pillow while he covered her naked body with his.

Every gust of wind blew her waist-long hair against his back, surrounding him with the scent of her.

His woman. His wife.

She probably didn't even realize the sensuality she emitted by her small gestures, but he did.

His cock swelled even more each time she closed her eyes and lifted her face to the sun, her obvious enjoyment in the warmth of it on her face enthralling him.

Her smile had to be the most beautiful thing he ever saw.

It was a smile of pleasure and of sensual delight.

A look he would very much like to see on her face as he took her.

She looked at Hawke now, who'd moved closer at her soft cry. Leaning away from Phoenix and toward his brother, she covered herself again with the shawl, hiding her beautiful hair.

It was apparent that she trusted Hawke. She gazed at him as if the sun rose and set with him, her habit of looking toward his oldest brother and moving closer to him whenever she felt threatened creating an unfamiliar clenching in Phoenix's stomach.

Accompanying it was a slow, simmering anger and the almost overwhelming desire to grab her arm and yank her back against him.

Jealousy.

The look in Hawke's eyes stopped him, the change in his oldest brother nothing short of astounding.

Hawke had always been quiet, usually answering with one word or a grunt whenever possible. He spoke to Sarah in a crooning voice, though, using the same tone he used when dealing with the horses.

Hawke watched her almost constantly, the usual hard glint in his eyes absent, replaced with concern, fascination, and a possessiveness Phoenix never would have believed if he hadn't seen it with his own eyes.

As Hart and Gideon approached, Phoenix glanced at Blade to see if he noticed the change in their brother, only to find Blade moving closer to the buckboard and staring at Sarah.

Blade looked slightly dazed, his eyes glittering with emotion as his gaze settled on Sarah's face.

He glanced at Phoenix before quickly looking away, all emotion gone by the time he faced the approaching riders.

Hart's eyes remained hidden beneath his hat, but the flash of surprise in them was unmistakable when he saw Sarah. Facing her, he touched the brim. "Ma'am." Averting his gaze, he moved to ride on the other side of Hawke. "Wondered what was takin' you so long."

Hawke nodded, but said nothing, his lips twitching.

Gideon tipped his hat in Sarah's direction, grinning as he took a position on the other side of Blade. "A real beauty. You kidnap her, Blade, or did Phoenix win her at a poker game?"

Amused, Phoenix glanced at Sarah, delighted that even with the shawl covering part of her face, he could see her flush. "Neither. Hawke found her at the train station."

Gideon's smile fell, his brows going up. His eyes sharpened with interest as he turned to get another look at Sarah, blinking when Phoenix shot him a dark look. "No kidding. Is she one of the brides Eb and Jeremiah advertised for?"

"Sure is." Phoenix glanced between Gideon and Hart to see their reactions. "Ours."

When both men whipped their heads around to face him, Phoenix grinned, aware of Hawke and Blade stiffening on either side of him. "We married her last night."

Gideon turned back to Blade, his eyes wide. "All three of you?"

Blade nodded. "Yes. Her name's Sarah. Sarah Royal." His voice held pride, but also a hint of disbelief, and he kept glancing toward Sarah as if expecting her to disappear. "We're expecting trouble—a man looking for her. We'll let everyone know about it when we get to the ranch."

Hart grunted. "Trouble ain't nothin' new to us. Give us a chance to practice our aim." He turned to half smile at Sarah. "Looks like you three are the ones who are in trouble. Remind me to hide next time Eb and Jeremiah want to send someone to town. Matrimony seems to be contagious, and if it got Hawke, none of us is safe."

# Chapter Six

Sarah clutched her bundle close, grimacing at the rough wool blanket from her bed beneath her hands instead of the soft material she'd held most of the day.

She followed Hawke, pausing on the small wooden porch when he held out a hand in a silent command for her to remain there.

He'd done the same thing when they'd entered the hotel lobby the night before, and Blade had also walked into the hotel room ahead of her.

It was a little thing—a stupid thing that shouldn't have mattered, but she'd seen men open doors for women and allow them to go first back in Waco.

She'd seen it everywhere except in the saloon, and the rooms upstairs. She'd asked her mother about it once, and been told that men did that sort of thing to show his respect for the woman he was with— a respect the men who visited the saloon didn't have for the women working there.

Just minutes ago, the ranch bosses, Eb and Jeremiah Tyler, had opened the door for their beautiful wife and kept an arm wrapped around her as they led her outside, the two men obviously anxious to see what had kept Hawke, Blade, and Phoenix so long.

Their wife, Maggie, had been very welcoming, and had even taken her to the large building where they stored their supplies for the ranch.

Giggling, Maggie looked back toward where the men unloaded the buckboard. "I just wanted a chance to talk to you alone. It's nice to see another woman around here, but I have to tell you, I didn't expect the Royal brothers to ever get married."

Sarah liked the other woman immediately, and hoped that she'd found a friend. "They said as much. I don't know why they married me, but I'm glad they did. Are there any other women around here?"

"Just one. Savannah. She was my best friend back home." With a smile at her husbands, she stood aside as the men started toward the supply building. "We'd better get out of the way before we get run over."

Despite the fact that his arms were laden with bags of flour, Eb bent to nuzzle his wife. "I'd never run over you. Sometimes I wish I could stick you in my pocket to keep you safe. Go back to the house. You can talk to your new friend tomorrow. Hawke and the others look anxious to be with her."

Jeremiah slapped Maggie's bottom as he passed her. "We've been out on the ranch all day, and I'm anxious to be with my wife, too."

Stepping aside, he let her pass, the love shining in his eyes making Sarah feel like an interloper.

The two hard-looking men who owned the ranch obviously loved their wife, their affection for her apparent in every look. Their smiles for Sarah made her feel welcome, and they moved aside so she could pass through the doorway before them.

It hurt to realize that neither Hawke nor Blade seemed to feel that Sarah deserved that kind of respect.

Her mother had told her that men came to the bordello because their wives didn't like sex.

It made her wonder if that was the only kind of woman men respected. So if she didn't like sex, maybe Hawke, Blade, and Phoenix would eventually come to respect her.

"Is something wrong?"

Startled by Hawke's deep voice, Sarah jolted, whipping to face him. Surprised to find his eyes filled with concern, she took a steadying breath and forced a smile. "No. Of course not."

Hawke's eyes narrowed. "I don't care to be lied to—especially from my wife. Come on inside so we can get you settled. I thought you trusted me."

Not knowing what to say, she nodded, her face burning. Trembling, she followed Hawke past another large building and to a small cabin that set back among the trees. Her stomach clenched when Hawke strode through the door ahead of her.

"Something wrong?"

Shaking her head, Sarah walked through the door Hawke held open for her, blinking as her eyes adjusted to the darker interior.

Once her eyes adjusted, she looked around the small cabin, immediately feeling right at home. The walls, made of thick wood, appeared to be strong and heavy enough to withstand even the harshest storm.

Several lamps sat on various wooden tables, tables that appeared to have been handmade.

She'd bet anything that her husbands had made them themselves.

One table held a ceramic bowl and pitcher, painted in a variety of bright colors instead of the plain gray chipped one she'd had back home.

Besides the heavy-looking kitchen table and chairs, there were three stuffed mattresses on the floor.

Wondering where she would sleep, she averted her gaze, her face burning. "It's very nice. Very clean." It was very much like the men themselves. Sturdy and warm. Solid.

Blade went to the other side of the room and came back with a large basket. "Here's a basket for your things. We'll pick up another one the next time we're in town."

Finding herself alone with them in such confined quarters, and aware of their sharp scrutiny, she pulled her shawl more closely around herself. "Thank you."

Hawke ran a hand over her hair, sending a shiver through her. "It's even silkier than I thought it would be."

Her nipples tingled in reaction, and fighting the urge to lean into his touch, she pulled the bundle tighter against her chest. "It feels good to be clean again."

Carrying her new bathtub, Blade and Phoenix followed her inside, glancing at her before settling the tub in front of the fireplace. Blade straightened and strode toward her with a smile. "We'll fix a bath for you later. I know I could use one." Reaching out, he slid his fingers through her hair, lifting her chin with his other hand when she tried to avert her gaze. "It *is* soft."

Bending, he touched his lips to hers and, to her surprise, took the bundle from her arms, tossed it aside, and slid a hand over her breast.

Gasping at the shock of pleasure, she jerked away, right into Hawke's solidness. Meeting Blade's look of surprise, she shifted restlessly and crossed her arms over her chest. "I-I'm sorry. You surprised me."

Raising a brow, Blade smiled. "This time you won't have that as an excuse. I'm going to touch your breast now." His eyes narrowed, his smile sending a shiver of pleasure through her, one that she desperately struggled to hide. "You're very responsive. I want to see how sensitive your nipples are. Seeing them poking at the front of your shirt is making my mouth water."

Sarah couldn't believe he'd noticed, especially with the bundle in front of her, but she'd begun to understand that her husbands missed very little.

Trembling with anticipation, she held her breath, the tingling sensation in her nipples nothing short of wicked. Instinctively lifting her hands to cover them, she sucked in another breath when Blade caught her wrists in his.

"No. I'm your husband, and it's my right to touch you. It's my right to see you. I won't hurt you." Surprising her further, he took both of her wrists in his and held them behind her back, making it impossible to protect herself. "You're going to have to get used to being touched because you're going to be touched often, and by all three of us."

Instead of covering her breast with his hand the way he had the first time, he unbuttoned several buttons with a slow confidence that made her heart race. "I wanted to watch you take your bath last night, but you were scared and tired. Tonight, I'll bathe you myself. You need to get used to my touch."

Hawke's hands closed over her shoulders at the same time that Phoenix moved in beside her. "We won't allow you to hide anything from us, including whatever's bothering you."

Phoenix reached out to touch her hair. "If you're scared, all you have to do is tell us. I'm sure a lot of things are going to be new for you, and you're going to be scared, but you're our wife now. We won't hurt you and will protect you at all costs." He flicked a glance at Blade. "Stop torturing us. Move her shirt aside."

Although Blade spoke to his brother, his eyes never left hers. "Patience, Phoenix." Running the tip of his finger just inside her loosened shirt, he tightened his hold on her wrists. "Nice and slow. Take the time to savor."

"She's scared of men, and had good reason to be." Hawke pressed his cheek to her temple, watching Blade's hand over her shoulder. "She's beautiful, isn't she? She's shaking. Are you scared, Sarah?"

Before she could form an answer, Blade spoke again. "She's a little skittish, but she's getting aroused." He smiled again. "It's in her eyes. She has no idea what's going on inside her yet."

Aghast that he could see so much, Sarah hurriedly lowered her gaze, sucking in another breath when Blade lifted her chin higher.

"No. None of that. There's no reason to hide, and Hawke already told you we won't allow it."

Moving slowly, Blade bent his head. "I'm going to kiss you. It's not going to be a quick kiss like the ones we gave you in town."

A dark brow went up, the challenge in his eyes unmistakable. "You *do* know that this is going to be a real marriage, don't you?"

Gulping, Sarah nodded, bracing herself for whatever he wanted to do. Whatever he had planned had to be better than what she would have faced if she'd stayed in Waco. Aware that all three men watched her, she took a deep breath and let it out slowly. "Yes. I'm ready."

Blade's grin sent a surge of something warm and unfamiliar through her, the stirring between her thighs both alarming and exciting. "You're not even close to being ready, Sarah."

Not knowing what he meant, she said nothing, unwilling to make even more of a fool of herself.

The intense tingling in her nipples made her restless, but she forced herself to remain still when Blade released her wrists and his hands closed on her waist.

"Easy, Blade." Hawke rubbed her shoulders, his presence giving her the confidence she needed.

The hands at her waist tightened as Blade bent his head and touched his lips to hers, the sharp pleasure of his lips moving on hers startling a gasp from her.

Pressing his advantage, he slid his tongue between her lips, exploring her mouth with a possessiveness that caused a funny sensation in her knees, making her feel as if she might fall. Without meaning to, she lifted her hands to his shoulders for support, the feel of hard muscle beneath the smooth buckskin enticing her to lean into him.

The sound of a moan shocked her—especially when she realized that it came from her.

She vaguely remembered that allowing her to see that she enjoyed this wouldn't gain her respect, but she found her desire to resist swept away in the warm rush of sensation.

Blade's tongue swept her mouth again and again, pausing to tangle with hers in an exciting dance that she couldn't resist.

He tasted so good. So clean. So warm and inviting that she found herself touching her tongue to his, thrilling at his deep groan.

Cupping her breast, he ran his thumb back and forth over her nipple through the material of her shirt, the surge of heat to her slit startling a cry from her.

Blade lifted his head, his eyes hooded as they searched hers. "So soft. So responsive. See? There's no reason to be afraid. We'll go as slow as you need, but the sooner you come to terms that you're married to all of us, the better. Right now, you feel safer with Hawke holding on to you, but eventually, you and I will spend time alone."

Smiling, he reached for the next button, his eyes sharp on hers. "I want to see a little more." His smile held both hunger and a tenderness that made the tingling in her nipples and slit even stronger.

"Yes." A strange sense of yearning consumed her, a heat that came from deep within her, demanding satisfaction.

She wanted to be touched in ways that she'd never dreamed she'd want to be touched.

Her body felt different—tight—as if her skin had become too small to contain it.

She wanted to rip her clothes off, to bare herself to him. She needed him to touch her nipples and secret place between her legs, and to relieve the unbearable ache he'd caused.

Letting out a cry of frustration, she arched, leaning back against Hawke. "Please." She no longer cared that he knew that she wanted to be touched. She ached so badly, it no longer mattered.

Blade's slow smile and the appreciation in his eyes made the yearning even stronger. "Feels good, doesn't it?" He undid another button, and then another, pausing between each one to slide his fingertip inside and slowly caress the upper curve of her breast, each time getting closer and closer to her aching nipple.

Sarah gasped when another button came loose and then another, squeezing her eyes closed and crying out again when Phoenix touched her other breast. "Too hot. Everything feels too tight. I need something." A sob escaped, and she reached back to hold on to Hawke. "Help me. I don't know what's happening."

Phoenix leaned closer, waiting for Hawke to straighten before bending to touch his lips to hers. "You're becoming aroused." He kissed her again, deepening his kiss the way Blade had as Blade finished unbuttoning her shirt. "Guess what? It's going to get worse."

The feel of the sides of her shirt parting drew another gasp from her. Her eyes flew open just as Phoenix lowered his head, the attention to her nipple creating such an intense rush of heat that it startled another cry from her.

Phoenix's kiss tasted different than Blade's, but it made her just as dizzy. Hotter. Hungrier. His fingers moved continuously over her nipple, making her wish he'd remove the binding so she could feel his fingers on her bare flesh. He shocked her by nibbling at her lips, whispering her name before he took her mouth again.

Blade sighed. "So beautiful—and all ours."

Phoenix lifted his head, staring down at her with narrowed eyes. Frowning, he tugged the material binding her breasts the rest of the way free. "Is this part of making yourself look too young to work for Rose?"

"Y-yes." Sarah closed her eyes against the pleasure of the fingertip sliding back and forth over her nipple.

The intense heat shocked her, the feel of flesh on flesh nothing short of incredible.

Phoenix laughed softly, bending to touch his lips to hers again, brushing them with his own in a teasing way that made the muscles in her stomach quiver. "There's no reason to hide anymore. Let's unwrap you and see just what you've been hiding."

Hawke slid her shirt, still tucked into her skirt, from her shoulders to pool at her waist while both Blade and Phoenix began to unwrap the material she'd used to bind herself. Sliding his hands back up her arms and to her shoulders, Hawke began to softly caress her, urging her to lean back against him. "So soft." He kissed the top of her head, his lips lingering in her hair. "Our wife."

Blade and Phoenix worked the material free, leaving her naked from the waist up and completely exposed to a man's gaze for the first time in her life.

It was scary. Freeing. Confusing. Exciting.

Watching her with hooded eyes, Blade reached out and touched a fingertip to her nipple, moving slowly while watching her reaction. "Look at you. My wife."

Biting her lip, she tried to swallow a moan at the delicious hunger that increased with every stroke of his finger, but it escaped before she could prevent it.

"*Our* wife." Phoenix's eyes glittered with hunger as he reached out to touch her other nipple with his fingertip, his touch so light, she couldn't keep from arching against him for a firmer caress. He lifted his gaze to Hawke's. "If I'd let you talk me out of marrying her, I'd be kicking myself in the ass right now."

Blade pulled out one of the chairs at the table and dropped into it, pulling her onto his lap to straddle him. "Look at her eyes."

Sarah lowered her gaze again, knowing that if she let them see how much she liked being touched in such a decadent way, they'd never be able to respect her.

Moving to stand beside her, Hawke lifted her chin, staring down into her eyes. "She's not afraid anymore. She's aroused."

Sarah stiffened, fighting the hunger that grew with every touch. "No! I'm not aroused."

*Oh, God! How could anything feel this good?*

Phoenix wrapped his arms around her and bent low, touching his lips to her nipple, tightening his hold when she jolted and cried out. "Oh, no?"

Blade began to work her skirt up, sliding his hand slowly up her leg. "Oh, yes. You are. But, my darling wife, there's one sure way to find out."

Hawke bent to brush his lips against hers. "I'm more interested in why she's trying to hide it from us. I hope it's not out of fear."

Firming his hold on her chin, he reached down to stroke the nipple Blade had released. "When we know her body as intimately as we know our own, and know what pleases her, she won't be able to hide anything."

Sarah gripped Hawke's forearm, the unfamiliar sensations raging through her so overwhelming she couldn't catch her breath. She wanted something and didn't even know what, but she trusted Hawke to know. "Hawke. Please. Help me."

Crying out again when Blade lifted her and settled her at the edge of the table, she writhed restlessly, grateful for Hawke's solid warmth closing in behind her. She tried to close her legs against Blade's slow, wicked caress, but he and Phoenix held her thighs parted wide while he continued to slide his free hand higher.

Keeping an arm around her from behind, Hawke tilted her head back against his shoulder and watched her face while his finger tightened slightly on her nipple. His eyes flared with heat when she cried out and gripped him tighter, a slow smile curving his lips. "You're ours now. We'll take care of you. Blade, lift that skirt out of the way. I want to see her pussy while you make her come."

Shocked that the man who'd been so gentle to her would say such a wicked thing, she looked up at him, stunned at the sharp hunger in his eyes.

Hawke closed his finger on her nipple, sharpening the hunger and making her slit tingle hotter. "You know what I'm talking about, don't you?"

Sarah nodded, swallowing a cry. "Yes. I've heard the girls talk— oh!"

Blade pushed the material of her skirt aside, baring her mound. "You're about to experience some things for yourself. Hmm. Beautiful."

Phoenix lifted his head, running his thumb over her damp nipple while reaching down to stroke her thigh. "Damn." His gaze lifted to hers briefly before settling on her slit again. "Such a pretty pussy. Let's pet her and see if we can make her purr."

"Oh, God!" Her body screamed with hunger, every touch much more intimate and arousing than she'd anticipated.

She'd never have imagined that this kind of pleasure existed.

She'd never have imagined that she'd ever allow herself to be touched this way.

Still, she wanted more, and fought to hide it, a fight she feared she couldn't win.

With a groan, Blade sat in the seat in front of her and pushed her thighs wider, spreading her legs and pulling her forward until her bottom rested at the edge of the table. "I want to see her better."

Hawke moved to support her back, his hands covering her breasts. "Push her knees back, but be gentle with her."

Phoenix gripped her left knee and pulled it back, while Blade did the same with the other.

With his eyes steady on hers, Blade ran a finger through her slit. "You're soaking wet, darlin'. You still want to try to convince me that you aren't aroused?"

Mortified, Sarah looked away, only to have Blade turn her face back to his.

"It's nothing to be embarrassed about. It's supposed to happen. It means you like the way we're touching you."

"I can't. I'm not supposed to like it." Her stomach tightened at the thought that she could be just like her mother.

Hawke tightened his fingers on her nipple again, the shock of need to her slit making her jolt. Sill, Hawke held her steady. "We're your husbands. There's nothing wrong with letting us touch you this way. You're not sharing your body with everyone. Only us."

Blade touched her between her thighs again, using his finger to caress her slit, the sensation so alarming that she arched and reached for Hawke again. "Oh, God!" She tried to close her thighs, but Blade and Phoenix held her knees firmly pressed wide.

Blade made a sound in his throat, a crooning sound that vibrated over her skin as he slid a fingertip into her. "Easy. I won't hurt you." His eyes narrowed, his expression hard as he pushed at something inside her, creating a burning sensation that had her crying out again and grabbing at Hawke. "She's still a virgin."

Hawke's voice lowered again, becoming soft and silky. "Easy, Sarah. He's only using his finger to explore you a little. Tonight, when we go to bed, my cock's going there."

Her pussy clenched on Blade's finger, making it feel even tighter. "It burns."

Blade said something low under his breath. "It'll only hurt the first time." He slid his finger free, lifting his gaze to Hawke's. "She's so damned responsive. I've got to taste her."

Phoenix ran his hand up her thigh and under her, his fingers clenching on her bottom as he lifted her. "Do it. Make her come. I want to watch her. While she's aroused, I'm going to see if she's just as responsive somewhere else."

Blade stood, his gaze holding hers for several long seconds while he caressed her folds. "I'm going to use my mouth on you. It won't hurt. As a matter of fact, it's gonna feel real good."

With Hawke's hands on her breasts, his fingers dancing over her nipples, Blade's attention to her slit, and Phoenix's fingers firm on her bottom, Sarah didn't know how long she could attempt to appear unaffected.

Supporting her weight, Hawke focused his attention on her nipple, his eyes unreadable. "I've got her, Blade. Go ahead."

Sarah sucked in a breath, the sight of Blade lowering his head between her legs making her heart beat so fast so thought it might burst. "Oh, God!"

The first swipe of his tongue over her sensitive flesh felt so raw and wicked that she couldn't help but cry out and try to jerk away, but Hawke's hold kept her in place.

To have such a private place on display and touched both thrilled and alarmed her, the pleasure so intense she fought it.

Blade concentrated his attention on an extremely sensitive bundle of nerves that had her bucking on the table, her cries filling the cabin.

She'd lost the fight, but didn't care. It felt too good to be touched this way—every slide of their fingers building the pleasure to a point she didn't know if she could bear.

She wanted it to go on and on forever.

The feeling of being wanted—of being cherished for the first time in her life—brought a lump to her throat.

They wanted her, but they made her feel special.

Phoenix gripped her bottom, the caress of his finger over her bottom hole taking the raw sexuality to new heights.

She fought to escape it, but their firm hold and the pleasure of Blade's tongue made escape impossible.

Blade slid the tip of his tongue into her pussy opening, the carnal act almost more than she could stand.

Hawke groaned from behind her, tilting her head back again. "So sweet. So giving. Taking her virginity will be a great honor."

Sarah opened her eyes to stare into Hawke's, holding onto him—the only solid thing in her world.

A strange pressure continued to build inside her, and she shamelessly writhed on the table, desperate for something that remained just out of reach. "I can't stand it. Please. Something's happening."

Hawke's eyes narrowed to slits, his jaw clenching as he tugged at her nipple. "Let it happen, little one."

Phoenix lifted her knee higher and adjusted his hold on her bottom. "Easy, honey. Don't be scared. If I'm right about you, it's going to feel good. If it doesn't, I'll stop. I promise."

Sarah sucked in another breath, shaking even harder at the feel of the tip of Phoenix's finger pushing into her bottom hole.

"What are you doing? Oh, God!"

The slide of Blade's tongue on her clit had to be the most incredible pleasure in the world, the pleasure made even sharper by the feel of Phoenix's finger moving just inside her forbidden opening.

Without warning, the tingling heat and pressure exploded in a shower of tingling sparks that seemed to shower her in sensation.

Her body jerked, shaking so hard that it scared her. "Hawke!"

Hawke's eyes flared, the heat in them mesmerizing. "I've got you. We've all got you. Your clit's very sensitive, Sarah. We can give you a lot of pleasure by caressing it. There are many things we can do to you to give you pleasure. Trust us, Sarah. We won't hurt you."

The pleasure intensified—so good she thought she might die of it. Crying out, she threw her head back, wrapping her arms around Hawke's neck, thrilling when he groaned and caught her against him.

"Easy. You're safe. Just let it happen." Hawke's deep voice seemed to vibrate over her, the warmth and strength in his voice and his hold providing a safe haven that eased some of her fears.

When he pulled her closer with a hand cupped at the back of her head, she went willingly, burying her face against his neck. "Hawke."

Blade lifted his head, running his lips and hands over her thighs. "So sweet. Is she all right?"

"She's fine." Still holding her close, Hawke ran his hand up and down her back, the heat from his hand warming her cooling skin. "She's perfect."

Her face burned as Phoenix moved the finger against her bottom opening—the naughty feel of having Phoenix's finger inside her embarrassing now that the pleasure had begun to diminish. "Hawke?"

His lips brushed over her temple. "What is it, Sarah?"

Hiding her burning face against his chest, she fisted her hand in his shirt. "Phoenix. Oh, God. Why is he doing that?"

The hand at her back stilled. "Phoenix, what the hell are you doing to her?" The threat in his tone sent a chill through her.

Terrified that they'd fight, she shook her head at Hawke. "Please don't get mad. Please. Can I get dressed now?"

The awareness in her nipples, her slit, and her bottom made it difficult to look any of them in the eye, her face burning when Hawke lifted his head and gripped her chin to stare down at her.

Frowning, he ran his thumb over her cheek. "I'm not mad. I will know what's going on, though, especially when it concerns you." Releasing her, he turned to Phoenix. "What was she talking about?"

Blade looked up at Phoenix, and then at Hawke, before his gaze settled on hers, a smile playing at his lips. "Sharing her is gonna be a hell of a lot of fun."

Phoenix grinned, meeting Hawke's glower head on. "She liked the feel of my fingers brushing over her bottom." His gaze slid to hers. "Right before she came, I slid the tip of my finger into her."

Hawke stiffened, his arm tightening protectively around her. "You shouldn't have done that. I told you that she was scared."

Reaching out to touch her nipple, Phoenix grinned at her. "She didn't look scared to me. She liked it."

Pulling her shirt back up, Hawke helped ease her arms into the sleeves. "She's not one of your women in town, Phoenix. She's our wife." Something on her face must have upset Hawke, because he shot a glare at Phoenix and pulled her close again. "I'm sorry. That's in the past."

Phoenix smiled. "Stuck your foot in your mouth, didn't you, Hawke?" Reaching out, he started to button Sarah's shirt, his smile tender, but strained. "I won't be visiting those women in town again. You've really got my brother flummoxed. I can count the number of times that's happened on one hand."

Lifting her by the waist, Blade set her on her feet, letting her skirt fall again. "There's no point in causin' a scuffle. The three of us are going to have to work things out when Sarah's not around. No reason to get her upset. We're all gonna have different ideas about how to handle her, and it's not fair for her to be caught in the middle."

Phoenix finished buttoning her shirt and went to the pitcher to wash his hands. "Come on. I'm sure you're hungry. Let's go get some chow and introduce you to the others."

Sarah paused, looking back at Hawke, nervous about being with a lot of strangers without him by her side.

Hawke's eyes warmed, gleaming with satisfaction and pride. Reaching out, he draped her shawl over her shoulders and took her hand in his. "Phoenix is right. You need to eat, and I want you to meet some of the others, so you'll know who to go to if we're not around. When we get back, we'll get you settled for the night. We can all get baths."

Sarah nodded, remembering Blade's promise to bathe her. Swallowing heavily, she glanced at him, her face burning when he raised a brow. "It was nice of Maggie to give me some of the scented soaps she makes. I can't believe all the things they have stored in the supply building. It was real generous of her to offer to let me have more fabric."

Hawke frowned. "We'll give you what you need. I don't want charity."

Her stomach knotted at his sharp tone, a reminder that the three men she'd married now had complete power over her. Nodding, she turned away. "Of course."

Hawke said something under his breath in a language she didn't understand, and with a sigh, took several steps toward her. "Maggie Tyler is a fine woman, and very generous, but I—"

"We." Blade moved closer.

"—want to take care of you ourselves." Hawke's lips firmed. "We don't take handouts."

Phoenix shook his head. "You're both too hard-headed. You told her how we all watch out for each other, and then you tell her she can't take something Maggie offered in friendship."

"We can give her the things she needs." Hawke gestured toward the door. "Come on. Dinner's waiting."

# Chapter Seven

Nervous about meeting the others, and aware of the tension between her husbands, Sarah stayed close to Hawke as they entered the chow shack.

Intrigued and a little disconcerted by the satisfaction in their eyes, she smiled, her smile falling when Phoenix opened the door to the chow shack and went through first.

Although he pulled the door wide for her to enter and smiled when she passed him, he'd gone through first, confirming her belief that finding pleasure in their touch guaranteed that they wouldn't respect her.

Forcing a smile, she looked away from him to focus on the building she'd just entered.

Surprised to find it nearly filled with empty tables, she looked around, hoping to see Maggie. Her mouth watered at the incredible smells, her stomach growling at the unmistakable aroma of beef.

Taking her arm, Hawke led her to the front where a large feast waited. "We're late. Most everyone will have already eaten." Hawke took two metal plates from the pile and led her toward two serving tables piled with food. Stilling, he frowned and leaned closer, hovering protectively over her. "What wrong, Sarah?" He glanced around as if searching for a threat.

Shaking her head, she smiled up at him, embarrassed that her stomach growled. "It smells so good. I'd forgotten what beef smelled like."

The largest and meanest-looking man she'd ever seen stood behind the serving tables, using a huge knife to expertly carve a piece of beef so big that it took up half of the table. "It's a smell you're gonna get used to."

Even more alarmed by his gravelly voice, Sarah pulled her shawl more firmly around her. Watching him with the knife, Sarah gulped, pressing against Hawke.

The man turned his head, revealing a large scar that ran down the entire side of his face, giving him an even more sinister appearance. "Better hurry. More'll be comin' in soon."

With a supportive arm around her waist, Hawke nodded at the other man. "Sarah, this is Duke, the best cook around, and the only man on the ranch who can sneak up on me. Duke, this is Sarah—our wife."

Duke paused just long enough to nod in her direction, his bald head gleaming in the low light. "Ma'am." He went back to his carving, the huge muscles in his arms plainly visible in his short-sleeved shirt. "You're later than usual, but I figured you would be. There's still more comin' in though. Had a break in the fence at the south end and some of the herd broke loose. It's gonna be a long night."

Duke slid a thick piece of beef on each of their plates, not even glancing at Sarah. "Heard you got hitched. Appears those posters for brides is startin' to pay off." Something in his tone—a combination of sadness and fury—had Sarah stiffening and taking a hurried step back.

Blade closed in on her from behind, rubbing her shoulder. "It did for us."

Duke's lips twitched. "Thought you were supposed to bring the women back here. The bosses built that house for the single women to live in, and it's standing empty."

Blade scooped fried potatoes onto Sarah's plate and then his. "You never know."

Duke nodded and gestured for them to help themselves to a pile of steaming biscuits. "The bosses are happy the three of you finally got hitched, but now they have everyone arguin' 'bout who's goin' on the next run. Bunch of addle-minded cowboys if you ask me. Hart and Gideon are the only ones who have any brains."

Phoenix laughed at that, lifting a hand in acknowledgement when several of the men sitting at the tables behind them called out to him. "You don't want one of those women for yourself?"

Duke stilled, his entire body stiffening. "No. Not gonna go through that again."

"You were married before?" The question slipped out before she could prevent it, and she regretting it almost instantly when she felt both Hawke and Blade stiffen.

Phoenix helped himself to several biscuits, setting two on the edge of her plate as he whispered in her ear. "Duke doesn't talk about it. His wife was killed when another man took her as a hostage after a bank robbery. Duke was young and inexperienced. He ended up getting cut with his own knife when he went after they guy. Made up his mind to learn to use a knife to protect himself. He's deadly with 'em—more deadly than most men are with a gun."

Aware of their sharp attention, Sarah straightened, smiling an apology in Duke's direction. Seeing the huge man in a different light, and feeling sorry for him for what he went through, Sarah stared at him until he met her gaze. "Thank you, Duke. This looks delicious."

Nodding once, he looked away. "Eat good. I don't like people wastin' my food."

Touched by the brief glimpse of tenderness she'd seen in his eyes, she grinned. "I'm hungry enough to eat Hawke's horse."

To her surprise, Duke's lips twitched. "Well, there's a thought. I'll bet I could make a nice stew—"

"Stay away from my horse." Hawke glared at Duke over his shoulder as he led her to an empty table.

Uncomfortably aware of the attention she drew, she hunched her shoulders and hurried after Hawke.

Blade and Phoenix followed close behind, Blade's hand warm on her back. "Don't look so worried. You're safe here. They're just curious about you."

Nodding, Sarah sat on the hard wooden bench while Phoenix dropped onto the bench across from her.

Hawke set his plate and hers on the table. "Blade and I will go get some coffee. There's fresh milk if you want some."

"I'd love some!"

Hawke's gaze lingered on her lips for several long seconds before meeting hers again. "Eat, Sarah. I'll just be a minute."

Sarah watched him walk away, still unable to believe that such a man would marry her. With shaking hands, she cut into her steak, her mouth watering.

Phoenix spoke from the other side of the table. "Sarah, look at me."

Sarah lifted her gaze, her cheeks burning at his searching look.

Reaching across the table, he covered her hand with his, his smile playful. "I'll earn your trust."

The memory of what he'd done to her only minutes earlier had her cheeks burning even hotter. Lowering her head again, she stabbed her fork into her steak. "I trust you."

"No, you don't." Instead of the angry look she expected, Phoenix smiled again. "If Hawke hadn't been there, you never would have relaxed enough to enjoy my touch. I see the way you keep watching him. You were scared of coming in here, and didn't let more than six inches come between you. You rely on him to keep you safe. He's your security."

Still smiling, he broke a biscuit in half and used his knife to scoop butter from a crock on the table. "I'm your husband, too."

She glanced toward Hawke again. Realizing what she'd done, she sighed and lifted her gaze to Phoenix's. "I know that."

A dark brow went up. "Do you?"

"Of course."

He smiled, a smile that didn't reach his eyes. "Then you know that I'm going to want to spend time alone with you."

Nervous at the prospect, Sarah nodded again and took her first bite, a moan escaping at the explosion of flavor. "Oh, God. This is delicious."

Watching her, Phoenix grinned and placed the buttered biscuit on her plate. "Good, huh?" He touched her hand again, leaning forward as he took it in his. "You get so much pleasure from everything. It makes a man want to see just how much pleasure he can give you."

Hawke and Blade came back to the table, saving her from having to reply. Although neither spoke much as they ate, she could feel their scrutiny the entire time Phoenix asked her questions about her life back in Waco.

"What's your mother going to say when she finds out you're missing?"

Her stomach clenched at the question, and feeling slightly ill, she set her fork aside. "Willy was looking for me, so she'll know that I left with his money. I wish I could write to her and tell her I'm all right. I just hope he and Rose don't take their anger out on her."

Blade paused with his fork halfway to his mouth and lowered it again, leaning forward. "How do you know he was looking for you?"

Without meaning to, she leaned against Hawke, the memory of Willy's features twisted in rage sending a chill through her. "I saw him. I was already on the train and saw him riding down the street looking for me. He looked so mad. Enraged." Straightening, she picked up her fork and started pushing the last of her potatoes around on her plate. "When he couldn't find me, I'll bet he went back to the saloon and questioned my mother. Oh, God. I shouldn't have left her there."

Hawke made that crooning sound, wrapping an arm around her and pulling her into the safety of his embrace. "You can't be responsible for her. She should have been taking care of you."

Blade rubbed her back. "There's nothing to be done about it now. I'm sure she convinced Willy that she didn't know where you are. If you want to write to her, do it. It doesn't matter if she knows where you are now. No one can get near you here."

Sitting up, Sarah sighed and shook her head. "Willy's an outlaw. He's really good with a gun, and he doesn't care about killing anyone who gets in his way. He and his men are wanted, and even the sheriff wouldn't try to arrest them. He's a dangerous man, and you shouldn't underestimate him."

Phoenix handed her another biscuit. "We won't underestimate him, Sarah, but he's walking into something he won't understand. We're a family here. We've had to be, and we rely on each other to survive. We watch each other's backs. He won't get through us to you. Word is spreading about Willy and his gang, and everyone here is already on the lookout for strangers. That's one of the reasons that everyone is interested in seeing you, especially since you're one of us now. Don't worry. We'll take care of Willy and his men if they show up here. You have nothing to be afraid of."

Sarah picked up her fork again, worried that they seemed to be taking this so lightly. "You men are all alike. You won't listen, and I don't know how to convince you how dangerous he is. He's killed men before, and he will again. He's an excellent shot. I heard he even killed a man over a bottle of whiskey. The sheriff is terrified of him and won't lift a finger to stop him."

Rubbing her forehead, she stared down at her plate. "I caused trouble when I left, and now I've brought trouble here. I hate that. I just wanted to get away. I was so scared. I couldn't let Willy do that to me." Blinking back tears, she reached for her glass of milk, taking a sip to swallow the lump in her throat. "I shouldn't have let you talk me into marrying you. It's only going to bring you trouble."

And once it did, they'd blame her, and wouldn't want to be married to her anymore.

* * * *

Hawke pushed his plate and hers toward Phoenix to deal with. "We're married, and that's it. Since you're done eating, we'll go home. Hopefully a bath will calm you enough to get a good night's sleep."

Helping her to her feet, Hawke clenched his jaw when she stiffened, meeting both Blade's and Phoenix's looks of frustration and concern. "I'll take care of it."

With a nod in Duke's direction, he opened the door and went out, keeping Sarah's hand in his and her firmly close behind him so he could protect her body with his. Seeing no danger, he pulled her to his side, unsurprised that she trembled. "There's no reason to be scared. I won't hurt you."

"I know. I trust you. It's awfully dark."

"I know this yard like I know the back of my own hand. I don't want you to ever come out here at night alone, though."

The thought of her being a meal for one of the wild animals that came out at night sent a chill through him. "I'm gonna have to teach you to shoot. I want you to wear a gun whenever you leave the house. Wild animals roam around out here on occasion, and I don't want you to be caught alone to face them."

He didn't mention that Willy might be one of them.

He'd love to get his hands on the man who thought he could take her so coldly and without her permission.

He and the others had dealt with men like Willy before. They'd dealt with a hell of a lot worse, but he had no intention of telling his wife just how violent he could be.

How violent he and his brothers had had to be in order to survive.

He held her closer, regretting that he caused the shiver that went through her. "I don't mean to scare you, but I want you to be aware of the dangers. I want you to be alert and pay attention to your surroundings."

A coyote howled in the distance, the sound drawing a sharp cry from Sarah, who leapt at him, climbing up his body with a desperation that alarmed Hawke, while filling him with masculine satisfaction.

Wrapping her legs around his waist, she buried her face against his neck and fisted her hands in his hair. "What was that?"

Within thinking, he turned his head to kiss her hair, eager to dispel her fears. "Coyote. You'll hear them a lot at night, but they're too far away and rarely come close. You're all right, Sarah."

Cupping the back of her head, he clenched his other hand on her bottom. "You'll get used to the sounds here, but I want you to pay attention to them. I want you to learn them so you know when something's wrong."

She lifted her head slightly, looking around while gripping his neck tightly. "Are you sure he's not going to come after us?"

"I'm sure, little one." The endearment slipped off his tongue as naturally as breathing.

Still gripping his neck, Sarah pressed her face in his hair. "You have a gun, so you could shoot him if he came up to us, couldn't you?"

Amused, Hawke rubbed her hair, breathing in her sweet scent as he strode toward the cabin he shared with his brothers—and now her. "Yes, I could if I had to, but he's more scared of you than you are of him."

"That's not possible."

Pleased that her fear seemed to be easing, and aware that she lifted her head to stare at him, Hawke hid a smile.

Marrying Sarah had been an impulse, something Hawke rarely allowed, but he trusted his instincts.

His gut told him he'd made a decision that would change his life for the better.

Her eyes—as blue as a summer sky—captivated him.

Just listening to her soft voice made him hard.

She was everything a woman should be—everything he'd never expected to have.

Beautiful and passionate.

Brave and resourceful.

Sweet and shy.

And she belonged to him.

*His wife.*

He couldn't forget the way she'd looked and sounded in her passion, or the way she'd come apart in his arms.

She was his wife, and a virgin—an innocent that a man like him didn't deserve.

He understood that she regretted marrying them because she was trying to protect them, but he had to change her mind.

He couldn't stand even the smallest regret.

He'd never wanted anything more than he wanted her in his life, and no had qualms about using her passion to tie her to him.

Carrying her slight weight, Hawke cuddled her close and went through the door of the cabin. With the scent and feel of soft woman all around him, his cock got harder by the minute—a torture he never wanted to end.

He didn't deserve such a woman, but nothing on earth could keep him from taking her.

After kicking the door closed behind him, he made his way across the dark room, pausing next to his bed, reluctant to release her. "My bed is probably gonna be too hard for you, but I'll stuff it more when I get the chance. We ordered one while we were in Tulsa."

Her eyes went wide, barely visible in the low light of the moon shining in through the windows. "You didn't have to do that!"

Anxious to make love to her, he reluctantly lowered her to his mattress, running his hand over her hair before straightening. "I'll start a fire. It's a warm night, but I don't want you getting chilled from your bath."

And also give him enough light to see her.

With his cock throbbing with anticipation, he went to start the fire.

* * * *

Sitting back, Sarah reached down to remove her boots, struck by the intimacy of being in Hawke's bed.

The moonlight streaming in through the large windows allowed her to watch his tall form, which she did as she set her boots aside, curling her toes against the hard wooden floor.

He lit a lantern and set it in the middle of the table, every movement smooth and filled with a powerful grace that sent little shivers through her.

Glancing at her, he made his way to the fireplace. "The fire will warm the water for your bath, too. It's a warm enough night that bathing in cool water should feel good, though, especially when the fire warms the room even more."

A slight breeze blew in from the open windows, but it did nothing to ease the oppressive humidity in the air. She tossed her shawl aside before removing her socks, tucking her feet under her, and settled back to watch Hawke stoke the fire. She couldn't tear her gaze away from the sight of his broad shoulders and long black hair streaming down his back. "Yes. That'll feel good."

Setting her boots aside, Sarah wrapped her arms around her knees to watch her husband, mesmerized by his sheer size. Remembering how muscular her shoulders felt under her hands, she sighed. "You don't have to worry about giving up your bed for me. I'm used to sleeping on the floor."

As the fire licked at the logs, Blade and Phoenix came through the door, each carrying buckets of water. Both men stilled, their features hardening in anger.

Hawke straightened and turned, not even glancing at them. "You slept on the floor?"

"Of course." Wary of his tone, Sarah glanced at Blade, who appeared just as angry. "I made a pallet on the floor. There wasn't a need for me to have a mattress when I wasn't bringing men to my room." The thought of what would have happened if she hadn't run away had her pulling her shawl closer. "That probably would have changed if I'd stayed, but sleeping on the floor was better than the alternative."

Swallowing the lump in her throat, she forced a smile. "Willy would've thrown a fit if he had to be on the floor in the attic."

"Don't." Blade set the buckets aside and rushed to her side. "Don't think about it." Kneeling on the floor in front of her, he took her hands in his. "Don't think about what might have happened. It didn't happen. It won't happen. You're here now. We're your husbands now and we'll keep you safe. Just do what we say and you have nothing to fear from him, or anyone else."

Sarah blew out a breath, once again struck by the knowledge of how many lives would be affected by her actions. "I didn't think things through, and I'm afraid others might have to pay for my actions. My mother and I weren't close, but I don't want her to have to pay for what I did. Coming here sounded like my only chance, but I'm afraid I made a big mistake."

Hawke moved closer, lighting another lamp on the table next to his bed before lowering himself to the empty space next to her. "It wasn't."

Phoenix set the buckets on the fireplace next to the others. "I don't think she believes we can protect her."

Unlacing moccasins that went all the way to his knees, Hawke held her gaze. "She has no reason to believe us. She'll learn." He stripped out of his buckskin shirt, revealing a wide, muscular chest that gleamed like dark copper in the firelight. "Learning to trust us to protect her will take time, but once she realizes that we can, she won't be so scared anymore."

Standing again, Hawke turned to smile at her. "And once she gets used to our touch, she'll settle some."

Sarah wished she'd listened more to the girls back at the whorehouse. If she had, she'd know how to please them.

According to what she'd heard over the years, once a man had his pleasure, he lost interest in lovemaking.

If she could learn how to give them pleasure, she could distract them from touching her. They'd be so wrapped up in their own hungers that they wouldn't pay any attention to how much she liked their touch.

Then they'd respect her.

Hawke went to the fireplace and retrieved two of the buckets. "Blade'll bathe you. We'll get cleaned up and ready for bed." His eyes narrowed on hers. "You'll sleep with me tonight."

Blade slipped out of his own shirt, revealing a chest as wide and dark as Hawke's. "Phoenix, will you please go get the warm water Duke has waiting while I get Sarah ready for her bath?"

Phoenix grinned. "Of course. Go slow, though. I don't want to miss anything."

Shaking his head, Hawke walked on bare feet to her side, reaching out a hand for her. "Go get the water, Phoenix. We're not about to rush anything."

*  *  *  *

"No, we're gonna go nice and slow." Blade took Sarah's other hand, pulling her to his side. "Let's get you out of these clothes."

She nodded, her eyes wide as she looked back and forth between him and Hawke.

Wanting her attention focused on him, Blade gripped her shoulders, turning her to face him before reaching for the top button of her shirt again. "A nice warm bath will make you feel better."

Sarah smiled, shocking him when she reached out to touch his chest. "I feel better already. I'd like to learn how to please you. Will you teach me how?"

Troubled by the hesitancy in her eyes, Blade shared a look with Hawke over her head. "You're doing just fine. I like the feel of your hands on me."

She blew out a breath, obviously relieved. "Good. Show me more."

"In a hurry, huh?" Blade reached for the top button of her shirt, unsurprised that his hands shook. "Why don't you just relax and let me explore you?"

Sarah stiffened, biting her lip and pulling back slightly. "No!"

Confused and wondering what he'd done to scare her, Blade lifted her chin, frowning when she looked away. "What is it? What's wrong, Sarah? Did I scare you?"

He couldn't imagine what had frightened her, especially after she'd responded so beautifully earlier. When she tried to turn away, he tightened his grip, careful not to hurt her. "Tell me, honey."

The endearment brought a flash of pleasure to her eyes, a sharp reminder of how little affection she'd had in her life. "It's just that I want to please you, but you won't let me."

Amused and more than a little relieved, he smiled, holding her chin while he began unbuttoning her shirt again. "You please me just fine."

She closed her eyes when Hawke closed in behind her. "But I want to touch you."

"You will." Bending to touch his lips to hers, he finished unbuttoning her shirt, parting the sides just as Phoenix walked back in.

"Well, isn't that a beautiful sight?"

Straightening, Blade smiled at the awe in his brother's voice. Looking down, he pulled her shirt from her skirt, cupping her breasts while Hawke slid the shirt from her shoulders. "Yes. It certainly is."

His cock jumped, the sight of Sarah's body gleaming in the faint light as arousing as a fantasy. "You're so beautiful. Let's get you out of these clothes so I can see the rest of you."

He slid his hands from her breasts to the fastening of her skirt, watching her eyes flutter closed when Hawke replaced his hands with his own. "You like that, don't you?"

Her hands slid to his shoulders and tightened, a moan escaping just as her skirt puddled at her feet. "I—um. I don't know. Please. Um. You don't need to touch me. Let me—oh, God."

"Oh, I need to touch you very much." Watching her face, Blade smiled at the picture she made. Every moment he spent with her, he found himself drawn even deeper.

She gasped when Hawke's fingers closed on her nipples, arching into the fingers Blade held over her slit. "But it's not good this way. I'm supposed to make you feel good."

With sudden understanding, he flicked a glance at Hawke and then at Phoenix, struggling not to show his anger. Keeping his voice low and soothing, he forced a smile. "She's trying to treat us the way Rose, her mother, and the women back in Waco treated the men who came to visit them." Slipping his finger through her folds, he smiled at her gasp. "I can't blame her for that."

"No!" Gripping his wrist, she writhed in Hawke's embrace. "I don't want to be like them. Hell and tarnation! I'm never gonna get this right."

To Blade's shocked delight, Hawke released her breast to deliver a sharp slap to her shapely bottom. "I won't tolerate any bad language from you."

Phoenix moved closer, sliding his fingers into her hair. "This is gonna be a hell of a lot more fun than I'd thought."

Hawke frowned. "It's more than just fun. She's our wife and our responsibility. I won't have her swearing, and I sure as hell won't tolerate being lied to anymore."

The misery and confusion in her eyes knotted Blade's stomach. Gathering her against him, he lifted her and strode toward the tub. "Phoenix, fill the tub. I want to get her settled and get to the bottom of this."

"You don't have to get me settled!"

Blade didn't bother to hide his smile, rocking her gently while Hawke and Phoenix filled the tub and tested the water. "You're a fascinating woman—one I reckon it'll take the rest of my life to figure out. You steal an outlaw's gold, get on a train—alone—despite the fact that you've never been out of Waco, head to a town you've never heard of to marry a stranger."

He settled her in the tub, and taking her hand, he lifted it and began to soap it, slowly working his way up her arm. "You take on Hawke, when most grown men wouldn't even approach him, want to shoot Hart and Gideon, and give yourself to us when most women would have been hysterical."

Shifting his attention to her breasts, he let his soapy hands slide over them, paying particular attention to her nipples. "But the gift of some material and soap makes you cry, and getting pleasure upsets you."

Phoenix lifted her foot from the tub and began to wash it, smiling down at her. "You sure are a contrary woman." Lifting her leg higher, he grinned. "I'd rather deal with the spunk than with the tears."

"We all would." Staring down at her from above her head, Hawke ran a finger down her cheek. "We know that you like the way we touch you and know that you're aroused. Why are you tryin' to hide it?"

Phoenix rinsed her leg and hung it over the side of the tub before reaching for the other. "I wouldn't keep Hawke waitin' for an answer long, if I were you. When he uses that tone, his patience is runnin' out."

Dropping to his knees beside the tub, Hawke tilted her chin back and touched his lips to hers. "She'll learn about each of us herself. Won't you, little one?"

Smiling up at him, she sucked in a breath, squirming when Blade slid his hands lower and began washing her stomach. "I hope so."

Blade ran his fingers through the soft curls covering her mound, fascinated by her uninhibited response. "So, are you going to tell us what's bothering you, or do we have to force it out of you?"

Phoenix rinsed her other leg and draped it over the other side of the tub, and knelt between them. "Please make us force it out of you. I'd love the chance to spank your pretty bottom."

Slipping his hand between her legs, Blade shook his head. "If there's any spanking to be done, I'm gonna do it. Now, are you gonna talk to us, Sarah?"

\* \* \* \*

Sarah lost the struggle to keep her breathing even, a cry escaping when Blade's finger slipped between her folds. "Oh! How can this happen so fast?"

Blade pressed his finger more firmly against a spot that had her writhing in the tub, sloshing water over the side. "Your clit is really sensitive. We can give you a lot of pleasure by stroking it."

When the pleasure became almost unbearable, she grabbed his wrist, disappointed when he stopped stroking her clit and took her hand in his.

His eyes darkened, the smile playing at his lips filled with erotic intent. "Or I can arouse you and leave you like this."

Fighting to get her hand free, she cried out again when Hawke focused his attention on her nipples. "Oh!" Pressing her legs against the sides of the tub for leverage, Sarah arched almost completely out of the water.

Blade tightened his hold on her hand, lifting it to his lips. "Or, I can spank your little pussy if you misbehave."

Sarah froze, the image of Blade spanking such a sensitive place sending a rush of heat to her clit. "You c-can't spank me there." Her words came out in a breathless rush, the pressure on her nipples intensifying the heat between her thighs.

Blade tapped her clit, the shock making her jolt. "I certainly can— and will. Now, tell us what's going on in that pretty head."

Her cheeks burned, but found her attempt to avert her gaze thwarted by Hawke's fingers firming on her jaw. "I just wanted you to respect me." Shrugging, she closed her eyes, uneasy at the tense silence. "I know it's silly, especially with my background, but—"

"Open your eyes, Sarah."

Her eyes flew open at the icy command in Blade's voice, her gaze captured by his before she had the chance to look away.

Sliding his hand to her waist, he bent low until she saw nothing but him. "What have any of us done to you to make you think we don't respect you?"

Phoenix slid his hands up her thighs, sharing a look with Hawke before frowning down at her. "Is it because of what we did to you earlier? Because of what you're doing now?"

Hawke touched his lips to her hair. "You're our wife. I know that you have a different idea about what sex is, but if you thought that just because we didn't take you on our wedding night, that we weren't going to expect to have you in our beds, you're sadly mistaken."

Blade slid his hand over her belly. "We're your husbands. Did you really think that just because we're gentle with you that we wouldn't take you? That doesn't mean that we don't respect you. We all want you—very much."

Feeling foolish, Sarah moaned at the slide of Hawke's slippery hands over her breasts, sucking in a breath when Phoenix's hands moved higher on her thighs. "It's not that. I just wanted you to respect me enough to let me go through the door first."

Fighting the pleasure proved useless, her breath coming out in pants as they took her closer and closer to the edge. "I know. It's stupid, but—" She yelped when Hawke slid his hands under her arms and yanked her from the tub with one quick movement.

Spinning her to face him, he gripped her upper arms and lifted her to her toes. "You're not married to white men, Sarah. We're part Indian, too. That means we take a little from either side—things that make sense to us."

With a warning look, Blade pulled Sarah to his side, wrapping a large cloth around her. "We see how the white men let their woman go through a door in front of them, and it doesn't make a hell of a lot of sense to us. Our father and his people always went through the doorway before their women. If there's danger on the other side of the door, we meet it first."

Hawke made a sound in his throat that sounded suspiciously like a growl before he turned away muttering something about white men and their stupidity.

Shooting a grin at his brother, Blade gathered her close and began to dry her. "It seems stupid to us that a man would allow the woman he was protecting to go through a door first. We've had words with the others at times, especially when one of us went through a door before Maggie or Savannah, but that's the way we are."

From across the room, Hawke turned, his features like stone. "We're not like white men. We're half-breeds, remember?" He met Blade's glare with one of his own. "She's just going to have to get used to the fact that we're not like other men."

Understanding his sensitivity about being a half-breed, Sarah smiled. "Thank God. I like you just the way you are."

Hawke blinked. "You do?"

Nodding, she wrapped her arms around herself, embarrassed at being naked while all three of her husbands were still dressed. "Of course. You've been very kind to me. That's why it hurt so much to think you didn't respect me. I know it's silly, but—"

"It's not silly at all." Blade wrapped the cloth around her. "You just didn't understand why one of us goes through the door first. It's just our way. Do you feel better?"

"Much." Grinning, she leaned back against Blade, the knots in her stomach loosening. "If you don't respect me, you can't like me, and I want you to like me."

With a smile, Blade slid his hand inside the large, scratchy cloth. "We like you very much. Is that why you're so determined to give us pleasure—so we'll like you?"

Squirming, she sucked in a breath at the feel of his warm hands closing over her breasts. "Not exactly."

"Why, *exactly*?"

Lulled by the seduction in Blade's silky tone, Sarah lifted her arms to wrap them around his neck. Fascinated that every slide of his hands over her nipples sent an answering surge of hunger to her slit, Sarah moaned and watched Phoenix's approach, not minding at all when the towel fell away. "My mother said that the reason men came to the whorehouse was because their wives didn't like fulfilling their marital duties."

Phoenix frowned, his gaze raking over her. "So you wanted us to go to the whorehouse in Tulsa?"

"No!" Sarah didn't even want to imagine Hawke, Blade, or Phoenix in the arms of one of those women. Struggling to focus proved more difficult when Phoenix's hands closed over her hips, his thumbs stroking her abdomen while Blade continued to tug at her nipples. "I thought if you didn't think I liked it, you would respect me."

Blade applied pressure and tugged lightly at her nipples, groaning softly when she moaned. "God save us from thinking women."

Insulted, she gasped, a gasp that ended in a moan when Phoenix parted her folds and slid a finger over her clit, the resulting tingling sensation weakening her knees. "W–women who th–think too much get, um, themselves into t–trouble."

Leaning against the post in the center of the room, Hawke stared at her with eyes narrowed to slits. "Our woman used her wits to get out of trouble."

Straightening, he started toward her. "She's smart and has good instincts." He reached for the fastening of his leggings, his fingers working at the ties as he slowly closed the distance between them. "She has a sweet look about her, but she's no shrinking violet." He finished loosening his buckskin pants and shoved them down his legs, a small smile playing at his lips. "Are you, little one?"

Gasping at the sight of his cock, Sarah pushed back against Blade, her heart pounding. With Blade's hands massaging her breasts, and Phoenix's hand splayed over her abdomen, she trembled as she watched Hawke move closer. "Oh, God. I don't think it's gonna fit."

Her pussy clenched at the thought of something that big and hard going into her.

Remembering the incident with Willy, she swallowed heavily, lifting her gaze to Hawke's, alarmed to find the same need hardening his features.

The look in his eyes, though, gleamed with possessiveness instead of evil. He didn't seem the least embarrassed about his nakedness, and moved slowly as he approached her as if knowing of her curiosity and needed some time to adjust to his nakedness before he slid into bed with her.

Wondering if all three of them planned to take her, she turned to look at Blade and Phoenix.

Blade smiled faintly and bent to nuzzle her neck. "No. Only Hawke will take you tonight. The first time will hurt a little and you'll be sore afterward, so Phoenix and I will wait, but we want to be here when you lose your virginity. There'll be times when we each want to be alone with you, but most of the time, we'll be together when we take you."

Sarah gulped, watching Hawke circle to the other side of the bed out of the corner of her eye, while keeping an eye on both Blade and Phoenix. "You're going to watch us?"

Blade smiled. "Of course. If I can't be the one taking my wife's virginity, at least I'm going to watch."

Naked, Hawke was even more intimidating—all copper skin and hard muscle.

Powerful muscles bunched and shifted with every step, emphasizing his masculinity and making his long, thick cock even more threatening.

Gulping again, she lifted her gaze to his, reassured by the tenderness and affection in his eyes. "Will you show me what to do?"

From behind her, Blade groaned. "That's probably the most arousing thing I've ever heard a woman say before."

Hawke extended a hand, smiling faintly when she readily placed her hand in his. "I need to wash off first. Come wash my back."

\* \* \* \*

Hawke pulled her closer before climbing into the tub, moving slowly so as not to startle her. He'd seen the trepidation in her eyes, and hoped that letting her have the chance to touch him before he took her would ease some of her fears.

Bringing her hand to his lips seemed as natural as breathing, the delight in her eyes telling him that he'd made the right decision. "You said that you want to give us pleasure. It would give me a lot of pleasure to feel your hands on me."

Her smile held relief, and he could see the tenseness in her body ease. "I'd like to touch you." The hitch in her breath made his cock jump, his own body tightening at her nearness.

Confident that she was warm enough, he reached out to wrap a hand around her waist, keeping her beside him when she would have reached for the towel. "I want you naked. It's hot in here anyway. Get the other bar of soap from the shelf."

When she turned, he took advantage of the situation by running a hand over her lush ass. "I think I'm gonna like being bathed by a naked woman."

Phoenix stretched out on the floor, leaning back on his hands and watching Sarah's every move. "She's got a nice ass, doesn't she? Just knowing how tight she's gonna be has me close to comin' in my pants."

Hawke stiffened, automatically reaching for Sarah as she turned back and pulling her protectively to his side. "She's not one of the whores you're used to."

Blade dropped to the side of the tub, running his hands up and down Sarah's legs. "No, she's not. But that doesn't mean we have to treat her as if she's made of glass. After the way she responded earlier, I'm looking forward to exploring that passion."

Hawke hid a smile when Sarah soaped a cloth and began washing his arms and shoulders, intrigued and aroused at the sensuality in every movement.

Hawke slid under the water, water sloshing over the sides as he dunked his head. Sitting up again, he leaned back, pushing his hair over the side of the tub to let it drip on the floor. Delighted by the hunger in her eyes, but well aware of her innocence, Hawke braced an arm on each side of the tub, hoping to appear less threatening. "Would you wash my hair?"

Sarah gulped and lifted her gaze to his, her eyes alight with anticipation. "Of course."

Noticing that as her arousal grew, she appeared less and less self-conscious about her nakedness, Hawke shared a look with his brothers.

By unspoken agreement, all three of them had adopted non-threatening positions in an attempt to get their naked wife to settle some and get comfortable being naked in their presence.

Whenever she got within arm's reach of any of them, they reached out to touch her—soft caresses that drew moans from her.

Watching her lather her hands, he bit back a groan, struggling not to imagine her soap-slicked hands on his cock.

Setting the soap aside, she moved in behind him. "Are you ready?"

Sharing a smile with Blade, Hawke fisted his hands on the sides of the tub. "Very."

Sliding her hands through his hair, she sighed. "It's so soft."

Blade rose and slowly moved toward her. "Not as soft as yours."

Tilting his head back, Hawke watched Blade move in behind her, his hands coming around her to cover her breasts. "You like being naked in front of us, don't you?"

Sarah blushed, arching her breasts into Blade's hands while her hands firmed in Hawke's hair, scrubbing his scalp with increasing speed. "I can feel your eyes on me, but it doesn't feel the way it did when Willy looked at me."

Hawke dunked his head under the water again to rinse the soap away, quickly sitting up again. "Come here, little one."

Using one hand to sluice the water from his face, he snaked the other around her waist to pull her to his side. "That's because you know we won't hurt you. You're beginning to trust us, aren't you?"

Blade's eyes narrowed. "She trusted *you* from the start. For Phoenix and me, it's taking a little longer."

Sarah shrugged, wrapping her hand around Hawke's forearm. "I just feel safe with all of you, but kind of nervous at the same time."

Blade bent to nuzzle her neck, his fingers dancing over her nipples. "You *are* safe with us. We'd never hurt you." Sliding a hand down her body, he parted her folds, giving Hawke a clear view of her slit, which had him fighting not to spill his seed. "But you're smart enough to be nervous, because we're going to teach you things about yourself you've never even imagined."

His hand flattened and came down on her clit, eliciting a cry from her. "Like how good a little pain can feel."

Hawke cursed under his breath, fighting for control when moisture leaked from his cock. His balls tightened painfully when Sarah's shocked cry became a pleasure-filled moan and she began to rock her hips against Blade's hand.

Blade smiled down at her, his eyes filled with pride and possessiveness. "See, honey? That little sting only made the hunger stronger."

Watching her, Hawke hurriedly finished washing himself, anxious to sink his cock deep. Knowing that he had to be gentle with his virgin bride, he took several deep breaths in an effort to rein in his need. Rising to his feet, he glanced over at Phoenix's approach, his chest swelling at the wonder in his youngest brother's eyes. Holding out his hand, he stepped out of the tub. "Cloth. Now."

* * * *

Sarah gasped, stunned at the change in him.

Hawke went from patient watchfulness to hungry warrior in an instant.

Alarmed at the fierce hunger in his eyes and the power in the body that strode toward her, she attempted to step back, a whimper escaping when Blade's arms closed around her from behind.

"Easy, honey. Hawke wants you." His soft chuckle against her ear sent a shiver through her. "It looks like he can't wait anymore."

She gulped again, wrapping her arms around herself. "Hawke?"

To her surprise, he dropped to his knees in front of her. Without hesitation, his hands closed over her hips, his firm grip sending her off balance. "You know damned well I won't hurt you. I want a taste of what's mine."

Caught by Blade from behind, she cried out when Hawke parted her folds, her breath catching when Hawke touched his tongue to her clit.

Laughing softly, Phoenix bent to touch his tongue to her nipple. "Hawke looks pretty hungry. You'd better spread those thighs wide and give him what he wants."

Hawke licked her slit again, his eyes glittering and so dark they appeared black. "Don't try to scare her, Phoenix."

Fisting a hand in her hair, Blade pulled her head to the side and scraped his teeth over her neck. "No. That's my job."

Shocked at Hawke's raw hunger, and Blade's threatening tone, she cried out again, lost in pleasure and nerves. Shivers of delight raced up and down her spine, the attention to her clit and her nipple sharpening her arousal to a fever pitch. "God! I can't stop shaking. Please. Do something."

Hawke straightened, wrapped an arm around her, and sent her tumbling onto his bed. "I'm about to."

Hawke eased her to her back and reached out to touch his fingertip to her nipple, making it throb. "Yes, little one. You like my touch." He sounded so surprised by that, and she felt herself drawn closer. "Look at me." Staring down at her, his eyes gentled as he slid a hand down her body. "You tremble, but there's no fear in your eyes. Just desire."

Humbled that what she felt mattered to him, Sarah parted her legs wider and arched toward him, wanting him more with every passing second. "Yes. You make me feel things I never imagined." Sliding a hand into his long, damp hair, she tried to smile, but the slide of his finger over her clit made nothing but a cry of delight possible.

Brushing his lips over hers, he groaned and continued to caress her clit, making her hot all over. "All ours."

The reminder that Blade and Phoenix watched had her reaching for Hawke.

Wrapping her arms around his neck, she thrilled at the coolness of his long, straight hair gliding through her fingers. "It feels good to belong to you. I never thought I'd belong to anyone this way. You're so gentle with me."

Hawke's eyes narrowed, glittering with something that made her stomach flutter and sent a rush of moisture from her pussy. "It won't always be this gentle. There are times that I need more, and it'll be rougher, but I won't hurt you. I want you to remember that."

Sarah stiffened, but he covered her lips with his, the pressure forcing her to part her lips to allow him inside. Moaning at the feel of his tongue sliding against hers, she hung on to him as warm desire overtook her.

His kiss had a different taste than that of his brothers, the slow slide of his tongue over hers gentle, but demanding.

Lifting his head, he stared down at her with eyes narrowed to slits. "It doesn't mean I don't like you, or respect you. It means I want you too much to find the kind of pretty words and gentleness you need tonight."

Gripping his hair, she pulled him closer, lifting her hips in invitation. "I need *you*. I love the way it feels when you hold me." Her words came out in nothing more than a rush of breath, but the flare of heat in Hawke's eyes told her that he'd heard her. "Please. I want to be yours."

"You are." Lifting her face higher, he stared into her eyes while his fingers moved against her slit. "Make no mistake about that."

She writhed against him, needing more. She moved her thigh against his cock, stilling when she realized it felt as hard as iron.

Apprehensive now, but with a need that wouldn't be denied, Sarah whimpered, burying her face against his throat. She heard the splash of water, and turned her head slightly to find both Blade and Phoenix rinsing their naked soaped bodies with buckets full of water from the tub, soaking the wood floor.

Blade hurriedly ran the cloth over himself, wringing out his now loose hair before hurrying to her side. Reclining next to the mattress, he ran his hand over her other breast, tugging at her nipple. "You belong to all of us."

Sarah gasped when he lifted her hand to the pillow above her head, a move that left her breast unprotected and left her feeling even more vulnerable. "Oh, God. I don't know what to do."

Phoenix knelt behind Blade's legs, pulling her knee up and spreading her wider. "Let us worry about that. Just lie back and enjoy."

Hawke moved over her, covering her body with his. Bracing himself on his elbows, he cupped her face, his own just inches from hers. "I'm sorry that this first time is gonna hurt. I'll be as gentle as I can, but the first time always hurts for a virgin."

Swallowing a moan at the thought of Willy's evilness, she looked at each of them. "Thank God it's you. I don't even want to think about how—"

Hawke stiffened, his eyes going hard. "He didn't—and won't. It's just us. As slow and gentle as you need."

Reaching up with her right hand, she cupped his cheek, smiling at the flare of satisfaction in his eyes. "I trust you."

Phoenix lifted her leg, his lips warm as they ran over her calf. "Little by little, you'll learn to trust us, too."

Sarah couldn't look away from the intensity of Hawke's dark gaze as he positioned his cock at her pussy opening, trembling when he slid a hand under her bottom and lifted it. "Hawke?"

She wrapped her free leg around him, an instinctive movement that felt so natural, but that Hawke had apparently been waiting for.

Suddenly, he was completely between her legs, his powerful thighs pushing hers up and wider. "Easy, little one."

The feel of his cock against her pussy opening shocked her into stilling, the heat of it startling. "Hawke! Oh, God. It's there."

Blade murmured to her in a soothing tone before glancing at Hawke. "Be careful with her."

"Shut up, Blade." Groaning, he pushed his cock more firmly against her. "I know it's there, Sarah. Right against your hot little pussy. Easy, little one." Hawke brushed his lips over hers, nibbling softly at her bottom lip. "Taking a virgin requires patience." Lifting his head he smiled faintly, his smile filled with tension as he slid his fingers over her clit. "But our little one's more than ready to be taken, and I don't want to make her wait. She's getting ready to come and I want to take her before she does."

Taking her mouth with his in a kiss filled with tenderness, Hawke began to push his cock into her.

Whimpering when it started to burn, she bucked against him, gasping when the head of his cock pushed through her hymen and into her.

Aware of Blade's lips on her arm and his hand closing on hers, she stiffened, stunned by the hard fullness filling her.

Too big. Too hot. Too hard.

The slice of pain ripped through her, and a sob escaped as tears trickled from the corners of her eyes and into her hair.

He was inside her.

Swallowing her cry, Hawke groaned, his big body trembling against hers. He lifted his head, his eyes narrowed to slits as he stared down at her. "No more pain, little one." He kissed her tears away, not moving as though waiting for a sign from her.

As if to prove his point, he moved, pausing when she cried out in anticipation of more pain. "See? It won't hurt that way again. The hard part's over."

Blade released her hand and stood. "I have some more water next to the fireplace to warm."

Phoenix took Blade's place, taking her hand again and using his other to toy with her nipple. "She's so beautiful. I'll bet her pussy's tight as hell."

Hawke groaned when she involuntarily clenched on his cock. "It is." He began to move, withdrawing his cock until only the head remained inside her before plunging deep again. He watched her face the entire time, a small smile playing at his lips. "I told you it wouldn't hurt anymore. I'll go nice and slow, little one."

Slightly alarmed at the strain in his voice, Sarah gripped Phoenix's hand, unable to hold back her cries as the pleasure mounted, replacing the pain.

She felt a part of something more than herself—part of Hawke. She gripped him tighter, her eyes burning with tears.

She belonged.

"Hawke!" The sensations built to a fevered pitch, and the memory of the pleasure to come had her reaching for it.

"Yes, little one. I've got you."

"Please! Please make me yours."

"You are mine."

Sarah's breath caught when Hawke began to pump into her, the speed of his hard thrusts sending her spiraling into the world of pleasure she'd glimpsed earlier.

The tingling heat started at her slit and seemed to explode, showering in the delicious sparks of ecstasy.

Sarah panicked and clung to Hawke. "Oh! Oh, God. Hawke!"

"I love the way you say my name." Gathering her against him, he murmured something soft and crooning to her in a language she didn't understand.

Just the sound of his voice proved enough, the deep cadence of it giving her something to hold on to while the pleasure spun her out of control.

Hawke surged deep and stilled, gathering her close. "You're mine. You're always safe with me. I'd die to protect you. I'd kill for you."

He held her that way for what seemed an eternity, caressing her as she came down to earth again.

Holding her tightly against him, he slowly lowered her bottom to the bed. Bracing himself on his elbows, he ran his fingers through her hair as he stared down at her. "You all right?"

Sarah involuntarily clenched on his cock, fascinated by his look of indulgence, and still overwhelmed by his lovemaking.

Weak.

Lethargic.

Wonderful.

Smiling, she wiggled against him, giggling when he groaned. "Yes. I never really understood how it works. It's very intimate, isn't it?"

Hawke's lips twitched before he bent to touch them to hers. "Very much so."

Frowning, she squeezed Blade's hand, struck by the hunger in his eyes. "I don't understand how my mother and the others can do this for money." Her face burned when Hawke stiffened above her. "I mean—how can they do this with someone like Willy when he's so mean? I know they don't care about the men who take them. It's such an intimate thing to do with someone just because they hand you a coin or two."

Phoenix, looking decidedly uncomfortable, sighed and rubbed her leg. "It's different with you. Sometimes, it's just about the pleasure. It's just another body."

"That sounds awful!" She tried to imagine what it would be like with anyone other than her husbands, and found that she couldn't. "Just thinking about it makes me feel cold."

Hawke withdrew slowly, kneeling between her thighs. "It's not something you're ever going to have to worry about. You're our wife, and no other man is ever going to take you."

Blade came forward with a bucket, holding a cloth in his free hand. "The intimacy will get even stronger when we get to know each other better. Think about how that'll feel."

Self-conscious about her position, she nodded and started to sit up, but Phoenix, now reclining beside her on one elbow, flattened a hand on her stomach to keep her in place. "Just relax, honey."

Hawke dipped the cloth into the bucket and wrung it out, his gaze holding hers. "Be still so I can clean you up. You'll feel better."

Shaken, Sarah nodded, her cheeks burning hotter. "I can do it myself."

Hawke shook his head and ran the cloth gently over her slit, holding her steady when she flinched. "No."

She didn't expect him to do more than wipe her with it, but Hawke seemed in no hurry to finish.

Parting her folds, he wiped her thoroughly, every slow swipe of the warm cloth easing some of the soreness. He dipped the cloth in the water again and held it against her slit, his patience seemingly endless. "Does this feel better?"

Her face burned as she nodded. "Yes." She stared up at him, surprised that he appeared deep in thought. She glanced at Phoenix and then Blade, only to see both of them watching Hawke, their expressions thoughtful and slightly amused.

Both turned to her as if sensing her gaze, their reassuring smiles not reassuring at all.

Phoenix clasped her hand in his, brushing his lips over her fingers. "I never thought I'd see the day."

Although he whispered, Hawke must have heard it. It seemed to snap him out of his thoughts, and with a glare at Phoenix, he removed the warm cloth and tossed it into the bowl. "It's late."

Minutes later, she found herself tucked into bed—Hawke's hard body wrapped protectively around her from behind.

She watched Blade and Phoenix take the tub outside and dump it before bringing it back in, unable to tear her eyes away from the sight of their muscular bodies gleaming in the waning firelight.

Blade banked the fire, and turned to smile at her, his cock framed magnificently by the low fire burning behind him. "We don't need the fire anymore. Do you want me to leave a lantern lit for you? I don't want you to wake up in the night not knowing where you are."

Hawke groaned and pulled her closer. "She'll know, and I'll wake up if she does."

Phoenix fisted his cock, his eyes narrowed. "I'll be outside for a few minutes."

Blade chuckled at that. "Put it out of your mind."

"It's not my mind I'm worried about." Phoenix turned to glance back at her. "I want her too much to think about anything else."

His eyes met hers across the room, the hunger in them unmistakable. With a curse, he turned and went out the door, slamming it behind him.

Hawke flattened his hand on her stomach and pulled her closer, his nakedness warming her. "He's just aroused. Not mad. Go to sleep. Are you warm enough?"

Relieved at the tenderness in his touch and in his voice, Sarah turned her head toward him. "Yes. Thank you." Sleeping next to him was probably warmer than sleeping next to the fireplace.

"Keeping you warm is part of taking care of you. Go to sleep."

Chilled at his cold tone, Sarah turned back and nodded, watching the fire.

She didn't understand men—or Hawke—enough to know why he went from tenderness to hard anger without warning.

She couldn't deny, though, that she felt safer lying with him than she'd ever felt in her life.

Safe, warm, and too lethargic to move, she let her eyes flutter closed, and was asleep before Phoenix came back.

# Chapter Eight

Something was different.

Sarah woke with a sense of urgency, realizing almost immediately that Hawke no longer slept beside her.

He'd held her through the night, and each time she woke, he gathered her closer, murmuring to her that she was safe.

She hadn't slept so well in years.

"Good morning."

Recognizing Phoenix's voice at once, she sat up abruptly, clutching the soft blanket Hawke had covered her with in front of her. "Good morning."

Pushing her hair back from her face, she eyed him warily, remembering how tense he'd been when he'd stormed out the door the night before. "I never heard you come back in last night, but the last time I woke up, I saw you sleeping."

Instinctively looking around the cabin, she noticed that the fire had long ago gone out, and that both Blade's and Phoenix's beds had been straightened. Sunlight streamed through the windows, telling her that she'd slept well into the morning.

"So you looked for me last night?"

Sarah shrugged, pulling the blanket higher as he approached. "I felt guilty. I know you were hurting and it was my fault."

Phoenix grinned and moved closer, reaching for her hand as he crouched next to her. "If you're going to feel guilty every time you arouse me, you're going to spend way too much time feeling guilty. I'm aroused every time I'm near you."

He tugged at the blanket, pulling it from her fist to puddle at her waist. "I won't let you hide yourself from me, though."

Holding her breath, she watched him slowly lift his hand, the feel of it sliding up to cup her breast sending shivers of delight up and down her spine. "Oh."

"Yeah—oh." Running his hand over one breast and then the other, he paused to give her nipples the attention they ached for. "It's hard to believe that I have a wife." Fisting a hand in her hair, he pulled her head back slightly. Still caressing her breasts, he brushed his lips against hers. "We're alone. Just you and me. Hawke and Blade left hours ago. Are you afraid I'm going to attack you?"

When he lifted his head, she searched his features, trying to judge his mood. "No. Of course not."

"Well, that's a start, anyway." Frowning slightly, he ran his hand over the blanket covering her leg. "How are you feeling?"

Understanding his meaning, she averted her gaze, her face burning. "I'm fine."

Phoenix's eyes narrowed, a small smile playing at his lips. "I'm sure you must be sore, but you're embarrassed to tell me about it. I watched you lose your virginity, remember?"

To her embarrassment, her stomach growled. "I know."

Smiling, Phoenix tugged at her nipple and rose. "I fixed some coffee for you the way you like it. It's there on the table. There are a couple of biscuits filled with egg and bacon waiting for you. They won't be real hot, but I wrapped them in a napkin and put 'em next to the fire."

"Thank you." She expected him to leave to give her some privacy, but he merely crossed his arms over his chest and waited expectantly, a small smile playing at his lips.

Tucking the blanket around her, she wondered how she could get out of bed and to the table without revealing her nakedness.

Phoenix took the dilemma out of her hands, gripping her waist and lifting her to her feet with a show of strength that stunned her. "You're welcome. Would you be scared if I try to kiss you again?"

Sarah smiled, delighted that it mattered to him. "No. I'd like for you to kiss me." Wondering how he would react, she flattened a hand on his chest. "I'm sorry about yesterday."

He sucked in a breath, his eyes flaring with heat. "There's no reason to be sorry. I understand that you were scared." Still caressing her shoulder, he lifted her chin, staring down at her with eyes filled with hunger. "I *am* your husband."

"I know." Her breath caught again, her heart pounding faster.

He was so handsome that he could have had any woman he wanted, and for some reason, he'd chosen her.

Tilting her head, she bit her lip. "Why did you marry me? Did you do it just because Hawke and Blade did?"

His lips curved in a smile so beautiful it stole her breath. "No. I married you because I want you. Because I've never thought I could have a wife—and there you were."

Chilled, Sarah tried to pull away, but his fingers tightened on her chin. "So you only married me because you wanted a woman in your bed?"

Inclining his head, Phoenix smiled. "That's part of the reason. Women aren't exactly fallin' off trees out here."

"Your brother said the same thing. Is that why you share wives? For convenience?" She knew that people married for convenience and for security all the time, but she'd hoped for more with them.

"No. Eb and Jeremiah started this place because they both fell in love with the same woman and wanted a place where they could both have her. They didn't want anyone to be disrespectful to Maggie."

Sarah forced a smile, remembering the way Eb and Jeremiah had fussed over their wife and allowed her to go first. "I understand all about how people disrespect women. They treated all the women in the saloon like trash."

Phoenix's eyes hardened. "Even you?"

Shrugging, Sarah picked up the blanket and wrapped it around herself, suddenly chilled. "I lived there all my life. Of course, there were a few people that were real nice. Mrs. Anderson, the seamstress, is the one who taught me how to sew."

"You don't have to worry about that here. You're our wife, and if anyone treats you disrespectfully, I want to know about it." He touched his lips to hers, scraping his teeth over her bottom one and nipping gently. "Deal?"

"Deal." Sarah's answer came out breathless, the feel of his hand sliding under the blanket and down her side making it difficult to breathe.

Tugging the blanket, he bared her to the waist. Leaning back slightly, he ran a fingertip over her left nipple, lifting his gaze to hers. "You're very beautiful, and I care about you. Don't tell me you married me because you couldn't resist me. You didn't even know me. You married me for convenience and for protection."

Running the backs of his fingers down her cheek, he smiled faintly, but his eyes remained hard and cold. "Let's not lie to each other. Okay? Things will change between us when we get to know each other better." His eyes softened, the need in them unmistakable. "I don't mean to hurt you, but I don't want any lies between us. I want you very much, but I want you to want me, too."

Sarah stared into his eyes, marveling at the warmth that accompanied the hunger. "I'm your wife. You have the right to take me whenever you want to."

Phoenix frowned. "That's true. My brothers and I have a lot of rights where you're concerned, but I don't want sex from you out of duty."

Her stomach quivered, the slow slide of his fingertip over the upper curve of her breast making it increasingly difficult to follow the conversation. "I d-didn't think men cared about things like that." Without meaning to, she arched into his caress, loving the feel of his gentle touch. "I thought that men just wanted relief wherever they could find it."

Phoenix smiled, his pleasure at her silent demand for more of his touch glittering in his eyes. "Some do. I used to. I don't anymore." With a sigh, he bent to touch his lips to her nipple before straightening to kiss her lightly. "You're my wife, and having you want me is more important than ever. You're very beautiful. Very soft. I can't wait to explore every inch of you."

Pulling her close, he bent to nibble at her lips. "I can't wait to taste that pussy. I want to spread your thighs and bury my face between them. I want to hear those little cries you make when you come."

Sarah pressed her thighs together, fighting the wave of longing that washed over her. "I, um—"

Leading her to the table, Phoenix shook his head, his smile filled with devilish intent. "I know that you're starting to trust me, but it'll take time." He ran his hand over her hair, his eyes hooded. "For now, it's enough that you want me, but we can't do anything about that until you've healed some." Running the back of his hand over her breast, he captured her nipple between two fingers, squeezing lightly. "There are other ways to give each other pleasure. I can't wait to teach them to you."

Sarah gulped, biting back a moan at the rush of heat that centered at her slit. "I, um …"

Smiling again, he motioned for her to sit, waiting for her to pick up her cup before retrieving her breakfast. "I'll take mercy on you for now, but the first chance I get, you and I are going to play."

"Play?"

"Yep." Grinning, he tapped her nose. "Naked play. Something tells me you're gonna be real good at it, darlin'. Now, let's change the subject before my cock gets any harder. I waited for you to wake up because we didn't want you to wake up alone on your first day here."

Touched, she accepted the food and gripped his hand, fighting her arousal. "Thank you."

"You're welcome. Also, Maggie and Savannah are up at the house making soap. They're waiting for you."

"Oh!" Holding on to the blanket, she scrambled to her feet. "Do they need me to help them? My first day here and I'm already late." She rushed to her bundle and hurriedly tore through it for her other clothing. Since she had nothing clean to wear under her clothes, she stepped into her skirt and reached for her shirt. "I'm so sorry. You should have woken me up sooner. My first day here and I'm already doing things wrong."

Phoenix's hands closed on her shoulders from behind. "Stop it. You don't work for them." Turning her to face him, he nonchalantly buttoned her shirt, pausing to caress the upper curve of her breast. "Maggie and Savannah get together about once a month to make scented soaps. We bought some for you, remember? They like to do things together, and they wanted to include you. They both knew that you had a rough day yesterday, and didn't expect you to go up to the big house early. They just want to get to know you. They're happy to have another woman on the place, and wanted to include you."

Once he finished buttoning her shirt, he bent to touch his lips to hers. "We'll meet you for lunch, and since it's such a nice day, you can come with me this afternoon. I'll show you around the ranch. Now, come sit down and eat before it gets any colder than it already is."

After she finished dressing, she sat at the table and nibbled on her breakfast. "Where did you learn to speak English so well?"

His brow went up at that. "Because we're Indians, you think we wouldn't speak English?"

Mortified, and afraid she'd insulted him, she dropped the biscuit and reached for him. "I'm sorry. I didn't mean to insult you. I knew a few Indians in Waco, but none of them spoke English as well as you do."

Dropping into the seat next to her, he poured her a cup of water from the metal pitcher on the table. "Our father was Lakota, and left when we were young. Our parents were never married and he came and went as he wanted. One day he left and never came back. I think I was only one or two. Our mother was white, and she only spoke English. Hawke and Blade were older and learned his language, but after he left, no one spoke it any longer. When our mother died three years later, Hawke and Blade quit school, but made sure we all spoke English. Hawke and Blade only speak our father's language when they're upset."

She remembered hearing Hawke speak in a different tongue the night before, and vowed to pay more attention. "When your mother died, who took you in?"

He smiled coldly, staring into his cup. "No one. We're bastards and half-breeds. No one would have taken us in. Hawke was around ten, I think, and Blade was seven or eight. I think I was five."

Shocked, Sarah gasped. "I can't believe you were completely on your own! How did you survive?"

Phoenix's jaw clenched. "At least we had each other. How the hell did you survive being raised in such a rough place with no one to protect you? We survived the same way you did. We did what we had to do. Somehow, the thought of you doing it makes me sick to my stomach."

Breaking off another piece of the biscuit, Sarah chewed, eyeing Phoenix thoughtfully. "Can I ask you a question?"

"Of course." He leaned back in his chair and eyed her expectantly. "You can always come to me and ask me anything you want. You can ask me about sex. Anything."

Her face burned, but she had to know about Hawke's behavior the night before. "Last night, after Hawke… you know…" She took a sip of water to ease her dry throat, grateful when Phoenix finished her thought. "When he took your virginity?"

Her face burned at that. Nodding, she tore off another piece of biscuit, making crumbs all over the napkin in front of her. "He was so gentle and kind, even when he…and then afterward…"

Phoenix smiled faintly. "He was distant."

Sarah nodded, trying to hide how much Hawke's coldness had hurt. "I disappointed him, didn't I?"

"No. Just the opposite." Leaning forward, he took her hand in his. "You got too close."

Sarah blinked, setting her food aside. "Too close? I don't understand." She'd felt close to him, too, but now wondered if that was something that Hawke didn't want.

Phoenix smiled and leaned back again, picking up a cup of coffee that she hadn't seen. "You have to understand that Hawke doesn't allow himself to get close to anyone except Blade and me. He likes the others, but he keeps them at a distance. He talked to you in a way he doesn't talk to anyone except Blade and me. Hawke seldom puts two words together around the others." Lifting her chin, he ran his thumb over her bottom lip. "I saw the way he looked at you. He looked like he'd found heaven."

Sarah's stomach fluttered, the memory of the way Hawke had looked at her still making her weak in the knees.

"Then why—?"

Getting to his feet, Phoenix made his way to the window. "Hawke's a hard man. He took his responsibility to Blade and me seriously—and at a vulnerable age. He had to become a hard ass in a hurry. He had to in order to survive—and to protect us. You really shook him. He feels something for you, and Hawke isn't a man who takes things lightly."

Still uncomfortable at having three husbands, Sarah looked up at him through her lashes. "And you? Do you take things lightly?"

Grinning, he turned from the window. "A lot more than my brothers do. I certainly don't have a chip on my shoulder like Hawke does. He's very sensitive about being a bastard and a half-breed. I like to have fun, and Hawke doesn't know the meaning of the word."

Folding the remaining biscuit in the napkin, Sarah allowed a small smile. "I wonder if that's why he was so nice to me. I'm a bastard, too, and although I'm not a half-breed, I was raised in a saloon." Getting to her feet, she frowned. "How about Blade? He watches me, but I can't figure out what he's thinking."

Phoenix ran a hand through his hair before shoving a hat on it. "Blade can be as hard as Hawke, and as quiet. You definitely never want to be on his bad side. He likes to have fun, but my brother Blade has a dark side. He's not as forward with it as Hawke. Before you realize it, he's already got you in his trap."

He helped her with her shawl and opened the door. "Come on. We're burnin' daylight. After you spend the morning with the other women, I'll show you around the ranch and we can talk some more."

\* \* \* \*

Sarah cut another row of soap, glancing up at Maggie, who had her small son at her breast. She'd been thinking about Phoenix's words all morning, and had to struggle to focus on the other women's conversation.

"Sarah? Are you there, or are you still thinking about your wedding night?"

Sarah blinked, looking up at a beaming Maggie. "I'm sorry. I seem to be a little distracted this morning."

Savannah tied yet another bow around the soaps they'd been cutting. "Really? I never would have guessed. Please, don't be embarrassed. When I first married Wyatt and Hayes, I couldn't even carry on a conversation for weeks." Grinning, she shook her head. "There are still some days that it happens. I can't even imagine what having three would be like."

Maggie laughed softly at her friend and turned her attention back to Sarah. "I said that the soaps in the box are the ones going to town. You, Savannah, and I will split the rest for ourselves."

Sarah's face burned. "No, thank you." At Maggie's stunned look, Sarah rushed to explain. "Please don't be offended. For some reason, Hawke doesn't want me to take anything, and I don't want to do anything to upset him."

Shaking her head, Maggie smiled. "I understand. Believe me. Until you figure them out and learn how to get around them, you have to be careful. But I started making these soaps for myself. I only take them to town for a little extra money. I like buying things for Eb and Jeremiah, and I'm certainly not going to do it with their money. Just take them home. You'll figure out a way to get around him. Just pout."

Sarah sighed, remembering Hawke's distance the night before. "I can't imagine ever getting around Hawke."

Savannah laughed softly, and looked up from the box where she packed rows of the scented soap. "I thought that way, too. I figured it would be easy for Maggie to get around Eb and Jeremiah. She'd been doing it for years."

Sending a look of amusement in Maggie's direction, she reached for the soaps Sarah had just cut. "Wyatt and Hayes are both hard men. When I agreed to marry them, I knew they loved me, but I never thought they would love me the way Eb and Jeremiah love Maggie."

Blushing, she shook her head and started packing the other soaps. "There's nothing like having the heart of a strong man." Grinning, she looked at each of them. "Or strong *men*." She sighed again, staring at the far wall, obviously thinking of her two rugged husbands. "They'd do anything to make me happy. In turn, I'd do anything to make them happy." Shrugging, she went back to packing the box, sharing a look with Maggie. "Of course, they're really possessive and perhaps a little overprotective, but I know that they mean well. It's hard to argue with a man who would do anything to keep you safe."

Wrinkling her nose, she grinned. "Still, I manage to rile them up now and then."

Maggie lifted the baby onto her shoulder, rubbing his back when he began to fuss. "I used to think Eb and Jeremiah regretted bringing me here because they were so cold, but after I realized how worried they were about keeping me safe, I understood. How in the world is a woman supposed to resist a man like that?"

Sarah forced a smile. "I'm so happy for both of you, but I don't think it's ever going to be that way for me." When they looked at each other wide-eyed, she rushed to reassure them. "Not that I'm complaining. I'm just so grateful that they gave me a home. Feeling safe is something I'll never take for granted."

"Amen." Savannah turned back to her and smiled. "But I think you're in for a real surprise with those men you married. I saw the way Phoenix looked when he brought you here."

Maggie rose, placing the baby in the large padded basket in the corner of the kitchen before straightening and turning to her. "How's Hawke?"

Sarah didn't feel comfortable telling her new friends that Hawke had been the only one to make love to her. Shrugging, she cut into the large block of soap again. "He's been very kind to me. When I met him on the platform, he was so nice. So protective. I found myself telling him everything. I was going to leave again, but he talked me out of it."

Savannah frowned. "Why were you going to leave? After what you escaped from in Waco, I thought you'd be happy to come here. You said that you saw one of Eb's posters."

Remembering the relief she'd felt when she'd had a plan, Sarah smiled. "I did, and it seemed like the answer to my prayers. Once I got to the train station and Hawke told me about the ranch, I had second thoughts. If Willy Krenshaw comes here and causes trouble, I'll never forgive myself. You won't forgive me either, if one of your men gets hurt."

"Don't be ridiculous." Maggie touched her arm. "I can't believe you escaped the way you did. Good for you for stealing his gold. He deserved it." With a shiver, she turned away. "I can't imagine how scared you were. I'm just so glad you got away."

Setting the knife aside, Sarah wrapped her arms around herself, suddenly chilled. "I appreciate that, but I'm scared. You tolerate me now because Willy hasn't come yet. But he'll come for that gold. He'll hurt someone, and then you'll hate me." She dropped into a chair, choking back a sob. "You've been so nice to me. I've never had friends before."

Savannah jumped to her feet. "Oh, Sarah!"

Shaking her head, Sarah got to her feet again, wandering around the kitchen to keep Savannah from hugging her. If she let her, Sarah knew she'd break down for sure. Pausing next to the baby, she couldn't help but wonder what it would have been like to have one of her own. "I'll need that gold when I leave. I know I'll have to, and I'm dreading it."

She feared she'd never be safe again.

Dropping into a chair, Savannah smiled and shook her head. "Running away isn't the answer. You'd be alone, and even in more danger. Besides, I don't think Hawke, Blade, and Phoenix are going to let you go."

Maggie placed several more bars of soap in the box. "If Willy comes here, the men will take care of them."

Sarah moved again, too restless to stand still. "I wish I had your confidence."

Maggie smiled. "You would if you knew them better." Sharing a look with Savannah, she sighed. "I still get scared every time they go out, but I know how the men all watch out for each other. It helps more than you know."

She picked up the knife and cut the last of the soap with expert precision into perfectly even bars. "Eb and Jeremiah won this place in a poker game and knew just how they wanted things done around here. They made a home where the three of us could be together. They made a home where I would be safe. They hired the best men— men they could trust completely." Glancing at Sarah, she smiled. "They can be hard. Cold. Deadly, if necessary. They have to be, but they all have hearts of gold. They're very protective of us and each other."

Savannah ran a hand over her abdomen. "Now that I'm with child, I appreciate that more than ever. It can be a dangerous place, and we all need to count on each other. I heard Wyatt and Hayes talking last night. If Willy and his friends come, the men are ready for them. They have lookouts anyway so no one can sneak up on us. They're just staying a little sharper."

Maggie patted Sarah's shoulder. "It won't be the first time the men have dealt with trouble, and I can't imagine that it'll be the last." Grinning, she went to the coffee pot and poured each of them a fresh cup. "Now, let's talk about something more interesting. You say that you and Hawke actually *talked*? I don't think I've ever heard him say more than three or four words strung together since I came here."

Savannah gave her a sly grin. "Hawke usually nods, shakes his head, or grunts. He doesn't talk more than he has to. I can't wait to see the two of you together."

Maggie placed a cup of coffee in front of Sarah. "You haven't said much about Blade."

"I don't know what to say." She couldn't forget the look of possessiveness in his eyes the night before, or the satisfaction in his eyes as he watched Hawke make love to her.

Her nipples tingled with sensation every time she thought about the way he'd held her hand firmly above her head, or his firm caress as he tenderly explored her.

She didn't want to admit that she was nervous at the thought of being alone with him, or that it gave her a secret thrill to know that it would happen.

Her face burned under her new friends' expectant looks. "Blade hasn't really talked much. He's been very kind."

Savannah nodded. "They're all very kind—with each other, and with women." She raised a brow, running a hand over her abdomen. "As Willy and his gang will find out, they're not so kind when it comes to men who show up to make trouble."

Maggie wrapped up the remaining bars into three bundles, handing one to Savannah and one to Sarah before setting the other aside. "And they're nothing short of deadly when it comes to protecting their women—and you're one of the ranch women now, so you're under the protection of all the men here."

When Sarah started to speak, Maggie frowned and shook her head. "And if Hawke says something about you accepting the soaps, tell them they're payment for helping to make them. If that doesn't work, get Blade or Phoenix on your side and get around him that way."

Sarah eyed the burlap bundle, nervous about Hawke's reaction, but she didn't want Maggie and Savannah to think he was being mean. "He bought me so many nice things, so it's not like he doesn't want me to have them—"

"He's very proud." Savannah sipped her coffee, making a face. "I used to love this stuff." Setting it aside, she took Sarah's hand in hers. "Hawke and Blade are both very proud. Phoenix is a little more easy going because Hawke and Blade kinda raised him. Hawke's real sensitive about taking handouts and won't accept charity from anyone. If not for his brothers, he'd be a real loner."

The image of Hawke's eyes, warm and then distant, went through her mind. Lifting her gaze, Sarah forced a smile. "I'm grateful for whatever closeness he allows. He's a good man."

Maggie nodded. "They all are—but that doesn't mean they won't be firm enough to do whatever's necessary to protect what's theirs. I know things happened fast for all of you, but make no mistake, Sarah, Hawke, Blade, and Phoenix consider you theirs. They can be hard and cold about getting their way, but don't mistake that coldness for distance."

Sharing a look with Savannah, Maggie laughed softly. "Distance is the last thing these men want when it comes to their women."

# Chapter Nine

Sitting on the bench across from her in the crowded chow shack, Phoenix watched Sarah eat her dinner with gusto.

Her hands waved through the air as she talked excitedly about her morning to Hawke and Blade, who sat on either side of her. "Maggie and Savannah were so nice to me. You should see how many boxes of soap we made. The baby's so beautiful. Maggie wants to show me how to quilt. They're both so friendly. The morning just flew by."

Hawke's lips twitched. "Heard you got a late start."

She stilled, lowering her gaze. "Yes. I'm sorry." Sarah looked away, her face burning when she glanced at Phoenix.

Wrapping an arm around her shoulder, Hawke touched his lips to her hair in a show of affection so unlike his brother that if Phoenix hadn't seen it with his own eyes, he wouldn't have believed it. "You have nothing to be sorry for." Bending low, he touched his lips to her ear, his voice barely carrying to Phoenix. "It does a man good to know he can wear his woman out, and you were probably worn out anyway."

Blade grinned and bent to kiss her shoulder, keeping his voice low. "It was hard as hell to concentrate on work, though. We kept looking back at the house and thinking about you lying naked in bed."

Her blush made his cock stir, and when she glanced at him, she turned a fiery red.

Delighted with her, he watched her closely, noticing with no small amount of pleasure how often she looked in his direction.

The woman sitting before him had changed so much in the short time they'd known her, glowing with happiness at the small amount of attention and affection they'd shown her.

She'd become more animated, and eyed the other men with curiosity instead of the fear that had been in her eyes the night before. Her eyes danced with amusement, and although she seemed hesitant at times, and she tended to lean toward Hawke whenever she felt uneasy, she'd come a long way in such a short amount of time.

Phoenix smiled to himself, imagining what she'd been like when they grew closer.

After taking a sip of her milk, she wiped her mouth and smiled at each of them, her eyes sparkling. "It was such a lovely morning. It's so nice to have friends."

Gesturing for her to eat her stew, Hawke scooped up a spoonful of his own. "No friends in Waco?" He kept turning to look at her as if finding it hard to look away.

Sarah shrugged and looked down at her stew. "No. Not really, although Mrs. Anderson was kind. Most people don't want their daughter to talk to the daughter of a whore. Maggie and Savannah were both so nice to me."

Phoenix had a strong suspicion that few people had been.

Hawke's jaw clenched, but he said nothing.

Blade's eyes narrowed. "If anyone's *not* nice to you, I want to know about it."

Sarah's eyes went wide. "No. No. Everyone's been real nice. I don't want to cause any trouble."

"Anyone who treats women badly deserves all the trouble they get." Blade shot her a warning look, one that had her eyes going wide again. "If you don't tell me, and I find out about it, I'll turn you over my knee and paddle your bottom." Leaning close, he smiled coldly, but his eyes lit with anticipation. "Your *naked* bottom. I'll enjoy it, too."

Phoenix hid a smile at her look of shock. "Do it. I think our new bride would love something like that."

Hawke frowned at both of them. "You hit her and you're going to answer to me. She's been through enough."

Blade grinned, his eyes hooded as he turned Sarah's face to his. "I'm not lookin' to scare her that way. I have plans for something that I think she'll like. A little fear will only heighten her excitement. Her punishment won't hurt as much as the realization that she gets aroused when she's bare-assed over her husband's lap."

Dropping a kiss on her lips, he smiled again. "And she won't be able to hide it. Her thighs will be soaking wet with her sweet juices, and no matter how hard she fights it, she'll beg for more."

Sarah's face turned bright red, her eyes slightly unfocused—a telling sign that made Phoenix's cock jump in anticipation. "Never!"

Blade ran a hand over her hair before reaching for his spoon again. "Never is a very long time, honey."

Fascinated by her response to the erotic threat, and Hawke's own surprise, Phoenix gestured toward her plate, eager to put his own plans for her in action. "Eat. I want to show you something."

They all looked up when Maggie stopped beside their table, and he and his brothers started to stand before she waved them back down again.

Patting the back of the baby propped against her shoulder, Maggie Tyler had a confidence that she hadn't had when she'd come to the ranch almost two years earlier.

Grinning, Phoenix reached out to run a hand over the baby's soft hair. "He's getting big. Motherhood suits you."

"Yes, he is. He's gonna be as big as his daddies." Lifting her chin in challenge, she turned to glare at Hawke. "I tried to give Sarah some of the scented soaps, but she wouldn't take them. Is there something wrong with my soaps?"

The entire chow shack became silent, everyone apparently curious to see how Hawke would handle the boss's wife.

Hawke sat back, crossing his arms over his chest. "I don't take charity."

Maggie lifted a brow, showing the spunk that drove both Eb and Jeremiah crazy. "What does that have to do with giving soap to Sarah? She worked to help make them, and she's my friend. Friends do things for each other. Do you have a problem with your wife being my friend?" Her tone told him that he'd better not.

Shaking his head, Hawke sighed. "Of course not." He slid a look in Blade's direction. "I'd rather face a gun that an angry woman."

Looking pleased with herself, Maggie pressed her advantage. "Then why can't I give her some soap? Why can't I give her some of the material? She's giving me some of hers, or is that going to be a problem, too?"

Hawke reached for his cup of coffee, a small smile playing at his lips. "Motherhood has certainly changed you. That, and having your husbands wrapped around your little finger. Fine. She can accept the soaps and some material, but my brothers and I are responsible for our wife's needs."

Knowing that if one of the other ranch hands had approached Hawke and spoken to him in such a way, he would have been picking himself up from the floor, Phoenix hid a smile. "Thank you." He glanced at his smiling wife, willing to do anything to keep that smile on her face. "Sarah told us how kind you and Savannah were to her. We're grateful for that."

Maggie grinned. "We like her, and are both grateful for another woman on the place. We women are sorely outnumbered."

Carrying two trays, Eb approached, smiling indulgently at his wife. "That doesn't seem to curb your tongue any. I can't imagine having the ranch overrun with women. We'd spend so much time watching out for all of you that we'd never get any work done."

Frowning up at her husband, Maggie sighed. "Is that why you and the others came up with all those rules?"

Eb lifted a brow at her frown, obviously pleased at her look of apprehension. "Absolutely. If anything happened to you, I'd never forgive myself, so you're gonna pay dearly for disobeying us. Come on. You need to eat. You're grouchy, and if food doesn't sweeten that mood, I know something that will."

Sarah watched Maggie and Eb walk away before turning to Hawke. "What did she mean by rules? Is there something that I should know?"

Hawke swallowed his mouthful of stew before answering. "We've already talked about some of them. You're to obey us without question. It could save your life. You don't know the dangers here the way we do. You'll do what we tell you to keep you safe. You put yourself in danger or disobey us, and you'll get a red ass no matter how much you spit and sputter about it. I won't put up with any nonsense. We'll give you as much freedom as we can, but you won't be allowed to do anything that might put you in danger."

Sarah nodded, her gaze lowering. "I understand." She slid a glance at Blade. "You just can't wait to have an excuse to spank me."

Blade's brows went up, and he seemed to be clearly enjoying her sass. "I don't need an excuse. That ass belongs to me and I'll spank it whenever I want to. It's up to you whether it's a spanking designed to give pleasure, or one that'll make it hard to sit down again."

He picked up his cup of coffee and settled back, gesturing toward her lunch. "Finish eating and behave yourself. Hayes and Wyatt are making their way over."

Throughout the rest of the meal, Phoenix entertained himself by watching her, noticing that she scooted closer to Hawke—something that seemed to please Hawke enormously.

The lawmen asked questions, and with Hawke's urging, got Sarah to tell her story. They listened closely, their expressions hardening when she spoke about Willy.

Sipping his coffee, Wyatt sat forward, his smile tender. "That was a real brave thing you did. I'm just glad Hawke found you."

Sarah blushed again, looking up at Hawke through her lashes in a way that twisted Phoenix's gut. "So am I. I just can't help but think that comin' here was a mistake. Someone's gonna get hurt because of me."

Not trusting the resignation in her voice, Phoenix reached for her hand. "You're safe here. Let us worry about Willy Krenshaw and his gang."

Hayes smiled, a tender smile he reserved for the women. "We've been bored lately. We need trouble to keep us on our toes. You wouldn't want us to get lazy, would you?"

\* \* \* \*

Standing outside the chow shack several minutes later, Phoenix blinked, his smile falling. "What do you mean, you can't ride?"

He glanced at his brothers, unsurprised to find both of them watching Sarah.

Blushing adorably, Sarah glanced sideways at Hawke through her lashes before meeting Phoenix's gaze again. "I've never gone anywhere that I haven't walked. You know I was raised in a saloon. I never needed to ride. I've never had the chance to ride. I've never gone anywhere." Shrugging, she took a step back from Phoenix's restless horse. "To tell you the truth, I'm scared of horses. They're a lot bigger up close."

Hawke's eyes narrowed as took her hand. "I'm a lot bigger than you are, and you aren't scared of me. Are you?"

Shrugging again, she gave him a small smile, an intimate smile that made Phoenix grit his teeth. "Sometimes."

Hawke smiled back, a rare, gentle smile that only Sarah seemed able to bring out in him. "We'll have to see what we can do about that." Taking her hand, he pressed it lightly against Major's side, holding it there when Sarah tried to jerk her hand away. "Easy. Trust me. Feel his coat. See how he settled. He likes your touch." Although his eyes remained indulgent, he released her, but remained protectively close.

Phoenix could have sworn he heard his brother say something under his breath—something that sounded suspiciously like *so do I,* but he couldn't be sure.

Taking her hand in his, Blade placed it on his chest, holding it there the way Hawke had held it against Major. "I like your touch, too." Smiling at her gasp, Blade slid her hand inside his shirt, moving it against his chest. "Very nice. We'll teach you to ride—horses, and us."

* * * *

When the powerful horse shifted beside her, Sarah jolted and cried out, reaching for Hawke. "I'd never be able to control him, or you, enough to ride either one of you."

Throwing his head back, Blade laughed, yanking her back against him. His eyes glittered with pride and affection as he pulled her close. "That wasn't a request, *wife.*" Blade softened his tone, bending to touch his lips to hers. "You'll learn to ride because it could mean the difference between life and death. Hawke and I already have a horse picked out for you."

"You'll learn how to control *him.*" Blade touched his lips to her ear, smiling when she shivered. "But, in bed, I'm going to be the one controlling *you.*"

Sucking in a breath, Sarah slid a glance toward Hawke, who simply stared at her with unreadable hooded eyes. Looking back at Blade, she crossed her arms over her chest and lifted her chin—a defiant gesture that solidified Phoenix's plans for her. "Are you trying to scare me?"

Out of sight of any onlookers, Blade slid his hand over her breast. "No. Not this time." Running a hand over her back, he nuzzled her neck again. "I just want to make sure you're thinking about me today.

There'll be times when I make you nervous, but it'll only intensify the pleasure."

Hawke slid a hand down her hair. "We've got to get back to work. Behave yourself."

Phoenix closed in behind her, bending to touch his lips to her shoulder, slightly disgruntled that she didn't look at him the way she looked at his brothers. "Come on, Sarah. I want to show you something."

*And give you pleasure in a way that you'll never forget.*

* * * *

"It sure is a long way down." Sarah swallowed heavily and leaned back against Phoenix, grateful for his support. "Are you sure I won't fall?" Gripping his arm, she tried to stare straight ahead, but her gaze kept going to the ground below.

Tightening the arm beneath her breasts, he bent to nuzzle her neck, his warm lips sending a delicious thrill through her. "I won't let you fall, Sarah. Damn it, can't you trust me just a little?"

Struck by his tone, Sarah stiffened. "I'm sorry. I'm just a little scared. It's a lot different than being on the buckboard."

Phoenix sighed, running his hand over her arm. "I'm sorry for losing my temper, honey. It just makes me mad that you don't trust me to take care of you. For the first time in my life, I have someone to take care of. It means a lot to me, Sarah."

"I'm sorry." Turning her head, she rubbed it against his chest, loving the way his arms felt around her.

Despite his brief show of anger, he held her the way he would hold something precious. Keeping his arm wrapped around her, he slowed his horse to a walk, his arms tightening as he nuzzled her neck. "I'm the one who's sorry. I keep forgetting how much your life's changed over the last few days. Ours, too." Loosening his hold, he rubbed her stomach. "I'm a little impatient. I have a beautiful wife and I seem to be having a little trouble getting close to her."

Sarah looked up at him over her shoulder, her heart pounding furiously at his nearness. "Do you want to be close to me?"

He wore his hat low on his forehead, shading his eyes from the hot afternoon sun, which gave him a rakish look that made her heart beat faster.

He met her frown with one of his own. "Of course. You're my wife, just as much as you're Hawke's and Blade's wife."

Turning to face forward again, Sarah nodded, her heart sinking. "So the reason you want to be close to me is because you're competing with Hawke and Blade. You want me to feel the same way about you."

Phoenix fisted a hand in her hair and turned her back to face him, his eyes narrowed to slits as they raked over her features. "Yes, damn it! Something wrong with that?"

Sarah sighed. "Phoenix, I don't know what you want me to do. Hawke and Blade are serious about being married, but I think you're playing some kind of game. It's not a competition. I want you to want me because you want me. Not because you feel it's expected of you."

Phoenix's eyes went wide. "*I'm* playing a game? Hawke is one of the coldest men I've ever known, and you fall into his arms as if you've known him all your life! And I *don't* want you because I think it's expected. I want you because I want you, damn it!"

He crushed her mouth with his, his arms tightening around her. Sweeping her mouth with his devious tongue, Phoenix turned her on his lap, and with a groan, cupped her breast.

His kiss didn't have the smooth silkiness of Blade's, or the tenderness of Hawke's.

Phoenix's kiss was all hunger.

Drowning in sensation, Sarah clung to him, alarmed at the swift surge of desire. Dizzy from his kiss, she leaned into him, pressing her other breast against his chest.

He seemed to know the exact moment when she needed more, pushing the sides of her shirt aside and slipping his hand inside to close his fingers on her nipple. Swallowing her cries, he nipped at her lips before taking her mouth again.

Flames of need licked at her, so hot that she writhed against him.

Her pussy clenched incessantly in demand, his attention to her nipple sending sharp tugs of pleasure to her clit.

Lifting his head, he stared down at her, his breathing ragged. "Christ, I want you." Pushing her shirt aside further, he shifted his gaze to her breast, running his finger lightly back and forth over her nipple. "I swear, I could eat you alive. You think I don't want you? We'll just see about that."

Stopping at an outcropping of rock, he leaned her back over his arm and covered her breast completely with his hot, callused hand. "I know I want you more than I've ever wanted any other woman."

Straightening her on the saddle again, he dismounted and reached up, wrapping his hands around her waist. "We're about a mile west from the ranch and our cabin."

He lifted her from the horse, his strength once again astounding her. "We've set up a few places like this in case one of us gets caught in a storm or is hurt. It'll provide protection from the weather, and give you a place to hide if you need it. Everyone on the ranch knows about these places, and they're the first places we'll look if you're missing. Right now, though, you and I are going to create a storm of our own."

"How many of them are there?"

Phoenix shrugged. "Probably about two dozen, but most of them are farther away. It's a big ranch." Stopping, he turned her in his arms, sliding a hand down to her bottom. "One by one, we'll explore them all."

Sarah looked around, struck by the wide open space. "I'm sure there are all kinds of wild animals and snakes." Shivering in revulsion, she held the ends of her shirt closed as they approached what looked like a small cave.

"And there are some unfriendly Indians—not to mention men like Willy."

Frowning, she looked up at him. "Are they unfriendly with you, too?"

His eyes narrowed. "Why? Because I'm half-Indian? We don't all get along, you know, and Hawke, Blade, and I have never been part of a tribe. Come on. Let's get inside."

Worried that she'd insulted him, she tugged on his sleeve. "Phoenix, I'm sorry. I don't understand why you're angry. Don't you like being an Indian?"

He paused, his eyes going wide as he turned to her. "I'm not just an Indian. I'm a half-breed. Most people don't accept Indians or half-breeds. Neither the whites nor the Indians accept us."

"You seem to be accepted here and in Tulsa. Besides, being half white and half Indian isn't as bad as being raised in a whorehouse."

His lips thinned, his eyes shooting sparks. "Damn it, Sarah—"

Shaking her head, she stepped closer. "Look, I answered your questions because I thought you were interested in my life. Why do you get insulted whenever I ask you one?" To her horror, she started to cry. "You say you want to be closer to me, and then try to put distance between us." Turning away, she lifted her hands to cover her face, scrubbing away tears. "What am I doing here? I'm ruining everything. I don't know how to live on a ranch. I have three husbands and I don't even know how to be a wife to one. I don't know how to have friends. I don't want to insult them when they offer me something, but I don't want Hawke to get mad when I accept something. I lean on Hawke because makes me feel safe, but you get mad at that."

Phoenix caught her from behind, wrapping his arms around her and pulling her close. "Oh, honey. You've been through so much. Your entire world has changed, hasn't it?"

The panic in his voice had her turning in his arms, only to be caught up against him.

Running his hand down her back, he cupped the back of her head and pressed it against his chest. "To make matters worse, you're scared that Willy's going to find you. Oh, honey, I'm so sorry. Put it down to wanting you so much that I can't even think."

Straightening, he urged her head back to smile down at her. "I'm acting like a horse with a burr under its saddle. Poor thing. Please stop crying. I can't take it."

Sarah sniffed, eyeing him warily. "I'm not crying." Stunned that he seemed genuinely concerned, she smiled and laid her hands on his chest. "I want things to work between us, Phoenix. I'm proud to have you as my husband. I promise to try."

Phoenix smiled back, a gorgeous smile that weakened her knees. "I'm the one who's going to have to try harder. Come into the cave with me, and I'll show you how much I want you. No. Leave your shirt open. There's no one around except me to see you, and I can't stop looking at you."

Feeling decadent and more than a little naughty, Sarah smiled up at him again as he helped her up the rocks to the opening above.

Pausing at the entrance to allow her eyes to adjust, she pressed herself against his side. "Are there any snakes in here?"

Running a hand over her arm, he drew his gun. "I don't know. You stay put while I check."

Sarah watched him go into the cave, alarmed when he disappeared.

The cave was deeper than it appeared from outside, and when he'd been gone for several minutes, she began to get scared.

"Phoenix?"

"I'm coming." Seconds later, he appeared, holstering his gun as he approached. "No snakes. Come on in."

She stepped farther into the opening, stepping carefully over the uneven rocks. "Are you sure?"

Smiling, he took her hand and placed it on his chest. "Positive. I don't ever want you to go to the back of the cave, though. There's a huge hole in the middle, almost the entire size of the cave. It seems to go down hundreds of feet. You can't see it without a light."

Sarah shivered. "And you went in there?"

Phoenix grinned, a devilish grin that sent another kind of shiver through her. "I know where I'm going. As long as you walk around the edges, you're fine. There's about three feet of smooth rock all around the edges. I don't want to talk about that anymore. I want to show you just how damned much I want you and do something to you that I've been thinking about all day."

The temperature dropped with each step she took, making her nipples bead even tighter. "Sounds scary."

Phoenix appeared to notice, his look of appreciation warming her as he slid his hand into her shirt again. "It will be, and then it won't. I swear, darlin', I could spend all day admiring your breasts." Turning her, he hugged her from behind before his hands got busy with the rest of her buttons. "See the shelf over there?"

Her head had fallen back against his shoulder, her eyes fluttering closed. Jerking upright, she nodded, eyeing the rock formation that created a shelf. The feel of his fingers closing over her nipples had her leaning back against him for support, a moan escaping at the sharp pleasure. Nodding, she forced her eyes to stay open. "Hmm mmm."

Several canteens lined the shelf, along with two kerosene lamps.

Phoenix pushed her hair aside and with a low groan, brushed his lips over her neck while working her shirttails free of her skirt. "There's a box of matches up there, along with several blankets. Why don't we take one of those blankets down and make good use of it?"

"Phoenix. Oh, God."

He pulled her shirt free of her skirt, parting the sides to leave her breasts completely exposed. "You're so damned beautiful. You've got a fire inside you that burns me every time I get near you."

The hunger in his touch fueled her own. "Oh, Phoenix! That feels so good. You make me feel so naughty. I feel so free here."

His gravelly chuckle sent shivers over her over skin, heightening the awareness in her nipples and slit. "Free, you're not." His teeth scraped over the sensitive spot between her neck and shoulder as he stripped her shirt from her. "You're tied to us and we're never letting you go." He untied her skirt, letting it fall to puddle at her feet. "As for naughty—naughty is good. You can be as naughty as you want to be with me—and I'm going to teach you how to be even naughtier."

Releasing her, he went to the shelf and retrieved a blanket, throwing it over his shoulder before striding toward her again. Lifting her naked body high against his chest, he let his gaze rake over her. "As a matter of fact, I'm going to do my best to teach you to be *real* naughty."

He strode a little farther back in the cave where she could hear water dripping, and where she could see another entrance that would lead even farther. The cool air felt incredible on her heated body, the darkness heightening the sense of intimacy. "Riding with your body pressed against mine and my cock pressed against that ass drove me crazy. Do you know how much I want to take you there?"

Sarah sucked in a breath, her pussy clenching. "What are you saying? Surely, you can't mean that you want to …" Too embarrassed to put it into words, she buried her face against his shoulder, grateful for the darkness surrounding them.

She could barely see him in the low light, and hoped that he couldn't see that she blushed.

Phoenix chuckled again, but this time his soft laughter came out even rougher and filled with tension. "That's exactly what I mean."

He lowered her to her feet, shook out the blanket, and spread it on the rock floor. Once he finished, he reached for her, running his hands up and down her body. "I like having you naked and at my mercy. Stay right here."

Wrapping her arms around herself, Sarah watched Phoenix go, only to come back seconds later with her clothes.

"We'll use your clothes and mine to protect your knees." Turning to her, he drew her down to the blanket. "I was thinking about this all morning, and I stopped to get a tin of salve to grease that tight little bottom for my cock." Lifting her face to his, he drew his shirt off and arranged it on the blanket. "Any time you get scared, or something hurts, just tell me."

A cool breeze washed over her, the sound of water dripping increasing the unreality of the situation. Another shiver went through her, this one laced with sexual hunger. "I think I'm a little scared now. I've never heard of such a thing. Are you sure it'll work?"

Her bottom clenched, the awareness there feeling almost as if he touched her.

Phoenix groaned, rolling her to her side and settling in behind her. "I'm sure. We just need to go slow. We've got as long as it takes."

Sarah gasped at the slide of his finger through her slit, the friction against her throbbing clit nearly sending her over. "Oh!"

Slipping his finger inside her pussy, Phoenix groaned. "You're wet for me. Say my name."

Clenching on his finger, Sarah ran her hands over his chest, pressing her fingertips into the hard muscle she found there. "Phoenix."

It felt so good to be with him this way. So sexual, but with a closeness that hadn't been there before.

The intimacy seemed to grow with every kiss. Every caress. Every moan.

His lips brushed hers. "Again."

"Phoenix!" The finger inside her slid free, brushing over her clit. "Please."

Fisting a hand in her hair, he looked down her body and smiled. "Wearing just your boots, you're quite a sight." Circling her, he caught her shoulder when she would have turned. "No, Sarah. You stay right where you are. Things are about to get a little naughty."

Closing her eyes, she struggled to remain still as he circled her, her muscles trembling under his trailing fingertips. "I can't believe I'm doing this."

"Believe it." His voice came from directly in front of her, his body brushing her nipples as he leaned close and touched his lips to hers. "Say my name again."

Realizing that he wanted to make sure she wasn't pretending that he was Hawke or Blade, she smiled and opened her eyes. "Phoenix. I know who I'm with."

His eyes narrowed, but in the faint light she couldn't see them well enough to even guess at his thoughts. "Don't forget."

She sucked in a breath when he began to circle her again, crying out when he reached out to tap her nipple. "How could I forget?"

Trembling, she sucked in breath after breath, her entire body quivering with awareness under the slide of Phoenix's lips and fingertips.

Phoenix wrapped an arm around her from behind, his warm shoulder and chest forcing her to bend while he closed his teeth on the side of her neck. "I'm so hard I ache. I want you so damned much." He worked his finger slowly toward her puckered opening, his intent obvious. "You liked when I touched your tight little bottom before. You let me make you feel good. Will you trust me enough to do it again?"

Her bottom hole tingled, need brushing her fears away.

Pressing his finger against her bottom hole, he scraped his teeth over her neck and shoulder, his voice deeper and more gravelly than before. "I haven't been able to stop thinking about the way you responded. Spread your legs a little more. Yes. Good girl. Now a little more. That's it."

Shaking even harder, she clung to his forearm for support, shaken by how good it felt to have him touch her there. "Phoenix. Oh, God."

Bent in front of him with her thighs spread wide, she braced her hands against the smooth rock, alarmed by the heightened awareness in her puckered opening.

Phoenix withdrew his finger with a groan. "Be still, honey. I'm going to grease you up real good. Let's see if we can wake that bottom up like we did before."

Remembering the hunger—the yearning to have his finger deeper—Sarah moaned, her bottom and pussy clenching in anticipation.

Chuckling softly, Phoenix ran his finger, slick with salve, over her puckered opening. "Yes, you remember, don't you?" He pressed against her sensitive opening, and despite her instinctive effort to close against him, the salve and being spread wide allowed him to slide his finger into her with ease.

Feeling as wild and untamed as the land around her, she threw her head back and let out a cry of pleasure—a cry that seemed to echo off the rock walls. "Phoenix! Oh, God. It's deep. Oh, God. Please. It feels so strange."

His lips moved over her neck, back, and shoulders, the heat from them warming her all the way through. His words, gruff and filled with sexual tension, made her even hotter. "You are so damned beautiful. So exciting. My wife. I want to explore every damned inch of you. God, you're so soft. So responsive. Just feeling the way your ass is clenching on my finger is driving me crazy. I want to feel it on my cock."

Massaging her breast, he kept moving his finger in slow circles inside her bottom, creating a sharp hunger that had her spreading her thighs wider and lifting to her toes for more. "Phoenix!"

Groaning, he slid his hand to her waist again, nuzzling her neck in the way she'd learned she liked. "That's it. Say my name. I want to make sure you know who's touching you."

"Oh, Phoenix. How could I not know? It feels so different when you touch me."

His lovemaking had a different feel to it than Hawke's, his touch a different rhythm than Blade's.

Phoenix scraped his teeth over her neck, and with a harsh groan, squeezed her nipple lightly between his thumb and forefinger. "Different how?"

Ribbons of pleasure raced through her, her bottom clenching when he slid his finger free. "I don't know. Just different."

"Hmm. We'll have to talk about that. Right now, though, we have more important things to take care of. I'm going to put more salve in you, and I'm going to use two fingers this time. I'll go real slow, but I've got to stretch you a little to get your ass ready for my cock."

Her bottom clenched, the need to be filled strange and exciting.

"Down on your knees, honey." Supporting her weight, he eased her to her knees. "That's it. Keep your knees on the clothes and blankets so you don't hurt them." He scraped his teeth over her neck, sending another wave of longing through her. "You're so soft and tiny. I need to be careful with you."

Fisting her hands on either side of her head, she braced herself, her toes curling when he pressed a hand to the center of her back. "I don't want you to be careful. I want you to take me." Her pussy and ass kept clenching, while her clit tingled hotly for attention.

"Put your shoulders down, Sarah. Jesus, this ass is a thing of beauty." Phoenix's voice, barely a rasp, sent shivers up and down her spine.

Sarah cried out again at the burning sensation of having two fingers pushed into her, but found herself pushing back against him. "Phoenix! Oh, God. It burns."

"Do you want me to stop?" His voice, deep and rough with tension, came from just behind her ear.

Arching her back to give him better access, she lifted into his touch again. "No! I can't believe we're doing this." Her thighs shook as the pleasure grew, her voice becoming shaky and breathless. "I can't believe you're touching me there. Phoenix, are you sure this'll work?"

Sliding his hand from her breast, he pressed it against her back again, his firm fingers moving in and out of her with a slow deliberation that only made her want more. "It's not only going to work, honey, it's going to feel so good."

The need in his voice fueled her own, allowing a wildness she hadn't know existed inside her to break free.

Bucking restlessly, she threw her head back, her breath coming out in ragged moans. "Please. I ache so bad."

Straightening again, he ran his hand up and down her spine. "Hell, woman, you're gonna be the death of me."

Moaning in frustration when he pulled his fingers free, she clenched helplessly, crying out when the head of his cock pressed firmly against her puckered opening.

Her bottom burned as he worked the head of his cock into her, the shock of it rendering her immobile. "Oh, God. It's going in."

Phoenix growled, a low, gravelly, primitive sound that excited her even more. "Yes. Hell, you're tight." He pushed against her slick puckered opening, not stopping until the head of his cock forced the tight ring of muscle to give way. "Say my name."

Crying out at the full, stretched sensation, Sarah fisted her hands as a shudder raced through her. "Phoenix!"

Her clit tingled unbearably, the need for his touch so strong, she whimpered. "Please, Phoenix."

She felt wild, and Phoenix's low groans and curses made her feel even wilder.

Slowly rocking his hips, Phoenix pushed his cock deeper. "Hell, woman, you're killing me. Say my name again."

She cried out again at the burning, stretched feeling as he pushed his cock deeper into her ass, stunned at the overwhelming feeling of being taken there.

So wild.

So primitive.

"Phoenix. Oh, God." Alarmed at how solid his cock felt inside her, she stilled. "Phoenix? Please. Oh, God. It's so deep."

"Easy, honey." Bracing a hand on the ground, he pressed his lips against her neck. "You're mine now. I'm taking my wife. How can you think I don't want you?" His cock jumped inside her, the feel of it startling her. "You belong to me now, and I don't think I'll ever get enough of you."

Sobbing with hunger, she lifted her head and turned it toward him. "Phoenix. It feels too good. How can something so naughty this feel so good?"

"Because we want each other." He buried his face against her neck, his hand sliding down her body. "It's gonna get better."

Her stomach muscles quivered under his hand, her body tightening when his fingers slid over her mound. "Yes. Please. Oh, God. It's so hard. I feel so full. Oh!" She couldn't hold back her moans when he withdrew almost all the way before thrusting deep again. Jolting when his fingers slid over her clit, she started shaking harder, the pleasure too much to endure.

He groaned, his deep voice rumbling next to her ear. "Yes. So good. So tight. So sweet. Yes, honey. My cock's so damned hard. I can't hold out much longer. Hmm. You're soaking wet, love. Yes. Oh, yes. You like that."

The pleasure sharpened in her clit, and with a sob, she tried to close her legs, but couldn't. Shaking, she tried to grab his hand, the waves of pleasure growing and threatening to overtake her. "Phoenix!"

"I've got you, honey."

Without warning, the pleasure exploded, the heat and delicious tingling sensation coursing through her veins overwhelming her.

Caught in the grip of pleasure so intense it almost hurt, she barely registered Phoenix's low curse.

A low growl rumbled from his chest as his cock stilled inside her. His fingers slowed on her clit, drawing out her orgasm until she couldn't hold herself up anymore.

Phoenix caught her when she slumped, his voice low and crooning. "I've got you, honey. Just lie still and I'll take care of you."

She couldn't seem to move, each slide of his hand over her body creating little sizzles of heat, while somehow soothing her. "Oh, Phoenix. I'm so weak."

"You're okay, honey." Warm lips moved over her back. "I've got you. Yeah." His arms tightened around her, his lips pressed against her upper back. "I've got you."

They stayed that way for several long minutes, the sounds of their breathing and water dripping, and the caress of Phoenix's hands up and down her sides lulling her almost to sleep.

A moan escaped as he withdrew from her ass, her inner walls so sensitive that she clenched on him again. "Oooohhh!"

"Shh." Running his hand over her bottom, he turned her head until she faced him and studied her features. "I know, honey. Your bottom and clit are sensitive. Just stay here while I get something to clean you up and you'll feel better."

Smiling when he tossed the edges of the blanket over her cooling body, she burrowed deeper. "I can do it. Just let me lie here for a minute." Still trembling with the remnants of her orgasm, she closed her eyes, pillowing her head on his shirt and breathing in the warm, male scent of him. "Just a minute."

"Just rest, honey."

She must have drifted off, because the next thing she knew, he knelt beside her, soaking a cloth from his canteen. "Phoenix?"

"Shh." After cleaning her slit, he spread the cheeks of her bottom, chuckling softly and holding her when she squirmed. "There's no reason to be embarrassed. I'm your husband. It's my right to take care of you this way—to see you this way."

His smile held a new tender possessiveness that tripped her pulse. "You're my wife. You're going to spend the rest of your life with Hawke, Blade, and me, and if you're going to get embarrassed every time we're intimate, you're going to spend your entire life blushing."

Phoenix slid in next to her, pulling her close and pillowing her head on his chest. "You know you've gotten to me, don't you?"

Sarah smiled weakly, turning her face toward the fingers sliding over her cheek. "Does that mean you don't regret marrying me?"

His lips touched her hair. "Never. You're in my blood now. I thought you were beautiful from the beginning, but now I understand why Hawke and Blade are so enthralled with you. I didn't see what they saw, and now I understand why you didn't feel as close to me as you felt with them."

"They wanted to marry me. You only married me because they did."

"That's not true—not entirely." His fingers slid through her hair. "You interested me, but I didn't want to get attached to you. I really didn't think you'd stay."

Secretly pleased, she snuggled closer, loving the feel of his warm arms wrapped around her. "You were too busy watching the saloon girls to notice me."

Fisting a hand in her hair, he rolled her to her back, his eyes hooded. "Are you lookin' for compliments?" The sparkle of playfulness and affection in his eyes gave her the confidence to lift her face to kiss his chin.

She ran her finger over his bottom lip, thrilled when he kissed it. "Maybe. Maybe I just want to make sure that you're happy that you married me and that you aren't going to visit those women when you go back to town."

She watched his eyes, forcing a smile while holding her breath for his answer.

\* \* \* \*

Phoenix stared down at her, wondering what he'd ever done to deserve her. The feel of her soft curves under him had his cock stirring again, but the way she moved and the weakness in her voice told him that she'd had enough loving for now.

He could wait, now that he knew she wanted him, too.

Lying back, he closed her eyes, enjoying the feel of her in his arms. Smiling to himself, he realized that he hadn't even thought of the saloon since he left town, and even now, his body still trembling from the pleasure he'd found with his wife, he couldn't recall the faces of the women he'd bedded there.

Sarah's image was the only one he saw, every feature imprinted in his mind and wiping away the image of every other woman he'd ever known.

"You really like me?"

Phoenix's eyes snapped open. "Like?" Rising to his elbow, he leaned over her, his chest swelling with pride at the lingering pleasure still clouding her eyes. "I think it's a little more than like."

Touching his lips to hers again, he held her tight, surprised at how much pleasure he got just from kissing her. He fisted his hand in her hair to hold her head tilted, and sipped at her lips, quickly becoming addicted to her kisses.

Her shy attempt to kiss him back excited him more than the practiced moves of the whores in town, and gave him a feeling of masculine satisfaction that he'd never expected.

Lifting his head, he stared down at her, smiling at the picture she made with her eyes closed and her head tilted back. "No, sweetheart. I think I more than like you, and it scares the hell out of me."

# Chapter Ten

Leaning against the wooden fence, Blade looked up as he'd been doing every couple of seconds for the last hour, searching the horizon. "It's gonna be dark soon."

Hawke lifted his head from the barrel of water he'd dipped his face into to cool off. Throwing his head back, he pushed his long hair out of the way, and glanced in Blade's direction. "She's with Phoenix. He'll watch out for her."

Shifting restlessly, Blade looked out into the distance again, not believing his brother's cool nonchalance for an instant. Anyone who knew Hawke well would recognize the look of concern in his eyes. "Don't give me that. You're just as worried as I am. He doesn't feel for her what we do. Everything's a game to him."

Hawke shrugged, slipping his shirt on. "He'll change his tune, or I'll change it for him. Neither one of you had to marry her." Turning to Blade, he narrowed his eyes. "What is it that you think you feel for her?"

Amused at his brother's attitude, Blade turned to face him fully. "You know damned well she's gotten to me." His cock stirred with anticipation of the things he planned to do to her. "She's so damned sweet that I just want to take a bite out of her, and so passionate that I can't stop thinking about all the things I want to teach her. I never even dreamed we could have anyone like her. Hell, I never thought we'd share a woman. I just knew that I'd regret it if I didn't make her mine while I had the chance."

Hawke frowned and glanced into the distance again. "But do you care about her? I don't want you playing with her and hurting her feelings when she finds out it's just sex for you."

Insulted, and more than a little annoyed, he closed his hands into fists. "What the hell makes you think it's just sex for me?"

Hawke looked pointedly at Blade's hands, his lips twitching. "You're starting to love her, too, aren't you?"

Blade straightened, his pulse leaping when he saw Phoenix coming over the hill. "Yeah, but I'm sure as hell not gonna let her have the upper hand. Look at them together. She's gonna lead Phoenix around by the nose and you're not much better."

"Excuse me?" Hawke's dark brow went up.

Blade smiled, elated that his older brother had finally found a woman he could care for. "You heard me. I see you with her, and you've already fallen hard. You coddle her."

Turning to watch Phoenix approach, Hawke frowned. "She could use some coddling. I don't think she's ever had any tenderness in her life. Why the hell is she lying across Phoenix's lap that way? I hope he didn't let her get hurt."

Blade had already had the same thought and rushed toward his brother's horse, slowing when he heard her giggle. Pausing as the horse stopped next to him, he reached up for her, struck by the new intimacy between his wife and brother.

Unable to help himself, he gathered her against him and bent his head to touch his lips to her swollen ones. "I missed you. Did you have a nice ride?" Holding her, he took in her flushed cheeks and shy smile before lowering her to her feet.

She glanced at Phoenix before smiling up at him. "Yes, we had a nice ride. It was scary at first, but not so scary on the way home. Phoenix made sure I didn't have to look at the ground. I smell like horse now, though, and I'd better go get cleaned up."

Blade couldn't help but notice that she didn't walk as gracefully as she had before. Her walk had a stiffness to it and she winced a few times. Realizing what was wrong, he ran a hand down her back in sympathy. "You're sore, aren't you, honey? It was a new experience for you."

Her cheeks turned fiery red and she glanced at Phoenix. "How did you know? Oh, God. I hope you're not mad. It just sort of happened." Her words came out in a rush, the panic in her eyes confusing him. Snapping her mouth closed, she looked up at Phoenix, who threw his head back and laughed. "Oh. You're talking about riding the horse, aren't you?"

Blade turned to glare at his brother. "Something went on while you were gone, and I want to know what happened. Right now."

Hawke crossed his arms over his chest and shot a look at Phoenix. "So do I."

Phoenix kept his voice low, his eyes dancing as he slid from the horse and approached Sarah, completely ignoring his brothers. "Blade was referring to the fact that you were on horseback for the first time, not that I took your ass."

Intrigued at that piece of information, Blade lifted her chin, his cock thickening as he regarded her features.

She looked so damned innocent, but he'd already seen and felt her passion.

Remembering what Hawke had said to Maggie about having her husbands wrapped firmly around her finger, he blew out a breath, knowing that he'd have to be careful not to let his beautiful wife wrap her around his.

With a hand at her back, he led her to the house they shared with her, his mind spinning with plans for the evening ahead. "After supper, we'll go to the hot spring near here, and you can soak. Then, when we get home, I'll rub you down with some liniment."

Impatient to get her naked and get his hands on her, he spoke sharper than he'd intended. To make up for it, he wrapped an arm around her and smiled.

Her eyes lit up, delighting him. "Really? There's a hot spring near here? I've heard of them, but I've never actually seen one."

His lips twitched. "There really is."

She bit her swollen lip, and he reacted instinctively, bending to take it with his own, sliding his tongue over her bottom lip in an effort to ease the sting she must have caused.

Lifting his head, he couldn't help but smile. "Don't bite your lips. Save them for me to nibble on later."

Her blush sent a surge of masculine power through him. "Will we be able to get into the spring naked?"

Blade laughed at that. "Definitely naked."

"Will anyone be able to see us?"

Hawke spoke from behind her. "We'll all go. Wash your hands, but don't bother changing. We'll take some fresh clothes so we can all change afterward. Let's eat. You hardly touched a thing at lunch."

For Blade, the meal seemed to take forever. He ate hurriedly, anxious to get to the spring with Sarah.

Phoenix watched Sarah through the meal, the smiles he shared with her more intimate than earlier. Glancing at Blade, he chuckled. "What's your hurry?"

Blade glared back. "Just because you're satisfied doesn't mean the rest of us are."

Hawke looked up from where he, too, watched Sarah. "She's got to be tired and sore. She needs some rest."

Sarah blushed again. "Hawke, I'm all right. I am looking forward to the spring, though."

Blade shot a look at his older brother. "You act like I'm gonna attack her. She's my wife, too. Remember? Besides, I think I have a little more control than Phoenix."

Phoenix dropped his spoon and leaned forward, his eyes flashing with anger. "I have plenty of control, and I sure as hell didn't hurt her."

Hawke sighed in an uncharacteristic expression of frustration. "If you're gonna fight, don't do it around her. I don't want anyone making her feel like she's done something wrong." Turning, he held Sarah's gaze. "If she does, we'll all be included in letting her know it."

They ate in tense silence for several long minutes, the tension broken when Wyatt, Hayes, and Samantha joined them a short time later.

Samantha nudged Phoenix aside to sit across from Sarah, so Wyatt nudged a glowering Phoenix even farther down the wooden bench in order to sit next to his wife. Grinning, Sarah accepted the glass of milk from Wyatt. "I heard you're going to the hot spring tonight. You'll love it. It's so peaceful there."

Hayes grinned as he lowered himself to the seat on the other side of her. "Not for long." Wincing when Samantha made a show of kicking him hard under the table, he smiled in apology. "What do you expect? You don't think everybody know what goes on up there?"

The tension eased when the women started talking about the dresses Sarah would be making, only to increase again when they started talking about going into town together on the next trip.

Blade started to speak, Hawke already shaking his head. "Don't make plans for going to town yet, Sarah. Not until Willy's caught."

Wyatt frowned down at Samantha. "You're not going either. None of the women is leaving the ranch until this is over."

Dropping her spoon, Sarah lowered her head, her eyes full of apology when they met Savannah's. "I'm sorry. I didn't mean to bring trouble here. I've made a mess of everything."

Samantha slapped a hand on the table, much to the amusement of her husbands. "No! You haven't done anything wrong. It's that man who's after you that has a lot to answer for. I just hope I'm there when Wyatt and Hayes give him what he deserves!"

Wyatt blinked, his brows going up while he smiled indulgently at his obviously adored wife. "I didn't know you were so bloodthirsty, darlin'. I'm going to have to keep a closer eye on you—and no, you will absolutely not get anywhere near this outlaw. Drink your milk. You're eating for two now, remember?"

Hayes chuckled softly and reached across the table to lift Sarah's chin. "Don't feel bad. We're very much looking forward to meeting Willy."

Sarah sighed and dropped her head in her hands. "You don't understand." Lifting her head again, she looked around the table. "He's meaner than a snake. He's tough and he's got a short temper. He kills just for fun."

Blade ran a hand over her hair, surprised that she seemed so concerned about them facing someone as ridiculous as Willy Krenshaw. "Do we look like men who can't take care of themselves to you?"

She shook her head, but still looked apprehensive. "No. I have to say every man I've met here appears to be more than capable of taking care of himself."

Hawke grunted. "Themselves, their women, and the others. Go back to talkin' about your dresses."

Once everyone finished eating, Blade didn't linger over a cup of coffee the way he usually did.

Anxious to spend some time with Sarah, he hustled her out of the chow shack, leaving Hawke and Phoenix to deal with their dishes.

He led her to their house, his cock throbbing with a need he knew would have to go unsatisfied for now. "Come on. Let's get your nightgown and a blanket to cover you with that you can wear on the ride him, but you won't need either one tonight. You're sleeping with me."

Biting back a groan at the thought of spending the entire night with his beautiful, naked wife next to him and unable to do a thing to get some relief, he pushed the door of the small cabin open and ushered her inside. "Let's get your things together."

Gathering her things, he rolled them into the blanket and hurried her back outside. "Hurry. I'm sticky and sweaty and want to get cleaned up." Already aroused, he groaned as he thought of the hours of torture ahead of him.

Pausing in the doorway, he wrapped his free arm around her and yanked her close. "Even though I can't take you tonight, I want to see and hold you naked against me."

Her sharp intake of breath sent a surge of heat to his cock, testing his control. "Blade, I want that, too."

Seeing the honesty and need in her eyes, Blade nodded, running his thumb over her bottom lip. "Good." Turning her, they went back outside, only to find his brothers already on their horses and waiting.

Hawke moved closer and reached for Sarah. "Give her to me."

Blade smiled and handled up her nightgown, bundled in a blanket. "Not a chance. Here. You take this."

Hawke frowned, snatching the blanket from Blade's hand and tucking it into his saddlebag. "She rides with me on the way back."

Blade mounted his horse and reached down for her, settling her in front of him. Noticing her wince, he paused, frowning down at her. "Your thighs hurt, Sarah?"

He didn't give her time to answer, turning her in his arms and adjusting her across his lap. Leaning her back against his left arm, he used the right to push her skirt high.

Hawke moved in on his right, positioning the lantern he held over her legs to see them better in the waning light. "Looks like she's chafed some."

Phoenix rode up on his left, running a hand over Sarah's hair. "Yes, she is. That's why I rode back with her across my lap." Bending to touch his lips to her hair, Phoenix grinned and reached out to cup her breast. "One of the reasons."

Frowning, Hawke slid a gentle hand over her thighs. "I'll have to measure her for some buckskin leggings. They'll protect her skin better."

Sarah smiled, moving sensuously on his lap, her low moan like a stroke to his cock. "Are you going to dress me like an Indian?"

Hawke stilled, his eyes narrowing. "Do you have a problem with that?"

"Hmm." Holding onto Blade, she smiled when Hawke caught her foot and spread her legs wider. "Not at all. Then everyone will know I'm your woman."

Hawke smiled at that, his hard features softening as he ran a hand down her leg. "They'll know that anyway. Come on. Let's get going. The warm water will ease a lot of that soreness and make you feel better."

Blade held her securely as they started toward the spring, loving the feel of his woman in his arms.

With her head against his chest and her small hand flattened against him, she pulled at every protective instinct inside him, making him feel even more possessive. He'd never felt so much a man.

So needed.

Wiggling on his lap, she sat straighter and smiled at Hawke. "Can you teach me how to make clothes like yours? I can make some for myself and some more for you."

Knowing how much that would mean to his brother, Blade ran a hand down her back in gratitude.

Hawke glanced at her and shrugged. "Of course. I'll work with you. I need to make another pair of fur-lined moccasins for winter. You need some, too."

"I can't believe you sew them yourself."

Blade chuckled softly and shared a look with Hawke, who blew out the lantern. "Hawke and I can both make buckskins. Moccasins. Sew a cut, whatever."

He smiled again at her shiver. "Do you think cuts sew themselves?"

"I don't want to think about it. Do you really think you could teach me how to make moccasins for myself?"

Blade kissed her hair. "Sure. We've got enough hides stored to make quite a few things."

"It's so dark. I can't see a thing."

Phoenix chuckled. "Just listen, honey. Listen to the sounds around you. Don't worry. We know this land like the backs of our hands and there's enough moonlight to light our way. We're almost there. Listen. You can hear the water."

"I hear it. Oh, it sounds heavenly."

Blade hugged her closer. "It will be."

# Chapter Eleven

Sarah reached for Hawke, smiling up at him as he took her from Blade.

Eager to make him smile, she wrapped her arms around his neck and kissed him, giggling at his look of surprise. "Do you think that if I wore buckskins, I could pass for an Indian?"

Lowering her slowly to her feet, Hawke chuckled, something she'd learned was rare for him. Tugging at her braid, he held it up. "With blonde hair? Something tells me that no one would believe that."

He took her hand and turned, walking behind Phoenix, who led the way with a lantern he'd already lit. Blade lit another and handed it to Hawke before lighting one more.

When the spring came into view, Hawke released her hand. "Don't move. I wouldn't want you falling in."

He and the others moved away, placing the lanterns on the flat rocks surrounding the spring.

Despite the fact that the night air still had a warm, humid stickiness to it, steam rose from the water, giving the entire spring an unreal look, like in one of the fairy tales Mrs. Anderson in town used to read to her.

"It's so beautiful." She kept her voice low, not wanting to spoil the atmosphere. She looked up to find each of her husbands watching her, their lips curved into indulgent smiles. She smiled back before turning to scan their surroundings. "Are you sure no one will come here?"

Blade reached for her, his smile widening as he loosened her braid. "I'm sure. Anyone from the ranch coming this way will hear us long before they get here."

Lifting her chin, he dropped a soft kiss on her nose, his fingers busy on the buttons of her shirt. "They'll see the lanterns and will know we're here. Besides, we already told them we were coming here tonight and word spreads quickly on the ranch."

The feel of the warm night air caressing her breasts as he pulled the edges of her shirt aside had her reaching for him to steady herself. "This feels good already."

Blade smiled and untied her skirt, allowing it to puddle at her feet. "You're a very sensual woman, aren't you? You lift your face to the sun. You move into every touch. Even the air on your skin excites you."

Phoenix moved in beside her, kneeling at her feet as he stripped her out of her boots. Lifting her foot, he kissed her toes, sending sharp tingles of heat up her leg. "She loves it every time one of us touches her. Kinda makes you want to keep touching her, doesn't it?"

Blade ran a hand over her, pausing to tug at her nipples and smiling at her soft moan of pleasure. "I have plans to do just that." Taking her nipple between his thumb and forefinger, he gently squeezed. "I have all kinds of touching in mind."

Hawke moved in behind her. "Come on, little one. The water will feel good on your skin. Let me help you. The rocks can get slippery."

Turning, she gasped when she found herself pulled against Hawke's naked body.

Pressed against him and with the low light of the lanterns allowing her to see him clearly, she stood dumbstruck.

He was hard everywhere, every line of his body and sharp features solid and unforgiving. His cock jumped against her belly, emphasizing his masculinity even more.

Gulping, she pressed her hands against his chest, her breath coming in short pants as she lifted her gaze to his. A sob escaped at the tenderness in his eyes, a look that sharpened with concern.

Lifting her chin, he searched her features. "What is it, little one? You look scared. You're not scared of me, are you?"

Deciding to answer honestly, Sarah smiled faintly. "You have to admit, you're awfully scary looking. So strong. It would be so easy for you to hurt me if you wanted to."

Hawke smiled at that. "Yet you're afraid we can't handle your little outlaw." Taking her hand, he led her into the warm water—water that felt like heaven—while Blade and Phoenix stripped out of their own clothing. "For the record, I would never hurt a hair on your head, and you know it. Here. There's a ledge that goes most of the way around it."

When she started to lower herself onto the ledge, he lowered himself to the seat beside her. "Nope. You're too far away." Without warning, he tightened his hands on her waist and settled her on his lap.

The feel of his cock pressing against her bottom stole her breath. "Oh!"

Running his hands over her back and thighs, he laughed softly. "Yeah. Oh. I like having you on my lap. Now, why don't you just lean against me and let the water ease your sore muscles?"

Leaning against him, she watched Phoenix and Blade step into the spring, her pulse racing at the sight they made. She tried to reach for them, but Blade shook his head and took her hand in his. "No, love. Just close your eyes and let the water soothe you. I'm right here."

The combination of firm hands moving over her and the warm water caressing her body eased her aches and relaxed her muscles one by one until she felt as though she floated.

Then she realized that she was floating.

Blade's hands supported her shoulders, and Hawke had moved to the center of the small pool, supporting her bottom and thighs, but keeping them submerged.

Blade braced her shoulders against his chest, and with a groan, slid his hands up to cover her breasts. "So, you and Phoenix had a nice ride? I understand you stopped at the small cave."

The feel of his lips against her neck and his hands sliding over her breasts had her tilting her head to the side to give him better access, not bothering to open her eyes. "Hmmm."

Frustrated that he didn't give her nipples the attention they needed, she shifted restlessly, but it had no effect.

Opening her eyes, she sucked in a breath when she saw Phoenix standing directly in front of her, a half-smile playing at his lips as he parted her legs and lifted her knees to his shoulders. The ache in her nipples drove her crazy, and when she looked down at them, she realized that Blade held her so that just her nipples were out of the water. Even though the night remained warm, the water was much warmer—making the air on her nipples feel cooler by comparison.

It drove her crazy.

Running his fingers down the backs of her thighs to her bottom, Phoenix groaned. "Tell them what I did to you."

Blade slid his fingers over her nipples, drawing a cry from her. "Yes. Tell us what Phoenix did to you."

The brief attention he gave to her nipples in no way satisfied her. Instead, it left her aching for more. Her stomach muscles clenched at the slide of Hawke's hand over it, her thighs trembling at the feel of Phoenix's fingers moving over her still sensitive bottom hole. "He undressed me and turned me around, and bent me over. Oh!"

Hawke's hand moved slowly down her body, not stopping until her parted her folds. "Did you like that?"

"Yes. Oh, God. Please do something."

Blade chuckled, tugging her nipples once before releasing them again, increasing the awareness there. "We are doing something.

Several things at once. So you were bent over, with that pretty bottom stuck out. What happened then?"

Aroused beyond belief, she squirmed restlessly, desperate for Blade to stroke her nipples, desperate for Hawke to touch her clit, desperate for Phoenix to push his finger inside her. Her desperation made her angry, and she snapped. "You know what happened then! Why are you doing this to me?"

Hawke frowned. "Doing what, little one? We're just holding you, caressing you, and asking what happened with Phoenix." He turned his head, glaring at his youngest brother. "Did he hurt you? Did he use enough salve?"

Phoenix sighed and gathered her against him. "I know what I'm doing, Hawke. I used salve, and went slow. Ask Sarah if I hurt her. Believe it or not, Blade and I are well practiced in taking women that way, or do you think any of those girls in the saloon are willing to take a chance of getting pregnant by an Indian?"

Blade stiffened against her back, his hands massaging her shoulders. "Not a conversation to have in front of our wife, Phoenix."

Phoenix cursed again, and moved to the edge of the spring. "She knows I don't want anyone but her. I didn't hurt her. Check her out if you don't believe me."

Sarah gasped as she found herself turned and eased to her knees, a hand at her back pushing her down until her breasts were pressed against the smooth, wet rocks at the edge. Gulping at the awareness in her bottom when Blade grabbed one of the lanterns and held it behind her, she struggled to get up, but the firm hand at her back held her in place.

Hands moved over her bottom, parting her cheeks. Fingers ran over her bottom hole, one pushing slightly into her.

Hawke groaned. "She's very sensitive there, isn't she?"

Phoenix moved up to sit beside her, kissing her shoulder. "You have no idea."

Blade said something under his breath she didn't understand. "I'll get the salve. It'll help her feel better."

Sarah cried out. "If I felt any better, I'd go crazy! Listen, you sons of bitches, if you don't do something soon, I'm going to—"

Blade growled, a deep sound that seemed to come from his soul. "Watch your language." A hard hand came down on her bottom, making her jump. "You're not going to do a damned thing because there's nothing you can do about it. You belong to us, remember? In case you haven't noticed, we're a hell of a lot bigger and stronger than you are, and we're not going to be wrapped around your little finger like the other men on the ranch are with their wives. Behave yourself, or I'm going to give you a spanking that you won't ever forget."

Before she thought about the consequences of her actions, she turned to glare at him over her shoulder, the need to challenge him not to be denied. "Go ahead and do it! I'm not scared of you."

"Yes, you are, but not that we'll hurt you." Blade knelt on the lower ledge of the flat rock next to her and kissed her hair. "Phoenix said that you were upset earlier."

Although he hadn't phrased it as a question, she knew by his tone that he expected an answer.

Turning to watch Phoenix head to his horse, naked and wet, and retrieve the metal tin from his saddle bag, she moaned. "Phoenix and I talked about it." The feel of the cool rocks against her nipples threatened her sanity, and she found herself rubbing against them to get the friction they needed.

When she realized that her movements also wiggled her ass, she tried to stop, but couldn't.

The water splashed slightly when Phoenix eased down on the other side of her, his smile one of pure seduction. "Yes, we did." Setting the open tin in front of her, he ran a finger down her spine to her puckered opening. "She thought I didn't want her, and was afraid she wasn't a good wife. I told you the rest."

He handed the tin to Hawke. "Here, you check her out while I tell you why she was crying."

Stilling when Blade moved to stand behind her, Sarah sucked in a breath at the feel of her bottom cheeks being parted wide.

Phoenix reclined next to her, one hand supporting his head as he held himself propped on his elbow, while the other hand replaced Blade's on her back. "She knows better now."

Hawke chuckled. "It sounds like she's gotten to you, too. I'm glad you've decided to take this seriously." Running his finger over her forbidden opening, he touched his lips to her bottom. "Sarah hasn't been treated very well, and she hasn't had anyone to protect her. All that has changed."

Blade slid a hand under her hair and cupped the back of her neck, turning her face toward his. "This is a dangerous place and you have rules to follow now in order to keep you safe. I know you're not used to having anyone pay attention to you before, and have done what you could to be ignored, but that's not an option for you anymore."

Humbled by their concern, she smiled, loving the feel of Hawke's caress over her back and bottom. "I know it's dangerous here, but I feel so safe with you—safer than I've ever felt in my life. I can't tell you how much that means to me."

Blade's voice deepened, his expression hardening. "You're thinking about Willy. Anyone after you has to go through us to get to you. That's not going to happen."

Hawke parted her ass cheeks again. "So how did you like having your little bottom taken?"

Blushing, she tried to turn away, but Blade's hand in her hair prevented it. "I didn't even feel like myself."

"No?" Blade took the seat beside her again, keeping her face turned toward his. "So what does it feel like to be taken there?"

A shiver went up and down her spine, the sensation of a finger, thick with salve going into her bottom making it difficult to concentrate. "Oh, God!"

The knowledge that Hawke was the one pushing his finger deep made the sensation even sharper. "It feels so sinful. It's too private. I'm embarrassed that it feels so good."

Blade ran a thumb over her bottom lip. "There's nothing sinful about being taken by your husbands, and nothing to be embarrassed about. You're ours. That's the beginning and the end of it." Pressing at her bottom lip, he watched her closely, his eyes flaring each time she cried out. "How does it make you feel when one of us touches you the way Phoenix touched you earlier—the way Hawke's touching you now?"

Bending toward her, he brushed her lips with his. "Tell me."

Struggling against the increasing awareness in such a private place, she bit her lip and groaned. "It makes me feel so helpless, but not helpless like I was in Waco. Helpless like a woman. I don't know. It's hard to explain."

Especially when Hawke moved his finger inside her, and her brain stopped working.

Hawke withdrew his finger, pausing to kiss her bottom again. "She looks fine. I'm going to put some more salve into you, little one, and spread it around. I'm not hurting you, am I?"

"No." She didn't want to admit that Hawke's gentle, intimate touch had aroused her, especially since he'd concentrated his attention on her bottom.

Hawke slid his into her again, his touch firmer than before. He murmured softly to her when she cried out, the feel of being taken there making her tremble. "Easy, little one. I just want to spread the salve inside you. It'll make you feel better."

Gritting her teeth as the awareness and need for more continued to build, she threw her head back and wiggled, sucking in a breath when Blade cupped one breast while Phoenix cupped the other. "I can't believe what you do to me. Oh, God. How can it feel so good?"

Chuckling softly, Hawke moved his finger with more firmness, pressing against the walls of her bottom. "You *do* like this. Hmm. Just in case you haven't noticed, you do things to us, too."

She couldn't help but glanced down at Blade's cock, frustrated that she couldn't see it clearly beneath the swirling water. "I do?"

Blade closed his thumb and forefinger over her nipple, his gaze holding hers. "You do."

Hawke pressed a thumb against her clit, moving it slowly back and forth. "At times you unnerve the hell out of me."

Blade's eyes narrowed. "You're under my skin, but I won't let you wrap me around your finger." He tugged at her nipple, a slow smile spreading at her cry of pleasure. "Instead, I'm going to do whatever it takes to have you wrapped around mine."

Blade stroked her nipple while bending to touch his lips to her shoulder. "You had the privilege of taking her virginity, and Phoenix took her ass first. It's my turn to enjoy our wife and give her a taste of what she can expect from me." Although he spoke to Hawke, he never took his eyes from hers.

Sarah gulped, remembering what Willy had forced Rose to do as she'd rushed out of Rose's room. "I think I know what you want. Willy forced Rose to her knees and made her take his cock into her mouth. I ran out of the room, so I don't know what she did, but if you show me, I'll do my best."

A cold chill went through her, and her position had embarrassment taking over again.

Blade frowned, running his hands down her back. "You stiffened up and there's fear in your eyes. There's no need for that." His gaze flicked to Hawke's. "I've got her. She turns to you for protection, and it's about time she learned that she can come to me as well."

Hawke eased his finger from her bottom. "She's scared. I'm here, Sarah, but Blade's right. You're going to have to look to him and Phoenix for protection, too."

Blade turned her back to face him. "Look at me." He pushed her hair back from her forehead, his eyes glittering with something that stole her breath. "What you're talking about doesn't have to be the way you saw back in Waco."

Pulling her against him, he settled her on his lap, running a hand over her breast. "Sex can be a lot of things. Back in Waco, you saw women use it to make enough money to survive. It's not like that with us, is it?"

Lulled by his silky tone, Sarah looked up at him through her lashes, relaxing against him. "No. It isn't. I thought it would be. When Willy looked at him, I wanted to vomit, but when you look at me, and touch me, it gives me a mushy feeling inside."

Blade's lips twitched. "Well, I'm glad we make you mushy, but I was hoping for a little more than that. I guess we're gonna have to work harder."

Her face burned, his teasing smile relaxing her even more. Giggling, she slapped at him. "That's not what I meant."

He caught her hand in his before it hit his chest, smiling as he opened it to kiss her palm. "I know what you meant, honey."

He pushed her hair back from her forehead, as though he couldn't stop touching it. "I get that same feeling when you touch me."

"Really?" Frowning, she searched his face for any hint that he was still teasing her. Her stomach fluttered at the thought of having that kind of power over such a man.

Blade's features, clearly visible in the light from the lanterns on either side of him now, softened. "I don't get *mushy*. I get hard whenever you're around." Lifting her hands to his chest, he smiled. "Your touch definitely has an effect on me. I like the feel of your hands on me. I want to feel more."

Gulping, Sarah slid a glance to her left to find both Phoenix and Hawke watching the scene playing out in front of them. Turning back to Blade, she gulped again. "I make you feel that way?"

"Yes, Sarah. You do. I'm your husband and lover now." His eyes narrowed when her hands moved over his chest to his shoulders. "Don't you like it when I touch you?"

Nodding, Sarah ran her hands down his arms, pausing now and then to press her fingertips against solid muscle. "The women at the saloon—?"

"They don't exist anymore. There's only you. Our wife." Bending his head, he touched his lips to hers, his cock jumping against her thigh. "You're everything I ever wanted—and more."

He took her mouth slowly, as though savoring every second of their kiss.

Dizzy, she slid her hands over his chest and shoulders, clinging to him.

He sipped at her lips with a gentleness that ripped through her defenses, only to nip at them and strengthen his hold as if to remind her that he was in charge.

He built the pleasure in stages, the rhythm of his kiss changing from slow seduction to heat and demand. One kiss flowed into another, until she didn't know where one began and the other ended. When he lifted his head, she forced her eyes open, desperate to see his face.

Her breath caught at the need glittering in his eyes, her pulse tripping at the way his hands tightened on her waist.

Lifting her from his lap, he glanced at Phoenix, who moved to stand behind her. "I don't want you to do anything you're not willing to do, and if you get scared about something, I want you to tell me." Raising himself from the water, he sat on the outer ledge of the spring. "There'll be times when you're nervous, but in a good way. If it's in a bad way, I want you to tell us."

The tenderness in his eyes and in his tone wiped away the last of her trepidation, while the sight of his body and jutting cock filled her with a sense of excitement and anticipation. His cock seemed to grow under her gaze. "Do you want to touch me?"

Sarah shivered and leaned toward him while Phoenix slid his hands to her breasts and steadied her. "You won't mind?"

Blade smiled, a smile filled with tension. "Come here. I want to feel your hands on my cock."

Unable to resist the challenge and need in his eyes, Sarah slowly moved forward, flattening her hands on his thighs to steady herself. Smiling when his thighs tensed beneath her hands, she positioned herself between his powerful legs. "Are you sure I won't hurt you?"

Blade's jaw clenched. "Just a soft touch. I'll tell you what to do."

Phoenix tugged at her nipples. "Go on, Sarah. He's dying for you to touch him."

Mesmerized by the sight of his thick cock, and fascinated by the sight of his dark, sleek skin, Sarah knelt on the flat rock, the surface of the water just below her breasts. With her left hand on his thigh, she reached out the right, watching his face as she gently stroked his cock.

His deep groan startled her into pulling her hand back. His body bowed, the tension in it alarming.

Reaching out, he took her hand in his, pulling her back. "Son of a bitch. Don't stop, honey. It feels good. Too damned good."

"Did I hurt you?"

"You're killing me." Opening his eyes, he smiled. "Do it again."

Confident now, and filled with a sense of feminine power, she reached for him again, this time with both hands. Running her hands up and down the length of his cock, she watched him, amazed at the groans of pleasure that poured out of him.

Slowing her strokes, she took the time to explore him, marveling that something so hard could feel so velvety in her hands. She lifted her gaze to his again, smiling to find him watching her. "It's so hard, but so soft. I like touching you."

Feeling like the luckiest woman in the world, she smiled tremulously. "It's different, isn't it?"

Holding her face between his large hands, he ran his thumbs over her cheeks. "Tell me how it's different. Don't you dare cry." Taking both of her hands in his, he kissed her palms. "Tell me what's going through that pretty head of yours."

Aware of Hawke's and Phoenix's sharp attention, Sarah sighed and glanced at each of them. "It's so different. So wonderful. There's no disgust in your eyes when I touch you. I can't believe I can give you the kind of pleasure you give me." Pulling her hands from his, she smiled and reached for his cock again. "Please. Show me how to please you. It's so exciting to see that you like the way I touch you. Show me. Show me what to do."

She didn't want to sound silly and tell him that the affection and warmth in his eyes made her feel special, especially after he'd already claimed to fight the emotion that would wrap him around her finger.

An emotion she no longer could fight, and didn't really want to.

His jaw clenched, his eyes narrowing. "You really are trying to kill me, aren't you?" With another deep groan, he curved his hand around hers and guided her movements, the pleasure in his eyes filling her with a satisfaction and sense of connection to him that stunned her.

"Yes, honey. Just like that. Squeeze just a little bit. Oh, hell." Throwing his head back, he released her hands and braced a hand on either side of his hips. "Slow down, Sarah, or I'm going to spill my seed too early. Damn it, Phoenix! Distract her."

Phoenix chuckled softly against her neck, his hands sliding from her breasts and under the water to her slit. "She's distracted, but it seems our wife is also a determined little thing. She's really liking turning you into *mush*."

Hawke lowered himself into the water and onto the flat rock next to Blade, his hooded gaze raking over her. "Yes, well, now that she's seen the effect she has on all three of us, I'm afraid we're going to have quite a battle on our hands." With a soft smile, a smile she'd already realized was reserved just for her, he reached out to touch a fingertip to her nipple. "She's got a sense of power now, one that I doubt she's ever had before."

Phoenix groaned and slid his fingers through her slit, and with a scrape of his teeth over her shoulder, slipped a finger into her pussy. "I like it. Yes." He moved his finger in slow strokes while sliding his thumb back and forth over her clit. "She wants to give as good as she gets. It's a good thing there are three of us, so we can distract her."

He stroked her clit, his hands firming when she started to writhe against him. "Look at Blade's face, Sarah. He's fighting not to come. Why don't you take his cock into your mouth and see what happens to him?"

Blade growled and reached for her, gripping her shoulders and pulling her toward his cock. "You're definitely killing me." He spoke through gritted teeth, each word sounding as if it had been dragged from him. "I don't want her to do anything that reminds her of *him*."

Sarah smiled, her blood bubbling with anticipation. "I want to."

Blade held firm when she tried to lean forward. "No. Maybe one day, but not now."

Glancing at Hawke for guidance, she bit back a moan when Phoenix started moving his fingers again.

Hawke inclined his head slightly, the look of hunger in his eyes sending another surge of heat through her. Closing his fingers on her nipple, he slid his hand under the water and began to stroke his cock.

Guided by instinct and hunger, she pushed Blade's hands aside, knowing that she could only because he allowed it. "Please, Blade. I want to. I need to feel the beauty of it, not the ugliness."

Running his hands through her hair, Blade groaned again. "Just a little. I don't want to come in your mouth. I want to be in that sweet pussy. You're not sore anymore, and I want to take my wife."

Her pussy clenched on Phoenix's finger. "Yes!"

Bending her head, she touched her tongue to the head of Blade's cock, thrilling at his deep groan. Delighted with the clean, masculine taste of him, she did it again.

The finger at her clit moved faster, her arousal wiping away the last lingering traces of embarrassment.

Her body trembled with the need for release, a release she knew they could give her.

Hungry for them, she moved against the cock at her back, inwardly smiling at Phoenix's sharp intake of breath.

Using the fingers of one hand to keep her folds parted, he used the fingers of his other to slide slowly over her clit. "Trying to tease me, are you, darlin'?"

Rocking her hips to get him to move faster, she lifted from Blade's cock. "I don't know how to tease."

The sight of Hawke's hand moving over his cock had her reaching for him as she bent her head and took Blade's cock deeper into her mouth.

"Suck on him, Sarah." Phoenix's voice sounded as if he'd swallowed glass, and she couldn't help but notice that his cock hardened even more against her lower back.

Smiling around Blade's cock at their low sounds of hunger, she fought her own desire to concentrate on their pleasure.

Within seconds, though, she found her efforts thwarted.

Blade lifted her from his cock with another one of those low groans that made her stomach muscles quiver, pulled her out of the water with apparent ease, and settled her on his lap. "You're too damned good at that."

Hawke turned away, taking his cock into his hand again. "She's good with her hand, too."

Blade lifted her several inches and lowered her onto his cock, impaling her on its thick length, crooning to her when she cried out. His hands closed on her waist. "Hawke, salve her ass again. I know some of it must have worn off under the water, and I want to see how our little wife reacts to having something in her pussy and ass at the same time."

Lifting his hands to her breasts, he tugged at her nipples, his eyes flaring at her cry. "She'll be ready soon for two of us to take her at once."

Gripping Blade's shoulders, Sarah tried to rock her hips. "Oh, God. I can't even imagine it. Is that really possible?"

Blade tightened his hold. "Yes, when you're ready." Pushing her hair back again, he smiled. "You liked sucking my cock, didn't you, love?"

Smiling, she pressed her breasts against his chest, sucking in a breath at the heat on her nipples. "Yes." Lifting her face to his, she followed her instincts again and kissed his jaw, gasping when his cock jumped inside her. "You, Hawke, and Phoenix make me feel wanted, but you also make me feel as if you care about me." She felt so full, each stroke of his cock forcing her inner walls to stretch to accommodate him.

Hawke kissed her shoulder from behind. "That's because we do."

Blade smiled and bent to brush her lips with his. "I'd cut my own hands off before I'd hurt you. You're becoming more important to me by the minute."

She felt so full, each stroke of his cock forcing her inner walls to stretch to accommodate him. Every bump and ridge that she'd felt on her tongue now provided a delicious friction inside her, one that had her body tightening.

Phoenix moved in beside her, watching her intently as he ran soothing hands over her back and leg. "That's a girl. Damn if you aren't beautiful."

Stiffening at the feel of Hawke's finger pressing into her bottom, Sarah cried out and bucked, but Blade controlled her movements, holding her by the waist as he kept thrusting into her. "Oh, God. It's happening again."

The tingling sensation made her dizzy, the feel of something moving in both her ass and pussy so overwhelming that she no longer had control of herself.

Blade groaned and moved faster. "Yeah, you like having something in your pussy and ass at the same time. That's good, because you've got three husbands who want you all the damned time."

Her toes curled, her cries filled with desperation. "It feels strange. Oh, God. It's too much. It tingles everywhere. Please. It's too strong. I think something's wrong."

Nothing could ever feel this good. Every inch of her body screamed with a pleasure that made her feel clumsy and weak. She shook uncontrollably and struggled to hold on to Blade's slippery shoulders. "Oh, God. Something's happening to me!"

Sliding his hands forward, Blade wrapped his arms around her and pulled her close, slowing his strokes. Fisting a hand in her hair, he held her head tilted back and stared into her eyes. "I've got you. Just let go." Brushing his lips over hers, he watched her closely, his eyes narrowed to slits. He thrust into her three more times in rapid succession before thrusting deep and stilling.

Sarah fisted her hands in his hair, holding on to the only solid thing she could, another wave washing over her at the feel of his cock pulsing inside her. "Blade. Don't let go of me. Oh!"

Panicked, she tightened her grip on Blade, who seemed to understand at once.

Smiling tenderly, he ran his hands up and down her spine, his gaze sharpening even more. "It's all right. You're all right. Yes, love. Breathe. That's it. Again. That's my girl."

Hawke slid his finger free and rushed to her side. "Is she all right?"

"Of course she's all right." Bending his head, Blade took her mouth in a slow, searing kiss, one that left her limp and shaking. "She's so passionate that it's hard for her to come down. She needs to know that we're here for her."

Hawke towered over her, his stance protective, his eyes dark with concern. "Of course we're here for her." He bent to touch his lips to hers, his hand running up and down her back. "You're ours, Sarah. For life. You can always depend on us to take care of you. You can always depend on us to keep you safe." Sliding his hands under her arms, he urged her to lean back against him. "Relax, honey. We've got you."

She moaned when Blade slid his cock free, too drowsy to move. Smiling at Phoenix, who came to stand next to her, she let out another moan at the feel of Blade's hands moving over her bottom and backs of her thighs, while Hawke held her shoulders. "So sleepy."

Phoenix smiled down at her, lathering one of her scented bars of soap between his palms. "Just lie there and relax while I wash you."

All three of them took turns washing her, their hands so gentle on her skin that she found herself dozing more than once.

Afterward, Blade carried her out of the water, and held her securely against his chest while Hawke dried her with care, his expression thoughtful. By the time he finished, Phoenix had finished dressing.

She leaned against him, grateful for his support as he dressed her. "You're awfully quiet. Is something wrong?"

Shaking his head, he buttoned her shirt. "No, Sarah. Nothing's wrong. Everything seems to be very right. You have quite an effect on Hawke and Blade, more than I'd anticipated."

Blade and Hawke finished dressing, each retrieving the lanterns before leading the way back to the horses.

Blade handed the lantern to Phoenix before mounting and reaching for her. "Yes, she's had quite an effect on us." Lifting her chin, he adjusted the light blanket Hawke threw over her. "But I can't let my feelings for her distract me. We have to protect her, no matter what it takes."

# Chapter Twelve

Phoenix watched Sarah sewing with Blade and Hawke, her laughter of delight filling their small cabin.

Her smile seemed to make the small cabin even brighter.

He could stand there and watch her all day.

It had been a week since the night at the spring, and since then, he felt as if his world had changed completely.

Everything they did now revolved around Sarah.

He'd never been happier.

Judging by the smiles on his brothers' faces, and their eagerness to get home at the end of the day, Hawke and Blade were just as happy.

Hawke's features relaxed into a smile more often, the sound of his laughter becoming more and more familiar.

Blade's darker side now revealed a sense of humor that hadn't been there before, and as he guided Sarah into some of his more wicked desires, he did it with a tenderness and patience that Phoenix never would have believed.

They talked, worked on deerskin clothes together, and took long walks around the ranch.

Sarah, Maggie, and Savannah had become fast friends, and Sarah had taken to gathering the flowers for soaps.

He slid his gaze to the fresh flowers she kept in a clay pot on one of the tables, breathing in the new scents that had somehow invaded the small cabin.

He'd always imagined having a woman to come home to each night, a woman to warm his bed and give him pleasure whenever he wanted it.

He'd never imagined all the little things that came with having a woman in the house.

Sarah had taken to drying flowers as well. His bedding even smelled like lavender.

Getting out of the cabin in the morning took longer than usual because they each took the time for a kiss and a cuddle with her before starting their day.

Even the sound of her bare feet on the wooden floor made him smile.

He'd never imagined sharing his wife with his brothers. When they'd married her, he'd assumed there'd be conflicts, but he hadn't thought about this indescribable need for intimacy with his wife—the need for a closeness that came from more than sex.

A closeness he'd never experienced.

An intimacy he'd never expected to have. To want.

To need.

Each day that passed, he found his feelings for her deepening.

He loved her.

Sitting on Blade's lap, she leaned trustingly against him, running her hands over the dress Hawke had just finished for her. "It's so beautiful. I'm going to wear it tomorrow."

The transformation in Hawke and Blade still astounded him.

His restless brothers seemed content—happy—to sit at the table with her while she sewed, their patience endless as they taught her how to make clothing from buckskin.

Hawke grinned, something he did more and more around her. "I'm glad you like it. It's more durable than the material you use for your skirts." He gestured toward the material she'd spread on the table to measure. "Make your skirts, but you need some fur-lined leggings for winter."

Sarah grinned. "They're gonna be so soft! I can't wait to wear them."

Blade cuddled her closer, running a hand over her hair, which she'd taken to wearing in a braid. "We'll start the moccasins tomorrow."

Phoenix clenched his jaw, wondering what he could do to get closer to her, to spend time with her.

He sure as hell couldn't sew.

Then he smiled.

Hawke and Blade were experts with the rifles they carried across their shoulders, and with the knives and tomahawks they wore attached to their belts.

Neither one of them, though, could shoot as well as Phoenix.

Drinking the last of his coffee, he moved to the table and took a seat on the other side of her. "I know she needs some things to wear, but I think it's time to teach her how to shoot. When she's here alone, I think she should have a gun with her, and know how to use it."

Sarah's smile never faltered, but Phoenix couldn't help but notice that she glanced at both Hawke and Blade as if seeking their approval.

Hawke nodded. "Good idea. Between shooting and working on her sewing, she'll be too busy to get into trouble."

His teasing tone may have fooled Sarah, but it didn't fool him.

Waiting for Willy to appear had everyone on the ranch on edge, a tension that grew worse with each passing day. They all knew he wouldn't give up his gold so easily.

They'd also learned from Hayes and Wyatt that Willy couldn't stand for anyone to get the better of him.

Sarah had done it in two ways—taking his gold and escaping his attention.

Willy Krenshaw would never stand for that, and would feel that he had to make Sarah pay for embarrassing him.

He should have come by now, and the fact that he hadn't made them all wonder what the outlaw had planned.

Eb and Jeremiah had reduced some of his and his brothers' chores so they could spend more time watching over her, and as each day passed, everyone worried more.

Sarah smiled up at Hawke. "I won't need to shoot anything. I'm real careful when I pick flowers, and don't go too far."

Phoenix got to his feet again, too restless to sit still. "But if something happens, I want you to know how to shoot. We'll go out first thing in the morning."

Sarah smoothed her hand over the material of her buckskin dress as if she couldn't stop touching it, looking from Hawke to Blade.

Phoenix snapped, slamming his hand on the table hard enough to knock her bolt of material to the floor. "Don't look at them. I'm your husband, too."

He regretted his tone as soon as the words left his mouth. Frustrated that the tension of waiting for Willy had gotten to him, allowing his jealousy to show, he ignored his brothers' sharp looks and leaned over the table until his nose almost touched Sarah's. "And you're sleeping with me tonight."

Turning, he stormed out before he said something that would make things even worse.

\* \* \* \*

Sarah watched Phoenix leave, swallowing heavily as she looked up at Hawke. "Did I do something wrong?"

Running his hand over her back, Blade smiled. "No. You haven't done anything wrong." He ran a threatening hand down to her bottom and tapped gently. "I'll be glad to let you know when you do."

Hawke went to the coffee pot on the small stove. "Phoenix is just a little upset. It's nothing for you to worry about. Are you going to the chow shack to help Duke?"

"Yes." Grinning, she jumped to her feet, anxious to learn more of Duke's brand of cooking. "Duke has really warmed up to me."

Pausing, she folded the material again, knowing that she wouldn't get to it again until the next day. "It's a shame that he doesn't have a woman. He's such a nice man, but he seems so lonely."

Hawke's brows went up as he slid a glance at Blade, who scrubbed a hand over his mouth, his dark eyes dancing with amusement.

Blade got to his feet and took the material from her, dropping everything onto the small chest in the corner. "I'm sure you're the only person in the world who's ever called Duke *nice*. He's a hard man, Sarah, one who's already lost the woman he loves. He's very bitter about it, and has a bigger chip on his shoulder than Hawke's."

Hawke raised a brow at that, his eyes hard until he looked in Sarah's direction. "I'm just realistic."

Blade grinned. "You thought we'd never have a woman in our lives. Who's to say a woman doesn't show up here and do to Duke what Sarah did to us?"

Sarah started pulling on her boots, pausing to frown up at them. "What did I do to you?"

Blade closed the distance between them and bent to touch his lips to hers. "We're still trying to figure that out. Come on. I'll walk you to the shack. Hawke and I have some things to look into. Stay with Duke until we get back."

* * * *

Sarah rolled out biscuits under Duke's watchful eye. "Duke, do you think you'll ever get married again?"

"No. Pay attention to what you're doing. If you make those biscuits too thin, they won't rise right and I'll get blamed."

Giggling, Sarah glanced over at him, once again amazed that a man who looked so fierce could be so sweet. "You know, you remind me a lot of Hawke and Blade. They're both big men, but they don't make a sound when they move. They also look scary as hell, but they're so nice." Wrinkling her nose at his scowl, she turned back to her work. "Like you."

Smiling at his growl, she started cutting out biscuits. "Don't growl at me. I'm not scared of you."

"You should be." Duke sighed and stirred the chili he'd been working on, not looking at her. "A long time ago I was a nice man. I'm not anymore. Life changed me, just like life changed your men. Life is ugly and cruel. Just because your men changed doesn't mean that I would."

Curious, she turned, leaning against the table. "How have they changed?"

Meeting her gaze, he smiled, a small rare smile that she'd begun to cherish. "They're not as hard now, especially Hawke." Shaking his head, he set the big spoon aside. "Don't get me wrong. No one could ever accuse any of your men of being soft, but Hawke has always been hard as stone. He's a good man to have at your side in a fight. He has a sixth sense about him that I've never known to be wrong."

Sarah blinked. "A sixth sense?"

Shrugging, Duke took the tray of biscuits from the table in front of her and slid an empty one in its place. "He seems to know things. He's always been able to size up people right away." He laughed softly. "Same thing he does with horses."

Shrugging again, he slid the tray of biscuits into the stone oven. "He seems to have a sense for danger, and he's been a bear lately, worried about you."

Shocked at that, Sarah set the rolling pin aside. "What? That's not true!"

"He won't let you see how worried he is, but all three of them are sick with it. We'll all be glad when Willy finally makes his appearance and we can deal with him once and for all."

He went back to his chili, tasting it and adding salt. "Just make sure you do what they say. If anything happens to you, Hawke will be ready to kill someone."

* * * *

Watching Hawke dig into his chili, Sarah thought about what Duke had said. "You're really worried about Willy, aren't you?"

All three of her husbands stilled, some unspoken communication passing between them. It lasted only a second, but she'd seen it—and it worried her.

Blade sighed and turned his attention back to his chili. "We told you that we can handle Willy. When he shows up, we'll take care of him. You just do what we say in the meantime. I want someone's eyes on you at all times until we've dealt with him."

Hawke's brow went up. "Don't you trust us to keep you safe?"

Nodding, Sarah picked at her biscuit. "Of course. I just don't like putting you in danger." Her stomach knotted at the thought of anyone on the ranch getting hurt because of Willy, but she didn't know what she could do to prevent it.

Phoenix looked up from where he'd been staring down into his coffee. "Anything that's a threat to you worries us. As much as I hate to admit it, we're impatient. I know I am, which is why I yelled this morning. We're used to meeting trouble head-on, not sitting around waiting for it."

Grimacing when she realized she'd crumbled her entire biscuit into her chili, Sarah picked up her spoon and began to stir it in. "I think I should go to Tulsa."

Whipping his head toward her, Phoenix blinked. "What?"

Hawke and Blade both stilled, lifting their heads to narrow their eyes at her in disapproval.

Waving away the lecture she sensed coming, she glanced at Blade and Hawke, hoping they would side with her. "Wait. Listen to me. He's probably in Tulsa, trying to figure out how to find us. He's mean, but he's not that smart. No."

With a sigh, she got to her feet, aware that she'd drawn the attention of several of the ranch hands. "He wouldn't have stayed in Tulsa waiting for us to go back to town. He's too impatient. If anything, he's lost somewhere between here and Tulsa. Maybe if we—"

"No." Hawke gathered his dishes and hers and got to his feet. "You're not going to do anything except what we tell you to do."

Phoenix rose, reaching for her hand, which she placed in his without hesitation. "I'll walk her back to the cabin. Give us a few minutes alone."

Hawke inclined his head. "We'll have another cup of coffee. Get things between you worked out." His eyes narrowed. "I mean it, Phoenix. Get whatever's wrong between you worked out."

Sarah's hand trembled in Phoenix's much larger one as they made their way outside. Once away from the others, she looked up at him, struggling to see his features in the faint light. "Are you mad at me?"

He squeezed her hand and kept walking, but not in the direction of their home. "No, honey. I'm mad at myself."

Surprised at that, she stopped, smiling when he also stopped and pulled her into his arms. "Why? It's something to do with me, but I don't know what." Her face burned, and grateful for the semi-darkness, she stared at the front of his shirt. "You've been quiet ever since we went to that cave. Even when you make love to me, you don't play anymore."

Phoenix sighed and threaded his hands through her hair, pulling her head back to look into her beautiful eyes. Running his thumbs over her cheeks, he smiled, a sad smile that tugged at her heart. "It's not that, although taking you opened my eyes. I've been doing a lot of thinking this week."

Sarah's heart dropped. Lifting her chin, she nodded. "I understand. You've decided that marrying me was a mistake after all."

"What?" Phoenix scrubbed a hand over his face. "Marrying you is the smartest thing I've ever done, honey. I've messed this up. I know it, but I don't know what the hell to do about it."

Shocked when he wrapped his arms around her and buried his face against her neck, she held on to him. "What is it? Please talk to me. Tell me what to do."

"Hell, woman, you drive me crazy." His lips moved against her neck, sending little shivers of delight through her. "I want you so much I ache, but I don't know how to get close to you the way Hawke and Blade have. I know how to give you pleasure, but I don't know how to talk to you."

Lifting his head, he brushed stray strands of her hair from her face. "I love to tease you, but I'm not good at saying all that other stuff."

Sarah cuddled against him, loving the feel of his hard arms wrapped around her. Leaning back, she looked up at him and grinned. "Now that I know you're just as nervous around me, I feel better."

Phoenix's eyes narrowed, a small smile playing at his lips. "You do, do you? You like having me all tangled up inside?" Leaning her back over his arm, he ran a hand over her breast. "How much better do you feel?"

Able to see through his teasing now, she ran a hand over his chest. "A lot better."

Straightening, he took her hand in his. "Let's go to the cabin and you can show me how much better."

As they made their way back, he lifted her hand to his lips. "I think I'm falling in love with you."

Sarah blinked, stopping abruptly. "You do?"

Reaching down, he patted her bottom. "Yes, brat. I do, and I can't say it's a comfortable fit." Taking her hand, he started toward the cabin again. "I've never felt like this before. Just be patient with me, all right? Hell, you have me jealous of my own brothers." Pausing again, he pulled her close, bending to brush his lips over hers. "I just look at you, and I can't think of anything else. I want you all the damned time, but I don't want you thinkin' that's all I want from you."

Lifting his head, he frowned. "I'm just worried that I'll say the wrong thing—something I never had to worry about before. Blade always knows the right thing to say, and Hawke hardly ever talked at all."

Running a hand over his chest, and warmed by his vulnerability, she smiled at his groan. "I like your teasing."

He smiled and led her toward the cabin, the lantern they'd left on the porch guiding their way. "Good, because I love to play with you, but I want you to know that I take this marriage seriously."

Sarah glanced over at the chow shack, smiling at the low drone of conversation coming from inside. She knew that Hawke and Blade would be coming out soon, and felt guilty for wanting a little time alone with Phoenix.

Still holding her hand, he made his way up the steps, smiling as he pushed the door open. "I'll show you just how much—hell! Get down!"

\* \* \* \*

Lifting his coffee cup to his mouth, Hawke stilled. "Something's wrong."

Aware of the sudden silence of the men all around him, he got to his feet, his heart pounding furiously at the sense of urgency. "I'm gonna go check outside."

Blade followed him, reaching out to grip his arm. "You're just nervous about Phoenix and Sarah being alone together."

Shaking off his brother's hand, he went outside, his gaze zeroing in on Sarah. "I won't interfere. Phoenix has to work out his own problems with her. Damn it."

He rubbed his neck where it itched, and carefully began to make his way around the chow shack. "It's not Phoenix and Sarah. Something's wrong. Something else. It's not right. Shut up."

His senses sharpened, his hearing becoming even more acute. Slicing a hand through the air when Blade started to speak again, he spun as Eb rounded the corner of the chow shack and approached.

Eb's gaze narrowed, his body tense. "What is it?"

Hawke gritted his teeth and reached for his gun, having left everything else at the cabin when they left. "I don't know. Something. Quiet. Birds are quiet. Nothing's moving. Neck itches." When his neck itched, danger was close. It had always been that way for him.

Eb eased his own gun from its holster. "I've never known you to be wrong, Hawke. If you say something's wrong, that's gospel as far as I'm concerned."

Hawke swallowed heavily, fear for Sarah tightening his gut. "I hope I'm wrong."

Making his way around the chow shack, he glanced in the direction of the cabin he shared with the others and nudged Blade, keeping his voice low. "Go check the other side of the chow shack, and then go get Sarah and take her inside. I'm going to check around the cabin."

The feeling that something was terribly wrong grew stronger, and hurrying his steps, he rushed around the side, sparing a glance for Phoenix and Sarah, still in the distance.

Nothing mattered more than Sarah's safety.

Slowing his steps, he approached one of the windows they'd left open in deference to the warm, humid night air. Crouching next to it, he held up a hand to signal for Eb to stop, but his boss hadn't gotten where he was standing back while others, especially his own men, were in danger.

Trusting Eb's abilities, he eased into position to look into the window while Eb did the same on the other side.

The scent of sweat and whiskey came to him on a breeze, sweeping away the womanly scents that Sarah had brought into their home.

His gut tightened in fury.

Not seeing anyone inside, he eased back and glanced at Eb. His eyes had adjusted to the darkness, allowing him to see his boss shake his head even in the moonlight.

Nodding, he crouched low and continued on, moving around the next corner and to the open window there. Slowly straightening, he held his breath, listening for any sound coming from inside.

Any movement.

Breathing. Anything.

He could be patient, and had the ability to sit for hours, but not when Sarah was in danger.

He reminded himself that she would be safe with Phoenix.

Her safety depended on his patience.

Taking a deep breath, he clenched his jaw.

His prey would soon become restless, and give himself away.

Hawke could wait, and when his prey moved, he would have him.

* * * *

Blade crept around the side of the chow shack, stilling when he heard the sound of ragged breathing coming from around the corner.

Crouching low, he slid his knife from the sheath attached to his thigh, his pulse racing with anticipation. He needed to get rid of the threat and get to Sarah.

He didn't dare yell out and give away his position, not knowing the danger.

But, he trusted Hawke's instincts with his life.

Peering around the corner, he saw that only one man stood in the moonlight, but Blade waited, taking the time to scan the area for others.

The man stood about twenty feet away, a gun in each hand. He crept toward the far end of the chow shack away from Blade, peeking around the corner.

Seeing no one else, Blade straightened, pressing his side against the chow shack in an effort to remain in the dark shadows. Easing away from the wall, he saw Phoenix and Sarah heading right, toward their cabin.

The man watched them, lifting his guns.

Blade rushed forward, his moccasins enabling him to cross the distance between him and the stranger without a sound. "Drop those pistols."

As the other man started to turn, Blade pressed his gun against the stranger's back, his knife against his neck. "I wouldn't. Drop them." He felt a presence behind him, but didn't bother turning.

Duke stepped forward as the other man tossed his guns to the ground, and flipped his knife around, hitting the other man in the head with the heavy handle, knocking him out.

Sparing a glance toward the open yard where he'd last seen his brother, Blade swallowed a curse when he saw that Phoenix and Sarah had reached the front porch of the cabin.

"You got him?"

"Of course. Go warn—"

"Hell! Get down!"

Blade's stomach lurched at the sound of his brother's voice, followed by a gunshot.

And then more.

Blade was already at a dead run by the time Phoenix started to fall.

\* \* \* \*

Sarah froze at Phoenix's shouted warning, staring in horror when an explosion sounded from inside and knocked Phoenix back.

Not until Phoenix shot back did she realize it had been a gunshot.

"Phoenix!" She ran toward him, horrified when he shot again and slid to the ground.

"Stay back!" Another shot rang out, and then another, which he answered with two more of his own.

The sudden silence terrified her, and with a sob, she grabbed the lantern and ran toward him, her heart in her throat when she saw the blood coating the front of his shirt. "Phoenix!"

Smoke and the scent of gunpowder filled the air, but she blocked them out to focus on Phoenix. "Phoenix! Oh, God. You're bleeding. You've been shot!"

"Damn it, Sarah!" He shoved her, knocking her away from the doorway. "I told you to stay back!"

What felt like bands of iron wrapped around her from behind, and she found herself yanked against an equally hard chest. Before she knew it, her feet left the ground and she found herself upside down over a wide shoulder, bouncing as Blade ran across the yard back to the chow shack.

"Put me down! Phoenix is hurt."

Blade's strides never slowed. "Phoenix is being tended to. Be still, damn it!"

Stilling at the panic in Blade's ragged voice, she gripped his shirt. "Blade? Oh, God! What happened?"

Suddenly, Duke was at her side, running alongside Blade. "Is she hurt?"

"I don't think so." Blade ran into the chow shack and set her on her feet so fast that her head spun.

Clutching him to steady herself, she looked up, struck by the change in both men.

Blade's features appeared to have been carved from stone, the rage and fear in his eyes giving him a savage appearance that left her shaking. He searched her features before lowering his gaze to rake over her, his hands moving over her arms and legs with a gentle thoroughness that was a sharp contrast to the wild look in his eyes. "Do you hurt anywhere, honey?"

He knelt in front of her, reaching under her skirt to run his hands up and down her legs. "I can't find anything. Sarah, look at me. Do you hurt anywhere?"

"No." Shaking her head, she looked from Blade to Duke and back again. "No. It happened so fast." She pressed a hand to her stomach. "Please. Phoenix is hurt. I want to go to him."

Duke looked furious enough to spit nails, his scar even more pronounced as anger hardened his features. "They'll be bringing him in here. Damn it, we need a full-time doctor."

Blade ran a hand over Sarah's back. "He'll be fine. Gideon went to find Will Prentice. He knows how to remove a bullet."

Just then, Hawke burst through the door, followed by Jeremiah and several others. Rushing to her side, Hawke gripped her by the shoulders, the storm in his eyes terrible to see. "Are you hurt?"

* * * *

Hawke had never been so scared in his life.

His heart still pounded nearly out of his chest and his hands shook, the realization of how important she'd become to him hitting him hard.

Running his hands over Sarah again, he glanced back to see Phoenix trying to shake off Eb's hold.

"Let go of me, damn it! I was shot in the shoulder. I sure as hell can walk on my own. I want to see Sarah."

Hawke stepped aside, knowing that he and the others would have a hell of a fight on their hands until Phoenix saw that Sarah was all right. "She's not hurt. You shoved her away from the door just before he fired again."

He didn't want to think about how close Sarah had come to being shot, or how many shots he and Eb had fired into the room to keep that from happening.

The intruder lay dead on his mattress—in the very spot Sarah had slept so trustingly the night before.

Clenching his jaw, he wrapped an arm around Sarah, wondering if he'd ever be able to let her out of his sight again.

"I need you to come with me, little one. You can see for yourself that Phoenix is all right." He'd already asked Jeremiah to bring the dead man out of the cabin, not wanting Sarah to have the memory of seeing him in the bed he shared with her.

"But I want to stay with Phoenix." The tears in her eyes broke his heart.

Wrapping his arms around her, he shot a meaningful look in Phoenix's direction. "We'll be right back. I need you to take a look at these men. I need to know who they are."

Phoenix made his way to one of the benches and sat, grimacing when Will walked through the door. "I'd be willing to bet that neither one of them was Willy. Sarah, honey, you know what Willy looks like. Are you strong enough to go check for me?"

Sarah lifted her chin. "Of course."

"Good girl." Blade inclined his head, silently saluting Phoenix. "I think you're right. I'd bet that Willy's still out there. He'll strike again."

Hawke kept an arm around Sarah, leading her outside, his insides clenched into hard knots. "We'll be ready for him."

Still shaken at how close he'd come to losing the woman he loved, he started toward the door, pausing when Duke stepped in front of him.

With a glance at Sarah, Duke clenched his jaw, his eyes screaming with grief. "I'm glad your woman's all right. I wasn't so lucky." A sad smile curved his lips. "I see that you've realized just how much she means to you. That happened too late for me. Keep her close."

He hadn't fully understood why Duke had become so hard and cold until now.

He hadn't understood the other man's anguish.

Looking down at Sarah, he took in her tear-stained cheeks, and the trust and love shining in her eyes. "I will. Very close."

She was everything to him—as vital to him as breathing—and he'd kill to keep her safe.

# Chapter Thirteen

Lying in the darkness on the pallet his brothers had made for him in the yard, Phoenix looked up at the stars, struggling to keep his eyes open. A low fire burned several yards away, providing just enough light for him to see his surroundings.

If he could only keep his eyes open.

His brothers had cleaned up the blood inside the cabin, but the scent of whiskey and gunpowder still lingered in the air. Leaving the cabin open to air out, they'd decided to sleep outside.

The mattress from the bed burned in the fire.

"Do you need anything?"

Phoenix forced a smile at the question Sarah had already asked in one form or another for the past hour, the pain in his shoulder making it difficult to get comfortable. "Just for you to go to sleep. You're wiggling all over the place."

"I'm sorry. It must hurt your shoulder."

Chuckling at that, Phoenix turned his head to meet her gaze. "Among other things. How do you expect me to sleep when you're wiggling your ass against me?"

He hoped by teasing her, she'd relax enough to get some sleep.

Blade turned from where he stood talking to Hawke several yards away. Approaching, he stood over Sarah, the tension at learning that Willy hadn't been one of the intruders pouring from him in waves.

"Go to sleep, honey. You're safe. There are men stationed all over the place."

Phoenix tried to sit up, but the laudanum they'd managed to pour down his throat left him too dizzy and weak to try. "Did the other guy wake up yet?"

Blade nodded grimly. "Yeah." Scrubbing a hand over his face, he glanced in the distance and sighed. "He didn't want to talk at first, but Duke changed his mind. Enjoyed it, too. Willy's out there, about a mile north. The plan was to kidnap Sarah and get her to lead them to the gold."

Blade held Phoenix's gaze for several long seconds, the message in them clear. "Said Willy's got a burr under his saddle because he had to ride here on horseback, and didn't like being in strange territory." His lips twitched. "Pity."

Phoenix glanced at Sarah, who sat staring north. "Yeah, a real shame."

Willy wanted more than just the gold. He wanted Sarah, and most likely wanted to get even with her for inconveniencing him.

Phoenix didn't even want to think about what Willy would do if he got his hands on her.

Forcing a smile in Sarah's direction, he ran a hand over her arm, not liking the look in her eyes, or how she kept avoiding their gazes. "Don't worry, honey. You're safe here. Go to sleep."

Sarah frowned, shaking her head. "I'm not scared for me. I'm worried about you. In case you've forgotten, you were shot just a few hours ago. You shouldn't be lying on the ground outside."

Phoenix smiled. "Well, I can't lie on the ground inside, now, can I?"

Whipping her head around, she slapped at his leg. "I'm serious, Phoenix. Please don't make fun of me, or make me feel stupid for caring about you. For the first time in my life, I feel cared for, and a part of something. Please don't take that away from me."

Blade raised a brow, chuckling softly. "You can't argue with that without sounding stupid, little brother, especially with that laudanum in you. Just shut up and let her fuss a little. It'll make you both feel better."

"I hope you remember that if you ever get hurt." Phoenix reached out and pulled her closer. His cock stirred briefly, but the laudanum kept his arousal at bay. "I'm not used to being fussed over. I'm fine. I don't want you to worry."

"Well, I am worried." She placed her hand lightly over his shoulder wound, her eyes dark with remembered horror. "This is my fault. I knew I would bring trouble here. I told you that Willy's dangerous. I really think I should just get the gold and go give it to him."

"No." The menace in Blade's tone sent had Sarah whipping around to face him. "You're not getting anywhere near him. No one can get to you here."

Sitting up again, Sarah leaned back to look up at Blade, her hands braced slightly behind each hip. "I know that." Averting her gaze, she shrugged, a delicate lift of her small shoulders. "It's probably stupid to say this under the circumstances, but I love this feeling."

\* \* \* \*

Kneeling beside her, Blade glanced at his brother, who'd finally lost the battle with the laudanum. "What feeling, love?" He reached out to run a hand over her braid, which had become loose and tousled. The knots in his stomach hadn't loosened since he'd heard the first gunshot, and he found he couldn't stop touching her, reassuring himself that she was safe.

Sarah smiled, leaning into his touch. "I feel so safe here. With you. Phoenix. Hawke." She glanced in the distance, her eyes lingering on Hawke, who accepted a cup of coffee from Duke, the two men deep in conversation.

As if sensing her attention, Hawke turned, meeting her gaze, every line of his body tensing. He scanned the area around her, and met

Blade's gaze with a raised brow before looking back at her again with a faint smile of reassurance.

Sarah smiled and leaned against Blade's chest, her eyes brimming with tears—and trust—as she looked up at him. "I feel so safe here—as if nothing can get to me. No drunks can barge into my room by accident and try to crawl into bed with me."

Blade gritted his teeth at the shiver that went through her, pulling her tighter against him. "No, love. The only men in your bed will be us. No one can get through us to get to you."

Sarah nodded, the single tear trickling down her cheek making his chest ache. "That almost cost Phoenix his life."

"My brothers and I would die to keep you safe. Without hesitation. Without regret." Cupping her cheek, he lifted her face for his kiss. "We're better able to handle danger than you are. I'll make you a deal. You let Hawke, Phoenix and me deal with the danger, and you concentrate on dealing with us."

He kissed her again, his chest swelling with pride that such an adorable and sweet woman belonged to him. "Go to sleep. We'll be close by, and if you or Phoenix needs us, just call out. We'll hear you."

* * * *

From the other side of the chow shack, Hawke sipped coffee, watching his wife over the rim of his cup.

The dark circles under her swollen eyes, proof that she hadn't gotten much sleep, made her appear even more fragile and delicate.

He and Blade had spent the night watching over her while watching out for Willy to make an appearance, and a sleepless night hadn't helped his temper at all.

Every man on the ranch worked in shifts, riding in wide circles around them, the tension on the ranch thick enough to cut with a knife.

Hayes and Wyatt had raced to the chow shack as soon as they heard gunshots, rushing back to get Savannah as soon as they realized what happened.

After settling their pregnant wife in the big house and under guard with Adam Marshall and Conal Jones, the two lawmen focused their attention on the outlaw Blade and Duke had captured. Once they'd gotten all the information they could, they'd loaded him and the dead man onto the backs of their horses and headed for Tulsa to turn them over to the sheriff there.

Out of the corner of his eye, Hawke watched Blade approach, his brother's attention on Sarah.

Frowning, Blade strolled to Hawke's side. "She looks exhausted."

Hawke sighed, watching her stare at the far wall. "She does."

"She didn't sleep much."

Not taking his eyes from Sarah, Hawke inclined his head. "She didn't."

She'd tossed and turned all night, alternately checking on Phoenix and staring into the fire they'd built. Even now, she stared at the far wall despite Maggie's and Savannah's efforts to get her attention.

Not even the baby seemed to interest her.

Blade set his cup down and crossed his arms over his chest. "She's got something on her mind."

"Or she's planning something." Hawke hoped his suspicions proved to be wrong, but he'd begun to understand his wife's daring, and her heart.

Glancing at him, Blade clenched his jaw, his eyes flashing. "Damn it. She feels guilty for Phoenix getting shot. She's planning to take the gold to that son of a bitch!"

"Yeah." Hawke set his cup aside and straightened, something inside him warming with satisfaction when she turned her head to look in their direction.

He didn't look away, holding her gaze for several long seconds before she averted hers, the combination of guilt, fear, and sadness in her eyes, visible even from this distance, confirming his suspicions. He lowered his voice even more, despite the fact that the conversation in the shack and their distance from the others prevented anyone from eavesdropping. "I'm gonna take her back to the cabin and have a little talk with her, and let her know she's not going anywhere."

Blade straightened and set his cup on the table with a thud, his eyes alight with anticipation. "I want to be a part of that conversation."

Hawke moved toward Sarah, unsurprised that she looked up when he took his first step toward her.

There'd been a connection between them from the first time he'd laid eyes on her—a connection he had every intention of using to keep her safe.

He loved her—more every day—and could no longer imagine a life without her.

She wanted to protect them, which made him love her even more.

He couldn't allow herself to put herself in danger to protect them, of course, something he would make very clear to her.

* * * *

Sarah stared at the far wall, letting Maggie's and Savannah's conversation wash over her as the scene that had taken place the previous night played over and over in her mind.

The sound of gunshots.

The image of Phoenix falling, his shirt soaked with blood.

The very real fear of someone getting hurt because of her had become a reality.

Phoenix was lucky. It could have been much worse.

The change in him had been phenomenal.

He'd gone from being a playful, fun-loving man to a hard-edged gunslinger in the blink of an eye. He'd stopped to check on her earlier, but seemed distracted, the glitter of anger in his eyes convincing her that getting shot had changed his mind about her.

He'd left over an hour earlier to go to the cabin, the need for sleep after losing so much blood plainly visible.

Hawke watched her from the far side of the building, his gaze following Phoenix as he left, his eyes unreadable. He didn't even look up when Blade walked up to him.

She could tell he was also tired, and heard from the others that he and Blade had been up all night, watching over her.

Out of the corner of her eye, Sarah watched Hawke approach, followed closely by Blade, the determination and anger in their eyes making her stomach clench.

They had to be mad as hell that she'd gotten their brother shot.

She couldn't say that she blamed them.

She'd brought a lot of trouble to the ranch they loved, and threatened the only people they cared about.

Taking the gold to Willy was the only way to make sure that the outlaw didn't hurt anyone else.

Aware of Hawke and Blade watching her from the other side of the sturdy wooden building, she glanced toward the doorway again, anxious for Phoenix to reappear.

There hadn't been any loose floorboards in the sturdy cabin, so she'd hidden the gold in the back of the drawer they'd given her to use.

She knew she couldn't get to it without waking Phoenix. Just the thought of looking at the anger in his eyes—anger she knew she deserved—made her stomach knot and her eyes burn with tears she didn't dare shed.

Forcing a smile at whatever Savannah seemed so happy about, Sarah looked straight ahead again, her smile falling at the purpose in Hawke's strides. Keeping track of their progress, she stiffened, fighting the urge to run.

"Sarah, come with us. We need to talk."

Gulping at Hawke's harsh tone, Sarah lifted her gaze to his, the knot in her stomach turning to ice when she saw his expression.

Hawke had a hard glint in his eyes that sent a chill all the way to her bones. His features appeared to have been carved in stone, so set and cold that she began shaking.

"Uh-oh." Savannah's voice, filled with amusement, barely penetrated through the roaring in her ears. "I know that look. Someone's about to put his foot down."

Savannah patted her arm, her voice lowering. "Don't look so scared. They'd never hurt you. You can handle them. They're probably just scared that you almost got hurt last night."

Maggie nudged her. "Go with them, honey. You need them right now and they need you."

Not wanting to get her new friends involved, or cause any more trouble than she already had, Sarah nodded and got to her feet, holding onto the edge of the table to steady herself.

Her knees shook so badly that she feared they wouldn't support her, and she found herself leaning heavily against Hawke as he led her away from the others and through the doorway.

Realizing what she was doing, she straightened, pulling away from him, only to bump into Blade who came up on her other side.

Whipping around to meet his steady glare, she swallowed heavily. "I understand why you're angry."

"Do you?" The silkiness in Blade's voice couldn't hide the simmering anger underneath.

Chilled despite the blaring heat of the sun directly overhead, Sarah rubbed her arms. "Yes. I don't blame you."

One of Blade's dark brows went up. "Well, that's a relief."

Grimacing at the dripping sarcasm, Sarah clamped her mouth shut and kept walking, noticing that ranch hands rode in the distance in every direction.

Rubbing her arms again, she glanced at Hawke, her stomach tight with nerves. "Stupid, huh?"

Still, she couldn't deny that coming here had been the best thing that had ever happened to her.

Hawke's jaw clenched. "On that, we agree."

Her breath caught, the agony of knowing she'd lost them so sharp that it took several long seconds to fully penetrate.

When it did, only willpower kept her from falling to her knees. Taking several deep breaths, she locked her knees and kept walking, fighting to hold back tears.

Suddenly, a strange calmness overtook her.

She'd already made her plans anyway.

She just needed to carry them out.

She'd cry buckets later, but for now she had something to do.

She opened her mouth to tell them that she would make her way back to Tulsa, when Hart and Gideon came riding hell bent for leather in their direction.

Gideon brought his horse to a stop only a few yards away, the horse rearing at his abrupt stop. "Tracks. About a mile out. They're close." Turning, they headed back in the direction they'd come from, their features hard and filled with determination.

Phoenix came running out of the cabin, blinking at the bright sunlight. "Son of a bitch!"

Hawke took off toward the stables, with Blade running hard beside him, Phoenix at their heels. Glancing over his shoulder, his features lined with fury, Hawke gestured toward the cabin. "Get inside and stay there!"

With her heart pounding in her throat, and her stomach churning with fear for them, Sarah raced into the cabin, rushing to the drawer they'd given her to use.

Blinking back the tears burning her eyes, she grabbed the blanket she'd taken from her room in Waco and started throwing her clothes inside.

She didn't know how long they'd be gone, and had to hope that she could find Willy before one of them got hurt.

*Please, God. Don't let them get hurt.*

Gathering the small bags of gold, she stuffed them into her pockets, not wanting Willy to have an excuse to look under her skirt.

A sob escaped as she jumped to her feet again, her hands shaking so badly that it took her several tries before she could tie the rope around the top of the bundle she'd made, a sharp reminder of the terror she'd felt when she'd escaped Waco.

Hearing the sound of pounding hooves, she looked up in time to watch Hawke, Blade, and Phoenix riding hard after Hart and Gideon.

*Please, God. Keep them safe. Let me find Willy first.*

She started to run out of the cabin, when the material lying across the back of one of the chairs caught her eye. Pausing just long enough to run her hand over the buckskin dress Hawke and Blade had spent nights making for her, she swallowed a sob.

It had all seemed so perfect. Too perfect. She should have known that a woman like her could never have that kind of happiness.

Another sob escaped, one that seemed to come from her soul, and then another as she forced herself to turn away from the beautiful dress.

The image of the way they'd smiled at her—the memories of the way they'd talked and teased her—would be impossible to turn away from, though.

She'd really believed that they loved her.

Never again.

She'd never again fall in love.

It hurt more than she could bear.

Brushing tears from her eyes, she opened the cabin door, looking around to see that only a handful of men stood in the distance, all of them looking in the direction the others had ridden.

She eased out, closing the door behind her and made her way across the porch and to the other side of the cabin, her heart pounding nearly out of her chest. Not taking her eyes from the men, she circled to the other side.

Pausing, she waited, and watched them glance toward the cabin. With a gasp, she pressed her back against the wall, tightening her arms around the bundle. Forcing her breathing to slow, even though she knew they wouldn't be able to hear her from this distance, she counted to fifty before daring to peer around the corner.

Holding her breath, she watched them head in the opposite direction, and with a silent good-bye to her new home, she started to run—determined to find Willy before they did.

* * * *

Holding the reins of his horse, Phoenix walked behind his brothers with the rest of the ranch hands, looking into the distance, and across a field where Hart and Gideon also tracked Willy and his increasingly smaller gang.

They'd caught another member of Willy's gang just a short time ago, when the outlaw's lame horse had kept him from escaping with the others.

Wyatt and Hayes had recognized him at once as a train robber from back east, and after questioning him, had tied him to a tree while everyone else tracked the others.

No one spoke, all eyes trained on Hawke and Blade.

Hawke straightened from where he'd crouched to investigate the tracks he'd found. "They're not far ahead of us. A few minutes." Grim-faced, Hawke mounted again and started out, every line in his body stiff with fury.

Phoenix mounted and closed in behind him, angry that tracking made their journey frustratingly slow.

Each step, though, took them closer to the deadly threat to their wife.

Her safety meant everything.

They rode for several miles, the tension in the small group growing when they realized that they'd begin to circle the ranch, getting closer and closer to the homes there.

Closer and closer to the women.

Closer to Sarah.

Even the knowledge that men remained at the ranch to watch out for them didn't ease Phoenix's fears.

Judging from the looks on Hawke's and Blade's faces, it didn't ease theirs, either.

Fighting the urge to race forward, he saw Hawke stiffen, sharing a look with Blade.

"What?" Leaning forward, he looked past them, his jaw clenching when he saw horses. "It's about time."

Hawke motioned for silence, and leapt from his horse without a sound, racing for the grove of trees to their left. "No. Hell." The fear in his voice sent a chill through Phoenix, the chill growing colder when he saw what Hawke saw.

Blade ran after him, holding up a hand, not taking his eyes from the sight of Sarah standing at the edge of a grassy field, holding the bundle in front of her that she'd brought from Waco. "We've got to move fast, and your boots will make too much noise. We need you all to stay here. We're going to be counting on your rifles."

Phoenix started after them, stopping abruptly when Hawke held out a hand again.

"No, Phoenix. We need the element of surprise. Your boots will make too much noise." He glanced at the other men, his eyes filled with terror. "Don't worry about us. Protect Sarah. She's trying to give the gold to Willy to keep us safe."

Phoenix cursed and moved into the trees, searching for the perfect position while Wyatt and Hayes hurriedly led the horses deeper into the trees and out of sight, coming back in only seconds.

Conal glanced at Phoenix, his expression grim. "She'll be all right. That bastard's not gonna get the chance to hurt her. I'm going to make my way into the rocks over there with Hayes."

Phoenix nodded, dropping to the ground with his rifle, aware that Adam and Wyatt moved to his left for a different angle.

His chest got tighter as Willy and the others approached Sarah on horseback. He counted four other riders beside the outlaw he suspected was Willy. To his surprise, one of the other riders appeared to be a woman.

Knowing how terrified Sarah would be of both Willy and the horses, he clenched his jaw, fear and pride at her bravery waging a war inside him.

Once they rescued her, he'd spend the rest of his life showing her how much he loved her—and never let her out of his sight again.

* * * *

Blade concentrated on speed and silence, while inwardly running through every prayer and curse word he knew. "I swear, once we get her, I'm gonna turn her over my knee until she can't sit down."

Hawke didn't even glance at him as both men crouched low and raced toward Sarah, their position behind the trees making it possible for them to remain unseen. "I'm gonna kill him with my bare hands. Christ, what the hell does she think she's doing?"

Blade kept running beside his brother, every step the outlaw took toward his wife striking terror into his heart. "You know damned well what she's doing. That little thing is going against an outlaw to protect us from him."

The idea that any of them needed protection from a man like Willy would have been amusing in other circumstances, but could prove deadly in this one.

It was something he had to make abundantly clear to his wife as soon as he got the chance.

*Please, God, let me have the chance.*

The outlaw and the others rode slowly toward Sarah, as if enjoying her fear and wanting to drag it out as long as possible.

Vowing to make the other man pay for scaring his wife, Blade clenched his jaw and reached for the war club strapped to his back, a curved wooden club wrapped in buckskin that he and Hawke always carried.

Running side by side, they burst through the tree line, coming up on the outlaws from behind.

Blade knew the moment Sarah saw them, and prayed that he and Hawke could reach the outlaws before they had a chance to get to her.

With his brother matching him step for step, they ran faster, the distance between him and the outlaw closing with every stride.

Hawke already had his club in one hand, his tomahawk in the other.

Neither one of them drew their guns, knowing that Phoenix would have his rifle at the ready.

His little brother never missed.

With so much at stake, he ran faster than he'd ever run before, every yard seeming to take forever. He ran past the other men, ignoring their shouts.

"So, you thought you could get away from me. You really think you'd get away with stealing my money? You're gonna pay for that, bitch. You're gonna pay on your back. You're gonna pay on your knees."

A fresh wave of fury raged through him, and with a scream of rage, he leapt at Willy.

* * * *

Sweat trickled down Sarah's back. She'd dropped her bundle to stick her hands into her deep pockets, closing her fists around the bag of coins in each one.

The thought of facing Willy hadn't scared her as much when she'd been with her husbands, but facing the outlaw now, she realized what a mistake she'd made in coming here.

Only the knowledge that giving him the gold would keep the others safe kept her from running.

Sarah spared a glance for the other riders, horrified to see that her mother rode with them.

Her mother's dress was torn, and she looked haggard. Her cheek had a mark on it as if she'd been hit, and the bruises on her arms and other cheek were plainly visible.

He threw his head back and laughed. "We've been talking about all the things we want to do to you. Your ma kept us satisfied on the way, but we're gettin' a little tired of her."

Blinking back tears before they could fall, Sarah lifted her chin. "I'm not a virgin anymore, Willy. I'm married. I don't think my husbands would appreciate your plans for me."

She wished things had been different, and her husbands would ride to her rescue, but Willy had ruined everything.

*She'd* ruined everything.

Willy's eyes narrowed. "You're lying."

She took a steadying breath and pulled the two small pouches from her pockets. "Take the gold and just go away. Leave my mother here with me."

"Not a chance. You're both coming with me." He pointed his gun at her. "As a matter of fact, I want to see what I'm getting. Strip. Right now."

"No."

Sarah gasped at the sight of Hawke and Blade running toward her, moving so fast she could only stare in shock.

Willy laughed. "Yes." He moved forward, his eyes gleaming. "So, you thought you could get away from me. You really think you'd get away with stealing my money? You're gonna pay for that, bitch. You're gonna pay on your back. You're gonna pay on your knees."

The roar of rage that came from Blade sent a chill down her spine, the shouts and unmistakable gunfire that followed stilling her into immobility.

Willy turned to her, jumping from the horse and raising his gun. "You're gonna die for this, bitch!"

Something hit her hard in the leg, making it buckle, but before she could fall, she felt herself slammed back to the ground when something simultaneously hit her shoulder and side.

It knocked the air from her lungs, making it impossible to draw a breath.

Seconds later, fire seemed to explode in her shoulder, leg, and side, increasing her panic.

Screams of rage and pain.

Feet pounding on the ground and coming closer.

She tried to lift her head, to fold herself into a ball against the pain, but she couldn't seem to make her muscles work.

She needed to see them. She needed to know that the men she loved were safe.

A tear trickled from the corner of her eye.

And then, nothing but black.

* * * *

Hawke ran to Sarah's side, fear gripping him by the throat and nearly choking him.

Willy had managed to get a shot off before Blade tackled him to the ground, while two of Willy's men shot at her even as Phoenix and the others opened fire.

Hawke had killed the other man with a hard club to the head, preventing him from firing his gun again, but the damage had already been done.

They'd failed her.

They hadn't been fast enough.

If she died, a part of him would die with her.

Kneeling over her, he resisted pulling her hard against him, forcing himself to remain calm to see to her injuries as Blade and Phoenix closed in on her from either side. "She's breathing."

Phoenix circled to her to her other side, and carefully worked her shirt free of her skirt. "Christ, she's covered in blood." He ripped off his shirt and pressed it against her side, grimacing when she moaned. "I didn't get them in time."

Hawke ripped her shirt from her shoulder and took Phoenix's bandana with hands that shook, and secured it against the wound in an effort to stop the blood. "You got them. She's alive."

Wyatt yelled from behind him. "Is she all right?"

Blade cursed and half turned to see Wyatt holding on to the woman who'd been riding with them. "She's alive. How about them?"

"They're all dead, except for the woman. She says she's Sarah's momma. Damn it, stop wiggling. She wants to come see her."

Hawke took the bandanna Phoenix had soaked from his canteen. "No." He felt too protective of her to allow anyone else near, especially someone whose motives he didn't trust.

Wyatt appeared at his side, but Hawke's focus on Sarah was so intense that he hadn't even heard the lawman approach, or seen him turn the woman over to Adam. "Oh, hell. Duke and Hayes are riding hell bent for leather to town for a doctor. Duke'll bring him back while Hayes explains what's going on to the sheriff in Tulsa. In the meantime, Eb went to get Will Prentice."

Hawke wanted to throw up. "We promised to protect her."

Wyatt moved to crouch beside Hawke, gripping Sarah's arm and thigh to turn her. "We all failed her. What the hell was she doing out here?"

Hawke took her hand, grimacing when she moaned. "Trying to give him back the gold so he wouldn't hurt us."

Wyatt turned to look at him over his shoulder, his eyes filled with pity and fury. "You're kidding."

Blade removed his buckskin shirt and folded it, gently lifted her head to slide it under it. "I wish he was. Christ, she's a hell of a woman."

Pressing the shirt against her wound again, Wyatt lifted the edge of the bandanna on her shoulder. "The shot in her side went clean through, but it looks like the bullet in her shoulder is still in her. It's gonna have to be removed. How about the one in her thigh?"

"Still inside." Hawke felt as if his heart was breaking, the pain in his chest almost unbearable. "She's so damned small." He should never have left her back at the cabin.

As all four of them tended to her, fighting to staunch the flow of blood, Phoenix cursed. "Why the hell did she think that bastard would just accept the gold she had left and leave?"

"She really took his gold?"

Hawke spared a glance at the woman who'd spoken, seeing that Adam remained poised to catch her if she ran toward them. "Yeah." Furious at the outlaws, and at himself, he lashed out. "She had to protect herself somehow."

Sarah's mother nodded. "I deserved that. In my defense, though, I'm a weak woman. Always have been. Not like Sarah." Tears rolled down her bruised cheek. "Please. I know I don't deserve it, but I'd like to come closer. I'd like her to know I'm here. I need to tell her that I love her before she—"

Leaping to his feet, Hawke strode toward her, seething with anger. "She's not gonna die, damn it, and if you say anything like that again, I'll tie you to a tree and let the wolves have you!"

Ignoring the startled look from Adam, he hurried back to Sarah again, the knots in his stomach getting tighter. "She's so white."

Blade straightened and stood. "She's lost a lot of blood. Let's get a fire started. Will is gonna need hot water and we're gonna have to sterilize the blade of the knife before we can dig the bullets out."

Hawke shared a look with the others and said what he knew they were all thinking. "And to cauterize if we can't get this blood stopped."

\* \* \* \*

Sarah woke slowly, wondering where she was. A strange lethargy made her feel as if she floated, and she thought back to the time she'd spent with Hawke, Blade, and Phoenix in the spring.

Hearing the unmistakable sounds of low voices, she tried to turn toward them, but her body wouldn't obey her.

She felt dizzy. Weak.

The only thing she seemed able to move was her right hand, and when she did, she encountered what felt like cool grass instead of warm water.

Pain in her side, shoulder, and thigh slowly let itself be known, and grew stronger with every passing second.

God, it hurt, throbbing with every beat of her heart.

She never knew something could hurt this much.

She kept moving her hand, loving the feel of coolness against her heated skin.

She tried to open her eyes, the feeling that something was very wrong taking hold of her and not letting go.

A wave of terror washed over her at the mental image of Hawke and Blade running toward her.

An ear-piercing scream of rage.

Shouts and gunshots.

*Oh, God. Were they dead?*

A sob escaped, and then another, the pain in her side and shoulder nothing compared to the agony in her heart.

"We're here, love. We're here." Blade's voice came to her as if from a great distance, low and gentle, but with a desperation she'd never heard in it before. "Don't thrash around. Easy, love. You'll open up those wounds again."

*Wounds?*

Had she been shot?

A hand pressed against her forehead, so cool and wonderful against her heated skin. "She's even warmer than before."

Struggling to fight her way through the fog surrounding her, she hung onto Blade's voice like a lifeline. "Blade?"

"Yes, love. It's me. Hawke and Phoenix are here with you, too."

The sound of water, followed by a cooler cloth being placed on her forehead drew another moan from her. "Are we dead?" She saw no other way of explaining the strange feeling that made her hurt while floating.

"No, little one. We're not dead. Open your eyes for me, Sarah."

The command in Hawke's voice had her fighting to open them, the need to see him again giving her the strength she hadn't known she possessed. "Can't."

"Yes, you can. Open your eyes right now, Sarah." The underlying fear in his harsh tone made her stomach clench, and using every ounce of willpower she possessed, she forced her eyes open to find herself staring into Hawke's dark ones.

Only inches from hers, his eyes narrowed, swirling with an emotion her brain struggled to identify.

He smiled tenderly, but his body remained tight with tension. "That's my girl. See? I knew you could do it."

Sarah tried to reach for him, but she couldn't quite drum up the energy. "You're not dead." The memory of the looks on their faces when they'd ridden out and the anger in their eyes came back in a rush.

He took the cloth from her forehead and she heard the sound of splashing water again. "No, little one. We're all all right."

Another hand touched her leg. "You're the only one of us who got hurt. I'm sorry I didn't shoot a second earlier. Willy and his men shot at you the same time we shot at them. I'm so sorry, honey." The self-disgust in Phoenix's voice had her turning her head to look at him, the effort taking the last of her strength.

"Willy?"

Phoenix's jaw clenched. "He and his men are all dead. Pity. I had some serious plans for them." His expression softened. "Honey, your momma's here."

Suddenly, she remembered seeing her mother and the evidence of her mistreatment. Another moan escaped, the pain in her side intensifying. "Why?"

Hawke rinsed the cloth again and ran it down her neck to her chest. "That sick bastard thought he could have both of you, and use each of you to intimidate the other. She's safe now. She wouldn't go to sleep until she saw that you were all right."

"Am I?"

"You're gonna be fine." Blade slid a hand under her neck, lifting her head, and cursing when she moaned at the sharp pain in her shoulder. "I'm sorry, love. I want you to drink some more water. You in a lot of pain?"

"Pain. Fuzzy."

Hawke rinsed the cloth out again. "That's the laudanum. It's wearing off. We're gonna need to give you a little more. We need for you to sleep and stop moving around. Will and Doc Stanton sewed you up real good and we don't want you ripping out their work."

She didn't care for the idea of being sewn up, but was thankful that she hadn't known about it at the time. "Wanna leave."

Phoenix touched his lips to a spot close to where pain radiated from her thigh. "Just sleep, honey. Eb's coming out with the buckboard in the morning. We'll go back to the cabin nice and slow so we don't rip anything open. We'll take care of everything."

The darkness couldn't be held at bay much longer, and she had to make sure they understood her before it took over again.

"No. Leave. Goin' to Cal–calforna. Made a mess of everythin'. Don't blame you for hatin' me."

The sudden silence that fell heavily around her spoke volumes.

The pain in her heart grew, a pain no amount of laudanum could take away.

A tear leaked from the corner of each eye, but she knew she didn't have the energy to brush them away.

She didn't even have the chance as darkness closed in on her once again.

# Chapter Fourteen

Phoenix cursed when Sarah passed out again, lifting his gaze to his brothers'. "So she really planned to give the gold to Willy and then leave us?"

Hawke rinsed the bandanna again and folded it before placing it on her forehead. "She had her bundle, didn't she?"

"I swear I don't understand what the hell she was thinking." Getting to his feet, Phoenix stared down at his wife, fighting back anger. "I'll never understand women. I thought she was starting to love us."

Blade sighed and trickled a little more laudanum into her mouth, while Hawke rubbed her throat to get her to swallow it. "She does love us—so much that she was willing to risk her own life to keep us from being hurt."

Phoenix cursed again, looking toward the fire where the doctor and Sarah's mother slept. "That's just crazy. Men like Willy Krenshaw are nothing but hot air and bluster. I can't believe she didn't think we could handle him and his gang." Turning back, he crouched next to her again. "You think she really loves us?"

Blade smiled, bending to touch his lips to Sarah's. "She does. She doesn't know how to trust, though. It's gonna take some time." Straightening, he sighed. "She loves us. Who the hell would have ever thought the three of us would have such a brave, sweet little thing to call our own?"

Phoenix appreciated his brother's attempt to lighten the mood. "Don't forget passionate."

Hawke stretched out next to her on her uninjured side, taking her hand in his. "Don't you even think about that for a long time. She's gonna need time to heal." Staring down at her, he lifted her hand to his lips. "She doesn't even seem to notice we're half-breeds. She doesn't seem to care. She actually loves us."

Lifting his gaze to Phoenix's again, he frowned. "We're gonna have to be patient until we can get her to trust us."

Phoenix stared down at her again, his stomach clenching when she shifted restlessly in her sleep and moaned in pain. "I can't stand to see her hurting like this. It makes me sick to my stomach." Frustrated that there was nothing around for him to take his anger on, he started pacing.

He paced well into the night, alternately walking the tree line and sitting by her side, staring at her as she slept restlessly between his brothers.

So little, to have made such a big impact on his life in such a short time.

By the time the sun rose and Eb arrived with the buckboard, he no longer felt as if he was falling in love with her.

He knew it for sure.

After settling her into the hammock they'd rigged for her in the back of the buckboard, they started back to the ranch, Phoenix sitting on one side of her while Blade sat on the other.

Eb kept glancing back at Sarah, his jaw clenched. "I can't believe this happened. I had people watching the cabin. She must have sneaked out. What the hell was she doing, sneaking out like that?" He waved his hand negligently. "I know *why* she did it. I just don't know how she got past the men." Turning to glance at each of them, he shook his head. "We're gonna have to watch them closer. I swear, if Maggie did something like that, I'd turn her over my knee and she wouldn't be able to sit down for a month."

Other than asking about Sarah, Hawke hadn't spoken since they started out.

He did now. "We'll handle her."

Phoenix rinsed the bandanna and placed it on her forehead again, trying to contain the fear that threatened to choke him. "If we get the chance. She's burnin' up."

*Don't die, Sarah. Please, honey, don't die.*

She'd filled empty holes inside him, and he hadn't even realized it until he'd seen her lying lifeless on the ground.

She'd made him better. Made him feel.

If he lost her now, he didn't know how he'd survive it.

\* \* \* \*

The pain woke her, so extreme that she couldn't even catch her breath.

She was hot—so hot and weighed down, as if a dozen blankets smothered her. She tried to push them away, but couldn't seem to move them.

Each small movement she made intensified the pain, so she gave up. "Please!"

She couldn't speak louder than a whisper, but heard what sounded like the scrape of a chair leg.

"It's okay, honey. I'm here."

*He was here. He would take care of her.*

Something touched her lips, and a foul-tasting liquid trickled into her mouth, leaving her no choice but to swallow it.

A cool cloth touched her forehead before darkness overtook her once again.

\* \* \* \*

Hawke rushed in with two more buckets of water. "How's she doing?" He dumped the water into the large tub, his insides clenched with fear.

Blade looked up and dipped the cloth into the bowl full of water at her bedside. "She's even hotter. We've got to get her fever down. She woke up again, crying and in pain. Are you about ready with that water?"

"Yeah." Hawke dropped the buckets and ran to her side as Phoenix came through the door with two more buckets.

"Duke warmed these up a little so she won't get too chilled. He's got more warming." Phoenix dumped the buckets of water into the tub and hovered as Blade lifted her and carried her to the tub. "We're not supposed to get her wounds wet."

Blade lowered her gently into the tub, his eyes wild. "If we don't get her damned temperature down, she's gonna die!"

\* \* \* \*

Hawke strode into the cabin after dealing with a horse that had gone wild and broken Conal's leg. It had been five days since Sarah had been shot, and she still had a fever.

He was scared to death.

Ridding himself of his gun belt, he rushed to her side. "How is she?" He let his gaze rake over her naked form stretched out on the new mattress they'd bought for her, pleased to see that no blood leaked through the cloth binding her injuries.

Phoenix rinsed out the bandanna and started wiping her down again. "She woke again a little while ago. She was restless and cried out in pain, so I gave her a little more of the laudanum. She looks like she's trying to push something off her."

Hawke knelt at her side, setting the bowl of soup onto the table next to him. "She's still feverish, so she's probably trying to push off blankets that aren't there."

Fear for her recovery had kept any of them from sleeping for days, and it had started to take a toll on all of them. "Let me get cleaned up and then we'll give her another sponge bath."

They'd dressed her in nothing but her nightgowns for days, but they'd quickly become soaked with sweat, so they hadn't bothered anymore. "We'll wash her and change the sheets. The doc said it would make her feel better. When's he due back?"

Phoenix frowned and wrung the cloth out again. "He'll be back at the end of the week. Eb and Jeremiah offered him a job here—offered him so much money the doc couldn't refuse—especially since he wants to have a fully stocked office. He'll live and work out of the house the mail-order brides were supposed to live in until they can build him his own place."

Hawke nodded grimly. "Why the hell doesn't she wake up?"

"Doc says it's the fever. Once it breaks, she should be fine."

Hawke understood the desperation in his brother's voice, and although he knew he and Phoenix were both thinking the same thing, neither one of them dared to voice it.

What if the fever didn't break? What if it took her?

Phoenix started to rinse the fresh bandanna, bending to touch his forehead to Sarah's chest. "She doesn't calm until she hears my voice."

Hawke nodded, taking Sarah's warm hand in his, once again shocked at how small and delicate it felt in his. "Blade and I noticed the same thing. If the doctor or one of the women tries to calm her, she just gets more agitated, but if one of us talks to her, she settles."

Phoenix lifted his head, his eyes bleak. "She really loves us. Christ, Hawke. We let her down. I swear, if she recovers—"

"*When* she recovers." The thought of losing her proved more than Hawke could bear. "We won't let her go. We told her she wasn't getting away from us. She's fighting it, and we'll just have to make sure we give her the strength to keep fighting." Smiling, he touched his lips to her fingers. "And when she gets better, she's going to understand, in no uncertain terms, that we'll do everything in our power to keep her here, and protect her. There won't be any other incidents like this again."

He turned at the sound of footsteps on the small front porch, his smile falling when he saw Sarah's mother coming in with a tray. The unmistakable smell of the soup Duke kept making by the gallon made his stomach rumble.

Edna set the tray on the table. "Why don't the two of you go eat while I feed Sarah? I want to give her a bath afterward—"

"We'll take care of it." Hawke fought back his anger at the woman who'd failed to protect Sarah when she'd needed it most.

Edna approached the bed, taking Sarah's other hand in hers as she sat gingerly next to her legs. "I know you don't like me much, but I *am* her mother. I protected her and took care of her the best I could. I made a living on my back to keep a roof over her head and food in her belly. I might not be the best mother in the world, but I didn't abandon her as so many of the other girls did with their own babies. I kept her with me."

Her eyes filled with tears, weakening Hawke's anger. "I did what I could for her. I tried. Doesn't that count for anything?"

Phoenix lifted his gaze to Hawke's, before focusing on Sarah again. "It counts for a lot. I'm just glad we found her when we did. We'll take care of her now. You should have gone back to Tulsa with the doctor. We'll pay for your train fare back to Waco."

Edna laughed humorlessly. "I can't go back there. Because of the trouble with Willy, Rose fired me." Her smile didn't reach her eyes. "Maybe I'll do what Sarah was planning. I could get lost in California—start over." She eyed each of them, smiling coldly. "But, I ain't leavin' until I talk to my daughter."

\* \* \* \*

Sarah lay propped against the headboard of the new bed her husbands had just assembled, watching Phoenix as he eased down on the bed to sit next to her. She tried to wave her hand, but it proved too much effort. "I can't believe you bought another bed."

Phoenix smiled, his gaze narrowing as he studied her features. "We wanted you to be comfortable while you healed, and that other bed wasn't an option. We burned it. You look tired."

"I'm fine. How's your shoulder?"

Phoenix lifted his arm, rotating it. "Fine. Doesn't even hurt. Now, lie back and go to sleep. You need to get your strength back."

It had been three weeks since she'd been shot, and it frustrated her that she didn't have any more energy than a newborn kitten.

Standing at the foot of the bed with his arms crossed over his chest, Blade looked every inch a warrior. "Yes. We have a few things to discuss about that little stunt you pulled."

Sarah wiggled restlessly, wincing at the pull to her side and thigh. "You've made your opinion of that real clear."

Blade's brow went up in that way that made her stomach flutter. "Have I?"

"You have." Sarah shrugged and closed her eyes again. "You said it was stupid, but I don't see it that way. I thought if I could give Willy the gold, he would leave and stop causing trouble." She opened her eyes when Phoenix stood, flicking her gaze to Blade's again.

His smile didn't reach his eyes, the remembered horror in them making her feel guilty as hell. "And we all know how that worked out."

* * * *

"Lily—"

"I thought we'd agreed that you would call me Mother now." Smiling faintly, she pushed her hair back. "Your men refuse to even call me Lily. They call me Edna. Feels strange to be called by my real name." Shaking her head, she blew out a breath. "But I want you to call me Mother."

Sarah smiled. "*Mother*, I want you to take the gold I took from Willy and use it to get to California."

Shaking her head, her mother rose from the bed. "No. It's better that you have it. I don't want you to be stuck the way I was. I want you to be able to get away if you need to."

"She won't need to." Hawke came through the doorway, frowning as he approached the foot of the bed. "Sarah stays where she is."

A shiver of delight went through Sarah at her husband's tone, the possessiveness in his eyes sending a rush of warmth through her that had nothing to do with a fever. "Oh, does she?"

He couldn't exactly be thought of as handsome. His features were too hard for that, but no one could deny his masculinity.

Fluttering her eyelashes in the way she'd seen her mother and the other girls do a thousand times, she struggled to hold back a laugh when his eyes narrowed with suspicion. "Are you going to make it worth my while?"

Hawke recovered quickly, a dark brow going up. "Let's put it this way. If you try running away again, or go anywhere without telling one of us, you're gonna find yourself in all kinds of trouble."

Sarah's mother whirled to confront him, backing off slightly when he took a step toward her. "If you hurt her, I'll—"

Hawke scowled at her before turning his attention back to Sarah, his lips twitching when his gaze met hers. "I'd cut my hands off before I hurt her and she knows it. That's why she's taunting me now." He smiled faintly, and moved to her side, lifting the sheet and the edges of her nightgown to check her healing injuries, eyeing them critically before lowering the sheet again. "Behave yourself. I'll be back in a little while."

Meeting her mother's gaze, Hawke straightened. "Take the gold. Sarah has the reward money from Willy and his gang."

"What?" Sarah gaped at him. "Reward money? I didn't do anything." She hadn't expected that. "You take it."

Hawke shrugged. "You drew him here." Lifting a hand when she would have objected, he shook his head. "Everyone involved agrees that you deserve it. It's yours to use as you wish."

Pausing at the doorway, he turned. "Unless, of course, you use it to try to run away again." He glanced at her mother, some unspoken message passing between them. "We won't let you go, Sarah, unless you're unhappy here. Are you?"

Anxious to get better so she could make love with him again, she grinned. "How can I be unhappy when I'm with the men I love?"

His smile, a flash of white against his dark skin, made her stomach flutter and her pussy clench with need. "You can't be. You won't be. Behave yourself. I won't be long."

She knew by the look in his eyes that if they'd been alone and she'd been healed, he would already be making love to her.

Shifting her legs restlessly, she pressed her thighs together at the ache that settled there.

It amazed her that she'd become so dependent on the closeness that lovemaking enhanced between them, and missed it terribly.

Once Hawke disappeared, her mother turned to her, a smile curving her lips. "That man sure does love you. Blade and Phoenix too. You should have seen them take care of you. Hell, they even argued with the doctor. I didn't know men were capable of such gentleness." Smiling, she moved closer. "You love them, don't you?"

"I do." Laughing softly, she winced at the slight pain in her side. "I didn't think anyone would ever fall in love with me."

"Because you were raised in a bordello?" Her mother shrugged. "Men want to have sex with whores, but they certainly don't want to marry them. I guess you would have been painted with the same brush." Picking at a thread on her dress, she looked up at Sarah through her lashes. "I heard what happened with Willy back in Waco. I'm sorry for it. If I'd known what he planned to do, I would have found a way to get you out of there."

She smiled, her eyes gleaming with pride. "You did it yourself even better. Stole his gold and lit out of town before he even suspected. I'm real proud of you. On top of that, you run straight into the arms of men like that. I'm happy as hell that you managed to find men who love you the way those three do."

Shaking her head, her mother got to her feet, moving slowly around the small cabin. "I'd give anything to have the love of one man, and you've got three. A home of your own."

Wiping away a tear, her mother nodded. "I'll take some of that gold, if you don't mind. I'm real happy that you've got security." Grinning, she shook her head again, appearing more relaxed than Sarah had even seen her look. "Three husbands. Amazing. You've got three men to look after you and keep you safe—three strong, fearless men who'd risk their life for you."

Sarah gulped, glancing toward the window. "I know. It's a little scary."

It was also very humbling.

Her mother smiled and lowered herself to sit on the bed next to her. "You should have seen them. They were so scared."

Sarah traced a pattern on the sheet. "I thought they wanted me to leave. Phoenix got shot because of me. I thought they blamed me for bringing trouble to the ranch."

Her mother surprised her by throwing her head back and laughing. "Doesn't look to me like they're the type to hide behind a woman's skirts. Nope. Those men'll meet trouble head on and enjoy the hell out of it."

She'd never forget how they'd looked when they'd ridden off to confront Willy and his gang, and knew that her mother was right. Blowing out a breath, she moved to a more comfortable position. "They looked so hard and cold when they rode out, like completely different men." Smiling, she leaned back with a sigh, missing her husbands. At least one of them had been with her at all times since she'd been shot, and had only started leaving her alone to spend some time with her mother, Savannah, and Maggie. "They've been nothing but gentle with me. I never dreamed they could be so dangerous. I heard what they did to Willy and his men."

"Without even breaking a sweat. None of them started sweating until they saw you fall." Her mother smiled, turning from where she'd been staring out the window. Although the bruises on her face had faded, Sarah knew she'd never forget them.

"Oh, baby, every man I've met since coming here is dangerous—the good kind of dangerous." Laughing softly, her mother braced herself against the wall, sighing as she leaned her head against the window. Her laughter stopped, but she wore a satisfied smile and a faraway look in her eyes that kept Sarah silent. "Such good men, and so kind to women. Even to me."

Struck by the look of peace and contentment that seemed to erase the harsh lines on her mother's face, Sarah just watched her, amazed that her mother looked at least ten years younger. She'd never seen her mother look so beautiful.

Her mother stood in silence for several long minutes before turning, her smile widening. "To know that you're happy and settled means the world to me. If your offer's still open, I have a chance to start over. It's more than I could have ever hoped for—for both of us."

Straightening, she smiled again as if she couldn't stop smiling, moving to the bed and sitting next to Sarah. She took Sarah's hand in hers in a motherly gesture that brought back happy memories that Sarah had long ago forgotten.

As a little girl, she'd play with her mother's sparkly jewelry and colorful feathers that she wore in her hair, while her mother looked on with a smile, a smile she hadn't seen in too many years.

Until now.

"Your men are *real* men—strong enough to handle any trouble that comes along, and secure enough in themselves to let you see how much they love you. I've heard about men like them all my life, but I've never met any. To know that you're surrounded by them, and have three of them who would die—or kill—for you makes anything seem possible. A new life for both of us."

Patting Sarah's hand, her mother rose again as if the excitement shining in her eyes made it impossible for her to sit still. "California! Thank you so much for makin' it possible for me to start over. Now that you're on the mend, I'm gonna go. Your men have put up with me long enough, and Duke said he's goin' to town tomorrow for more supplies. I heard Mrs. Tyler talking her husbands into goin' to town, too."

Shaking her head, her mother clasped her hands and laughed again. "Both of those men gave in to her and agreed to take her and the baby to town with Duke. I think they want to show off the baby. I'll tell you, girl, you sure ended up in an amazing place."

# Chapter Fifteen

Sitting on the small front porch of the cabin she shared with her husbands, Sarah thought about her mother's words as she looked up from the skirt she'd started hemming.

The sight of Phoenix approaching, brushing dirt from his chaps, filled her with a longing that seemed to grow stronger each day.

As soon as she lifted her face, he smiled at her, a grin that made her pulse leap even from several yards away.

Smiling, she sat back and admired his purposeful walk, her smile falling when he suddenly frowned.

"Are you allowed to be out here?" He took the stairs to the small porch two at a time to crouch beside her chair. "Shouldn't you be in bed?"

Setting her sewing aside, she reached out a hand to him, her heart lurching when he took it in his and sat at her feet. "The doctor said that I'm doing fine, and that he wants me to start moving more. He said fresh air would do me good. Besides, I'm bored and I want to see what's going on. I've been watching you trying to break that horse all morning. Are you all right?"

His hand slid up her leg to the exact spot the bullet had struck her thigh. "I'm fine. How about you? What did the doc say *exactly*?"

His tone and the warning gleam in his eyes told her that she'd better not lie to him.

She leaned forward, thrilled at his kiss, but humbled when he laid his head gently on her lap. Running her fingers through his hair, she smiled. "He said that I'm healing nicely. He wants me to move more now so I can build up my strength. Being in bed for so long has made me weak and stiff."

Feeling guilty, she kept stroking his hair, loving the silky texture against her fingers.

He hadn't been the same since the shooting, becoming quieter and more thoughtful. Even though he'd teased her out of her grouchiness while she'd been healing, there'd been an angry glint in his eyes from time to time, one that made her feel even guiltier.

Smiling faintly, she sighed, wishing she could get him to play again. "I'm sorry. I'm sure you, Hawke, and Blade must be disappointed."

Lifting his head, Phoenix turned to face her, frowning again. "Disappointed?"

Sarah's face burned. "Because we haven't been able to—you know—for over a month. I feel better now, so if you want to—"

"Are you out of your mind?" Phoenix jumped to his feet. "You've barely healed enough to get out of bed, and you think we're gonna jump you?" Slashing a hand through the air, he started pacing. "Christ, woman! You could drive a saint crazy."

A deep voice came from around the corner. "And you're not exactly a saint. Hell, none of us is. What's the problem?" Hawke approached from the other side of the cabin, pausing in front of the porch steps with his hands on his hips, frowning at her. "What the hell are you doing out of bed?"

"The doctor said—"

"The doctor said that he wanted you to get some fresh air and to move, but until you gain your strength, only if one of us is with you. Just getting dressed would have required quite a bit of moving around that you shouldn't have done on your own." His tone had an edge she didn't quite trust, one that had her shifting restlessly in her seat.

Gulping, she shrugged, hiding a wince when it tugged at her shoulder. "I was careful."

Phoenix folded his arms across his chest and leaned back against the railing. "I thought we'd discussed the fact that you're going to be more careful in the future."

"I *am* going to be more careful. Look at you! When you got shot in the shoulder, you couldn't stand to be fussed over and made to stay put. I've had a month of it! I'm bored. I want to be outside. I want to get back to my life. I hate feeling like an invalid and I won't let you keep treating me like I am. I want my husbands back. I want to make love again. I *hate* being a burden!"

Phoenix smiled and turned to share a look with Hawke over his shoulder. "She's feeling better."

Hawke nodded once, his eyes hardening. "I'm glad. She still has a way to go, though. But I'm going to tell you right now, Sarah Royal, that if you ever pull a damned fool stunt like that again, I'll turn you over my knee and whip your ass until you can't sit down!"

Sarah watched him turn and walk away, stunned by his violent response. "He's mad at me."

Phoenix nodded and lowered himself to the top step with a sigh. "We all were, because you scared the hell out of us. We were mad at you for putting yourself in danger. Mad at you for not trusting us to deal with Willy." Leaning back against the post, he held her gaze. "Mad at ourselves for not getting to you in time. So furious at Willy and his gang that we wanted to kill them again."

Touching her knee, he sighed again. "We never thought we'd have a woman in our lives. I liked to play too much to be tied down to one woman. Blade's too possessive. Hawke had a chip on his shoulder a mile wide, and didn't think any woman could ever love a man as hard and cold as he was."

Smiling, he took her hand, lifting his gaze to hers. "And then you came along. You trusted Hawke from the very beginning. The first day we met you, you huddled against him, as if he could save you from the world. You didn't flinch away from his touch, and you kept looking in his direction every time you felt uneasy." He laughed softly. "You still do. Even though you know damned well that he loves you, you're shaken because he's mad at you."

Staring out after Hawke, Phoenix sighed again. "Having the responsibility of a wife made playing seem so childish." Grinning, he turned back to her. "Don't get me wrong. I love playing with you, but seeing you get shot shook me real bad. I don't think I've ever been so scared in my life. You got shot because I wasn't fast enough on the trigger."

Sarah smiled and squeezed his hand, humbled by his admission. "Now you know how I felt when you got shot because of me. If you hadn't moved as fast as you did, you could have been killed." Her chest tightened and, blinking back tears, she squeezed his hand again. "I couldn't have lived with that."

Phoenix smiled and lifted her hand to his lips. "But I can take care of myself. You're defenseless here. It's our job to take care of you." Straightening, he turned as if sensing something, grinning at Blade's approach. "Uh-oh. Here comes Blade. He's changed a lot since we married you, too. Now that he has a woman he can possess, it seems like he can't get enough. When you were shot, he examined you every day. He sat and stared at you the way Hawke did, as if they could will you to get better."

Shaking his head, Phoenix watched his brother cross the large yard, his long strides eating up the ground. "Blade's been obsessed with checking you out, and wants to know every mark on you. Hell, he took the cloth out of your mother's hand when she was trying to bathe you." Laughing softly, he patted her hand. "Told her flat out that she was being too rough, and took over the job himself."

Leaning close, he lowered his voice. "Betcha the first thing he asks is why the hell you're out of bed."

* * * *

Blade strode toward Sarah, alarmed to find her sitting on the front porch. Sparing a glare for his smiling brother, he took the stairs two at a time, searching Sarah's features for any sign of pain or fatigue—something that had become a habit. She looked exhausted, the dark circles under her eyes and too-pale features alarming him. The way she moved spoke volumes about her weakness. "What the hell are you doing out of bed?"

Phoenix grinned and rose to his feet. "Told you. I'm gonna go join Hawke at the well and get cleaned up a little before dinner. Take it easy on her, Blade. She got checked out by the doc."

Blade's dark brow went up. "And you think I don't know that?" Bending, he gathered her against him, and straightened, holding her securely against his chest. "I make it my business to know everything about her."

The last few weeks had been scary as hell and he spent every available minute watching her, so afraid that he would lose her.

Her fever seemed to last forever, and had kept him and his brothers awake at night, fearing she'd die in her sleep if they didn't watch her.

When it finally broke, he and Hawke had bathed the sweat from her and then he'd gone outside, crying for the first time in his adult life.

Leaning her head against Blade's shoulder, she smiled up at him, so light and delicate in his arms that it unnerved him. "Now that Phoenix wears moccasins instead of cowboy boots, he thinks it's funny as hell to sneak up on me."

Blade gave her the smile he knew she expected and strode to the bed. "We're all used to being as quiet as possible so we didn't wake you. I want to see how you're healing."

Mindful of her injuries, he flattened his hand on her thigh and started to raise her skirt, stilling when she laid a hand over his to stop his progress. "Blade, please don't."

His stomach clenched, the thought that she'd changed her mind about him during her recovery scaring him to his bones.

She'd taught him that he could love so deeply.

He didn't think he'd ever find a woman who'd tie herself to a half-breed and embrace living in the middle of nowhere the way Sarah had.

His need for her grew, and went far beyond just physical. The closeness he'd established with her had fed a need inside him he hadn't even known he'd had.

She was everything he'd ever wanted in a woman—more than he could have ever dreamed of—wrapped in one adorable, desirable package.

And so frighteningly delicate.

The slight flare of panic in her eyes was like a kick to the gut.

She'd never objected to his touch before, and his heart clenched because she did now.

If she'd decided she didn't want him anymore, he didn't know how he'd survive it.

# Chapter Sixteen

Sarah's face burned under Blade's steady stare, and smoothed her hand over his in apology. "It's ugly."

Blade blinked, the tension she hadn't noticed before easing from his body.

Although she didn't understand the relief in his eyes, his slow smile took her breath away.

Turning his hand to take hers, he held her gaze, his eyes glittering with emotion. "Nothing about you could ever be anything but beautiful to me."

"You're just being nice." Not allowing herself to believe him, she averted her gaze, staring toward the window. "I was already damaged. This just makes it worse."

"Oh, love." Pressing her gently back against the pillows, he knelt on the floor beside her. "How could you ever think that?"

She involuntarily leaned into his touch when he pushed her hair back. "I've seen the way you, Hawke, and Phoenix look at my scars. You stare at them and then you get this look on your faces and turn away as if you can't bear to see them."

Blade wore the same expression now. "And you think it's because we think they're so ugly that we can't stand to look at them?"

"Yes. I under—" She snapped her mouth closed as he slashed a hand through the air and surged to his feet.

Blade's features hardened even more as he began to pace, his long braid flying with every turn. "You understand nothing! We failed! Do you understand that?" He strode back and forth across the small room, scrubbing his hand over his face. "We were supposed to keep you safe. We were supposed to protect you."

Stunned by his outburst, Sarah sat up again. "But you did protect me. You came to rescue me, and took care of me."

"Yes. But, you got hurt. Seeing those scars just reminds us that we didn't do our job. We didn't protect you." Rushing to her side, he knelt beside her, the glitter of emotion in his eyes leaving her staring up at him in stunned silence.

Shoving her skirt out of the way, he pressed his lips to her now healed wound, gathering her against him. "You could have died." His arms tightened around her as he pressed his face against her belly. "We came so close to losing you. I love you, and I almost lost you."

Shocked that his voice broke, Sarah blinked back tears. Running her hand over his sleek hair, she smiled. "You love me?"

Blade lifted his head, his eyes shimmering with unshed tears. He blinked, and they disappeared, only to be replaced with an incredulous look of disbelief. "Of course, I love you. Did getting shot addle your brains?" Rising to his feet, Blade started pacing again.

"How the hell could you not know that I love you?" He spun again, confronting Hawke as he came through the door. "How the hell can she think that we think her scars are ugly?"

Hawke's brows went up, his gaze zeroing in on hers. "Oh?"

Phoenix came through the door right behind Hawke, frowning at Blade before turning to her. "She thinks that? Has she seen the scars on us?"

Shrugging, Sarah picked at a thread on the sheet covering her. "That's different. You're men. I saw the way you looked at them—"

Hawke came closer, his hair dripping wet from where he'd obviously dunked it to cool off again. "And you thought it was because we thought they were ugly?" Shaking his head, he shared a look with his brothers. "It looks like we've failed her again."

To her surprise, Hawke stripped the sheet from the bed, and with a gentleness she hadn't expected, and an efficiency he'd obviously gained in the past several weeks, stripped her out of her clothes.

Meeting her gaze, he pressed her back against the pillows again and lowered his head. "I'll show you how ugly I think your scars are."

The chill of his wet hair on her breast and abdomen made her jolt, but the heat of his lips on the spot on her side where she'd been shot quickly warmed her again.

Blade smiled. "Let's join him." He moved to the other side of the bed and knelt beside her, bending his head to run his tongue over the scar on her thigh.

Phoenix knelt next to him, smiling as he lowered his head to the now healed bullet wound on her shoulder. Running his lips and tongue over it, he ran a hand over her hair. "Delicious."

Lifting his head, Hawke stroked her nipples with the ends of her hair, smiling at her gasp. "Does this feel like we think anything about you is ugly?"

Feeling their lips and tongues moving over the sensitized, newly healed flesh, Sarah moaned and writhed beneath them. "Oh, God." To have them all touch her this way made every erogenous zone in her body grow hot and tingle for attention.

"You really don't mind them?"

Blade lifted his head and spread her thighs, running his hand up and down her inner thigh with a gentle demand that made her pussy clench. "We mind because we didn't protect you. That won't happen in the future. You'll behave yourself and do everything in your power to protect yourself."

Hawke pressed another kiss to her side, running his tongue over her scar before lifting is head again to slide his tongue over her nipple, his expression hard. "Including doing what we tell you to do. If you go anywhere, at least one of us had better know about it, or if we're not around, tell one of the men here. Do you understand me?"

"Yes!" Sarah moaned again, writhing continuously under their hands and lips.

Blade's hand moved over her thigh as he traced his lips over the spot where she'd been shot.

Phoenix used his lips on the wound on her shoulder, running his hand over her breast and teasing her nipple, while Hawke moved his damp hair over the other.

Lifting his head from the wound on her side, Hawke stared into her eyes. "Once you get your strength back, I'm going to show you just how damned much I want you." Straightening, he reached for her other thigh and eased it back, watching her face as he spread her thighs wide. "In the meantime, I'm going to use my mouth on you. You're gonna take a damned nap. After you come a couple of times, maybe you won't fight it so much."

Holding her other thigh, Blade smiled down at her, a smile filled with wicked intent. "You get the first one. I'll take care of the second."

Hawke moved between her thighs and lowered his head to her slit. "Phoenix, get on the other side of her and help Blade hold her as still as possible. I don't want her thrashing around and hurting herself."

Sarah bucked at the slide of Hawke's tongue over her slit, but the three of them held firm, not allowing her to move more than an inch or two in any direction. "Hawke!" His hot mouth on her clit drove her wild, his lips closing over it as he flicked his tongue over it with a speed and firmness that sent her over in a rush of heat and pleasure. "Oh, God. Oh, God."

The muscles in her thighs tightened painfully as the sizzling heat washed over her, and although she pushed at Blade and Hawke, she couldn't budge either one of them. "It's too much. Oh, my God."

Lifting his head, Hawke licked his lips, shiny with her juices. "Already, little one? I was just getting started."

"My turn." Blade changed places with his brother, his eyes alight with anticipation. "Let's see if I can drag it out and make the second one last a little longer."

Phoenix bent to close his lips over her nipple while Hawke held her thighs, lowering his head to run his lips and tongue over her wounds. "She's already weak. Be easy with her."

Blade grinned. "So easy that she's gonna beg for relief."

Sarah moaned, never feeling more cherished. More wanted.

More adored.

Blade's tongue moved over her clit with a slow deliberation that sent her senses reeling. He teased her, running his tongue over the sensitized bundle of nerves, easing her back toward release when she hadn't even fully come down from the last orgasm.

"Blade. Please."

Lifting his head slightly, he chuckled, the sound vibrating over her clit. "Already begging, love? We're going to have to work on your endurance in more ways than one, aren't we?"

Phoenix lifted his head, staring down at her with eyes dark with hunger. "We're gonna have to work on her stamina for sure. Once we build her strength up, we're gonna have to see how long we can play with her without letting her come."

Hawke's hand slid from her belly to her breast, his eyes filled with tender indulgence. "Does this feel like we don't want you?"

Sarah tried to writhe, and found to her surprise that instead of frightening her, their firm holds excited her more.

Still holding her thigh, Hawke laughed softly and bent to touch his lips to hers. "You like being held this way. Interesting."

Blade slid his tongue into her pussy, groaning when she clenched on it. He teased her mercilessly, sliding it in and out of her until she bucked again. Lifting his head, he brushed his tongue over her clit. "We'll have to tie her to the bed sometime and have our way with her."

Just the thought of it sent another wave of need through her, a wave that washed over the others and combined into something so intense, she reached for Hawke. "Please, Hawke. I can't stand anymore."

Heat—sizzling heat—seemed to touch her everywhere, the pressure building inside her with every swipe of Blade's tongue.

Hawke's and Phoenix's attention to her nipples increased the pleasure until she thought she would burst.

She didn't have the strength to fight it, or them.

Resigned to allowing Blade to have his way, she whimpered and begged again for release. "Blade, please. I ache so bad." Her thighs trembled, every muscle in her body quivering with pleasure.

Lifting his head, Blade stared down at her, sliding a finger into her pussy as he stroked his thumb over her clit. "Are you going to take a nap without arguing?"

"Yes." She'd do anything to go over again, her breath catching in anticipation of the ecstasy ahead. "I promise."

Hawke tightened his fingers on her nipple. "And no more stupid stunts. We can handle any trouble that comes along, but I won't have you putting yourself in danger again."

"I promise. I'll do whatever you want." She was so close that every slide of Blade's finger sent a shiver through her. She clenched on his finger, wishing he would take her, but she knew none of them would until she got stronger.

Nothing else could have been a better incentive.

"Good girl. We're going to hold you to that. Now, be a good girl and stay still." Blade bent again, his hot mouth replacing his finger. Closing his lips over her clit, he began to suck it, the quick flicks of his tongue sending her over within seconds.

Crying out, she clung to Hawke and Phoenix, who watched her with eyes that glittered. "Yes! Oh, God." Her orgasm took the last of her energy, leaving her weak as the waves of pleasure washed over her.

They seemed to roll through her, sweeping her along in a rush of heat that she couldn't control.

"That's my girl." Blade's voice, filled with male satisfaction, seemed to come from a distance, the hands that moved over her and the soothing words of love and caring lulled her into a world of warm and happiness that she never wanted to leave.

* * * *

Blade felt her slump, and smiled as he lifted his head. "She's asleep." Licking his lips, he savored the taste of her and slid his hands up her thighs. Frowning, he covered her with the sheet, not wanting her to get chilled as the pleasure wore off. "I didn't expect that. I thought she knew how we felt."

Phoenix shrugged. "Women always want to hear the words."

Hawke nodded. "I'd like hearing the words myself. The only time she's ever said it was when I asked her if she was happy here. She asked me how she could be unhappy when she's with the men she loves."

Blade nodded. "She loves us. She's proven it over and over, but doesn't seem to recognize it in us."

Phoenix straightened the sheet over her and rose to his feet again. Staring down at her, he ran his hand over her hair. "Maybe she's scared."

Blade frowned. "Of what?"

Hawke sighed and ran a hand over her arm, smiling when she rolled toward him. "What the hell security has she ever had in her life? She's probably just scared that someone's gonna pull the rug out from under her. We're gonna have to be patient."

Blade nodded. "Yeah. She actually thought we wouldn't want her anymore after Phoenix got shot."

Phoenix sighed, looking up to meet Hawke's gaze. "And she sure as hell was shaken when you got mad at her for being on the porch instead of in bed. She seems to think that anytime one of us gets mad, it's at her, and that being mad at her means we don't love her anymore."

Hawke's stomach clenched, the reminder of the kind of life she'd had making him physically ill. "We can't really blame her for that. It sounds like she walked on eggshells her entire life, trying not to draw attention to herself. Now that she's here, she's got all kinds of attention. It's given her confidence in some ways, but not enough."

Phoenix bent to touch his lips to her hair, smiling at her soft sigh. "We're just gonna have to be patient and let her know that being mad at her doesn't mean we don't love her."

# Chapter Seventeen

Sarah smiled at the cheers and shouts of encouragement coming from the paddock. Deciding that she'd done enough sewing for now, she got up to stretch, pleased that she felt stronger now than she ever had in her life.

Duke appeared, studying her from the doorway of the chow shack. "You all right?"

Grinning, Sarah nodded, and bent to put her sewing back into the basket. "I'm great. I swear, I don't think I've ever felt this good in my entire life." Straightening, she wrinkled her nose at him. "Must be all that delicious food you make."

Duke grunted. "I just cook it. It's your men who practically force feed you. How about a glass of milk? Savannah's in here having some."

Another loud cheer had her turning. "Thanks, but no. I've been sitting too long. I want to go see what all the commotion's about. I'll be back in time to help with supper."

With a wave, she raced down the porch steps and around the corner, hurrying toward the paddock before whatever the men were cheering about was over.

As soon as she rounded the cabin, she could see men all around the fenced area. Even from this distance, she recognized Hawke and Blade. Dressed in buckskins, they stood out from the crowd, but she would have known their lean, muscular forms anywhere.

A crowd of men stood around the wooden fence, calling out shouts of encouragement.

238                                                                    *Lana Dare*

Curious and anxious to see Hawke and Blade again, she started toward them, her boots squishing in the mud from the thunderstorms of the night before. Holding her skirts up to keep them from getting muddy, she wished she'd worn her buckskin dress and leggings.

Grinning, she ran up to them, stunned that despite the shouts and cheers from the other men all around them, they somehow sensed her presence and turned in unison to face her.

Hawke smiled faintly, his eyes flaring as she placed her hand in his outstretched one. "Hello, love." His gaze raked over her as he pulled her to his side. "Something wrong?"

"No." Smiling up at Blade, she leaned against Hawke, loving the solid warmth of his body supporting hers. "I was sitting on the front porch sewing, and I heard a commotion. What's going on?" Her eyes widened when she saw that the great attraction was Phoenix riding a horse that bucked wildly. "Oh, dear Lord!"

Covering her eyes, she turned to press her face against Blade's chest, tightening her hand on Hawke's. "Every time I see one of you do this, it gives me chills."

Hawke slid a hand down her back, bending to touch his lips to her ear. "Imagine what I felt like when I looked up and saw you going head to head with an outlaw."

Turning her head, she stuck her tongue out of him. "I know. I know. I promised not to ever do anything like that again." Straightening, she watched Phoenix again. "Besides, I heard from Duke that you were real proud of my spunk."

Blade tugged at her braid. "Duke has a big mouth—and even though we thought you were brave, and appreciated that you wanted to defend us, I'd be real thankful if you never did anything like that again. It was brave. Stupid, but brave."

Aware of the other men glancing at them and smiling before turning their attention back to phoenix, she sighed. "I know. No more spunk."

Blade chuckled softly, not taking his eyes from Phoenix. "You can have all the spunk you want. In bed." He stiffed beside her when the horse spun Phoenix so fast it made her dizzy.

"Oh, God. He's gonna get thrown."

Aware of Blade's hard body warming her from behind, she cried out in fear when Phoenix was almost bucked off again. His grin flashed as he seemed to get the horse under control again, clearly enjoying himself.

\* \* \* \*

Blade ran a hand over her hair, once again stunned by the swell of pride that she belonged to his brothers and him.

"Phoenix!" Her shout of terror and the horror in her eyes, like a fist around his heart, had him whipping his head around to the enclosure just in time to see his younger brother fly through the air and land hard on the muddy ground.

Hawke had already started over the fence when Blade gripped Sarah shoulders. "Stay right here."

Blade vaulted over the fence as several ranch hands made their way toward his prone brother, each of them watching the wild horse warily. Knowing that only he and Hawke could handle the black stallion, he gritted his teeth and confident that Phoenix would be taken care of, took the rope attached to his belt and began to edge toward the clearly angry stallion.

Hawke approached from the other side, and working together, they kept the horse between them and away from the others.

Out of the corner of his eye, he saw the ranch hands help Phoenix to his feet, and blocked out the shouts of encouragement and focused on the task at hand.

Sarah cried out, and out of the corner of his eye, he saw her racing toward Phoenix and dangerously close to Hawke. It distracted him just as he released his rope, which landed over the stallion's head a split second after Hawke's.

The fear of seeing Sarah race to Phoenix's side distracted him just enough that if it weren't for Hawke's hold on the rope, Blade would have been trampled. It took several minutes before he and Hawke got the horse under control again, his fear strengthening to fury by the time he and Hawke had the horse back under control and secured in his stall.

After giving instructions, he turned away, his anger even hotter. The mental image of turning his wife over his lap and reddening her ass made him feel only slightly better.

Wiping his hands, he turned to his brother, unsurprised to see that Hawke's eyes glittered with the same fury. "She disobeyed me. I'll take care of it."

Hawke's lips thinned. "She's my wife, too. I'll be there and if you don't take care of it properly, I will. I want her to see our anger."

"Don't worry. I'll handle her. Before I do, let's go check on Phoenix. He hit hard."

Hawke grimaced. "He was showing off for Sarah. He let himself be distracted."

Blade smiled and shook his head, some of his anger melting away. "You see too much. She didn't seem to distract you, though."

"I knew where she was the entire time." Something came and went in his eyes, a glitter that disappeared as fast as it had appeared. "I was the only thing standing between her and the stallion. She needed me to do my job."

Blade cursed under his breath. "Hell."

"She put herself in danger. We can't have that."

Blade nodded, determined to teach his wife a lesson she wouldn't soon forget. "No. We can't."

# Chapter Eighteen

Dropping to the ground, Sarah gripped Phoenix's hand, fear tightening her stomach. "Phoenix! Are you all right?"

The other men tried to push her aside, but she wouldn't let go.

Phoenix shrugged off their help, smiling his thanks. "I'm fine, darlin'. You really don't think you're gonna get rid of me that easy, do you?" Wrapping his arm around her, he started toward the fence, limping slightly. "That's what I get for showing off."

Walking on the other side of him, Jeremiah scrubbed a hand over his face. "I'm sure Hawke and Blade are gonna have something to say about that, so I won't bother. Uh-oh. Well, it looks like someone's in for some trouble."

Pursing his lips, Jeremiah shook his head and narrowed his eyes at Sarah. "If Maggie had done what you just did, she'd be in big trouble. You ran out there and put yourself in danger. I'm *real* sure Hawke and Blade will have something to say about that. If not, I know the rest of us will."

Sarah's knees weakened, his dark stare making her mouth dry. "I'm sorry. I just wanted to get to Phoenix."

"No excuse." He looked back over his shoulder and nodded. "Yep. You're in trouble. Good. The women around here need a strong hand." Smiling, he shared a look with Phoenix. "They all seem to be a bit stubborn."

Sighing, Phoenix nodded and ran a hand down her back, warming her. "That's because they're spoiled."

Throwing his head back, Jeremiah laughed as he walked off. "That they are. I'm gonna go get the stallion settled. You take care of your woman."

Aware of Hawke and Blade following them back to the cabin, Sarah hurried her steps. "Maybe you should lie down a little while."

"What?" Phoenix hugged her close before releasing her with a curse. "Hell, I'm filthy. I'm getting dirt all over you, darlin'. I'm gonna go get cleaned up. Go back to the cabin with Hawke and Blade."

"I don't want to." She looked over her shoulder again, gulping at the angry looks directed at her. "I think I'll come with you."

Phoenix stopped, turning to her with a smile. "And you don't think they'll follow you? Hell, we're both gonna get an earful. Me for showing off, and you for jumping over that fence. Might as well get it over with." Leaning close, he whispered in her ear. "Go on. I'll give you a head start."

Turning to face his brothers, Phoenix nodded. "I know. I saw Sarah and was showing off. Couldn't help myself. Did you see how she ran? She's feeling better, don't you think?"

Sarah hurried toward the chow shack, hoping that Hawke and Blade would have a chance to cool down over supper.

She didn't get the chance to find out.

Appearing on either side of her, they each took one of her arms and changed direction again, heading straight to the cabin.

Once inside, they released her, and Blade ran a hand over her hair. "We need to have a talk."

Sarah shrugged and moved farther into the small room, shaking with nerves. "What do you want to talk about?"

After a lengthy silence, she turned to find Hawke and Blade both staring at her.

Hawke had his hip perched on the corner of the table with Blade standing beside him. Both men had their arms crossed over their chests.

Blade's hooded gaze raked over her, leaving a trail of heat in its wake. "Are you all right?"

Smiling, Sarah nodded. "Yes. Of course. Phoenix is the one who got hurt."

Hawke's brow went up. "Not hurt anywhere?"

Sarah gulped, knowing that when Hawke cut his sentences, he was upset. *Very* upset. "No. Not at all." She tried anther smile. "As a matter of fact, I feel better than I have in a long time. You were right. All that exercise and Duke's cooking was all I needed." Nervous at the way they were both looking at her, she shifted her feet, reaching out to fluff the pillows on the bed for something to do with her hands.

Blade's next words had her stilling again. "Good, then we can move on, and you can explain to me why you deliberately disobeyed me and went over the fence and straight into danger?"

Shivering at his icy tone and the cold calculation in his eyes, Sarah shrugged. "I, um, didn't think about it. I saw Phoenix fall and just wanted to get to him."

Blade unfolded his arms and took a step closer, a dark brow going up. "Even after I told you to stay where you were?"

*Uh oh.*

Sarah shrugged and attempted another smile. "I told you—I didn't think about it." Pushing out her bottom lip the way Maggie had shown her, she wrung her hands. "Poor Phoenix. Did you see the way he went flying through the air? He fell so hard." Lowering her gaze, she looked up then through her lashes. "I worry every day about all of you. You're always in danger."

Blade took a step closer, his eyes narrowed. "We can handle the danger. And, I know you didn't think about climbing over that fence. That's the problem. Things happen fast out here, and you have to learn to react." He took a step closer, his eyes narrowing again when she took a step back. "You're not used to this way of life and aren't experienced enough to be able to weigh your options or realize the consequences of each one. That's our job, and we've already stressed to you how important it is to obey us, haven't we?"

Unnerved by his anger, she wrapped her arms around herself. "Yes, but—"

"But within seconds of me telling you to stay put, you climb over the fence and into danger."

Her own temper flared. Taking a step toward him, she poked him in the chest. "What was I supposed to do? Phoenix was hurt."

Gripping her wrist, he whirled her around, the hand at her waist pulling her firmly back against him. "You were *supposed* to do what I told you to do."

Shivering at the feel of his body against hers, and the brush of his warm lips against her ear, Sarah dropped her head back against his chest. "I, um, wasn't in any danger." She laid a hand over his arm, and tilted her face toward his, her pulse leaping at the hard press of his cock against her back.

Blade nipped her earlobe, sending a sharp stab of pleasure to her nipples and clit. "Really? So you're an expert on danger around here?" His voice, so low and silky, lulled her into closing her eyes and leaning heavily against him. "Hmm. I didn't say that." Shocked that her skirt fell to the floor, she started to move, only to be yanked back against him.

"Do you know that only Hawke stood between you and that wild stallion?"

Her eyes flew open, her gaze whipping to Hawke's. Seeing the truth in his eyes, Sarah pushed out of Blade's hold and started toward him. "Oh, Hawke!"

Blade yanked her back, his voice low and filled with anger. "Do you know that he risked his life, knowing that only he stood between you and a wild horse?"

"Oh, God!" She reached for Hawke, stunned at the knowledge that she could have gotten him killed. "I had no idea. I'm so sorry."

She looked from Hawke to Blade and back again, and then to Phoenix as he came through the door. "It'll never happen again. I promise."

Hawke studied her features, his eyes unreadable. "I'm sure you didn't also realize that Blade was distracted by the sight of you running toward danger. He lost his concentration and almost got trampled."

Spinning back around, she gaped at Blade, horrified at what she'd done. "No. Oh, God." Shaking her head, she looked at each of them, her stomach in knots. "I didn't know. I'd never do anything to hurt any of you."

Blade's jaw clenched. "You not only put yourself in danger, but everyone out there. If I'd been hurt, Hawke might've been hurt, too, and then everyone out there—including you—would have been at the mercy of that hard-headed stallion."

Sarah gulped. "Oh, God. I'm so sorry."

Blade inclined his head. "You will be. You need to learn a lesson. I don't care how many times we have to do this to hammer the point home. Practicing obeying without question might just keep you from getting hurt in the future. You *will* do what we tell you to do. Without question. Without hesitation. Your life, our lives, and others' lives might very well depend on it."

Clasping her hands in front of her, she nodded. "It won't happen again."

Blade looked up from where he sat at the table, the air of confidence surrounding him steadying her. "You assured me that it wouldn't happen at all, but it did. Even when we explained how important it was—you chose to ignore me the first time I gave you a direct order. I'm afraid I don't believe you."

The enormity of what she'd done hit her hard. "I didn't ignore you."

She honestly hadn't thought before she'd reacted, something she now realized could be deadly in such a wild untamed place.

Walking toward her—stalking her—Blade raised a brow again. "You disobeyed me."

"I didn't mean to."

"Yet you did."

Glancing toward where Phoenix leaned back against the door, Sarah shuffled her feet, wishing she knew what to say. "I just wanted to get to Phoenix."

Hawke sighed. "We know that, but how can we be sure you won't run out in the middle of a shootout? How can we be sure that you won't follow one of us into a damned sinkhole or move when we tell you not to if there's a snake or wild animal?"

Seeing that she wouldn't get any help from Phoenix, she dropped to the side of the bed. "Oh, God."

Phoenix shrugged. "Sorry, honey. They're right. Your safety's the most important thing. I can't go through you getting hurt again."

Hawke crossed his arms over his chest again, looking like a warrior. "If we don't stick together, you won't have the security you need. Don't try to pit one of us against another. It won't work."

Blade moved to one window, closing it while Hawke closed another. "You're going to learn to obey us if I have to turn you over my knee every day to remind you."

Sarah gulped, eyeing Phoenix as he closed the last window, the realization that the only reason they would close them on such a warm day would be to keep others from hearing her cries. "But—"

"Take off your clothes."

Sarah gulped again at the hard edge in Blade's voice, and the look of iron determination in his eyes. "What?"

A muscle worked in Blade's jaw, but his eyes held a tenderness and daring. "You heard me, yet you question a direct order. That's one of those things we're supposed to be working on. Remember?"

Hawke turned from closing the window, crossing his arms over his chest. "Take them off right now, or I'll rip them off you."

"You wouldn't dare!"

Hawke's brow went up, and without hesitation, he stepped toward her.

"No! I just made this dress and you're not ruining it."

He stopped, eyeing her steadily. "You have one minute. Blade's going to administer your punishment because you disobeyed him, but my hands are itching to paddle your well-padded backside. Disobey me and it will."

She should have been terrified. Surprised that although she was nervous, she wasn't afraid, she eyed each of them warily, wondering if they'd actually spank her. Knowing that they wouldn't hurt her, and that she didn't appear to have much choice in the matter, she began to undress. She deserved it. She already felt guilty. She'd distracted Phoenix and he'd gotten hurt as a result.

She could have very well gotten others hurt as well,

Trembling with nerves of trepidation, she unbuttoned her blouse, aware of her three husbands' rapt attention. Pausing, she stared at Hawke, knowing that only he could stop this.

Hawke's brow went up went she hesitated. "Minute's almost up."

"You'd really rip them off me?"

Hawke's lips twitched. "And enjoy it."

Glaring at him, she threw off the rest of her clothes, and stood in the middle of the floor wearing just her boots, self-conscious that she stood there naked while they remained fully dressed. "There."

"Boots, too." Blade's gaze raked over her as he turned one of the chairs from the table and sat in it. "I don't want to get kicked with your boots when you're struggling to evade your spanking."

Lowering herself to the edge of the bed, she tugged off her boots, tossing them aside before wrapping her arms around herself, her body burning under their sharp gazes.

Despite their threats, she'd become aroused, and knew that as soon as they touched her, they'd realize it. Lifting her chin, she faced Blade. "There."

Blade lifted a hand, his eyes dancing with amusement. "Better. Come here."

Knowing that hesitating would just anger him, she got to her feet and started toward him, trying to hide her nervousness and arousal.

Holding her breath as she walked past Hawke, she let it out in a moan when Hawke reached out to trail a hand down her back to her bottom.

Leaning back, Blade smiled. "Over my lap. Now."

Sarah didn't dare look at either Hawke or Phoenix, her face burning as she lowered herself over Blade's lap.

Although the buckskin felt soft against her skin, the thighs beneath her were rock-hard.

She jumped at the feel of his hand sliding over her bottom, inwardly wincing when he chuckled.

"I barely touched you and you jumped. Are you nervous, love?"

Gulping, she stared at the floor, struggling to even her breathing. "I've never been spanked before."

One hand moved over her braid while the other caressed her clenched bottom. "Well, it looks like there's a lot of firsts for us, doesn't it?"

Hawke's feet came into her line of vision. "You don't seem particularly scared."

Fisting her hands in front of her, Sarah bit back a moan when Blade parted her thighs and slid a hand between them. "I know you won't hurt me. Oh!" She gasped as Blade plunged a finger into her.

Chuckling again, he stroked her pussy. "She's aroused."

Phoenix's boots came into view, and she knew that all three of them watched what Blade did to her. "So, you believe that we love you? You know that if we didn't love you, we wouldn't care so much about this."

Turning her head, she smiled up at him, feeling the love for her pouring off of them even now. "I know." Turning back to stare at the floor, she blew out a breath. "Just get it over with."

A hard slap landed on her bottom, one she hadn't expected because Blade's finger was still inside her. Gripping her hair, Hawke turned her to face him, his eyes glittering darkly. "You don't tell us how to punish you."

Blade laughed softly. "This is not a spanking that I'm just going to rush. Phoenix, get that wood I carved for her and get it ready."

Imagining that he wanted to use a piece of wood to spank her, Sarah began to struggle. "No. Please, just use your hand."

Blade stilled, turning her to face him. "Do you really think I would hit you with a piece of wood?" Shaking his head, he sighed. "Trust is still an issue with you, isn't it? What am I saying? Of course, it is. Baby, I would never hurt you like that. Ever. None of us would. If it's the last thing I do, I'll get your trust."

Hawke spoke from behind her, somewhere near her feet. "We'll get there. In the meantime, she needs to learn a lesson. She needs to understand that a threat to her safety isn't something any of us is ever gonna overlook. Give it to me, Phoenix."

Sarah gasped when Blade slid his finger free, clenching her bottom when he parted her ass cheeks. "What are you doing?"

A sharp slap landed on her bottom and then another. "Quiet. I don't care how tight you clench your sweet ass, this is going in." Blade's voice had taken on a silky, no-nonsense tone that sent a chill through her.

The chill travelled up and down her spine when he parted her ass cheeks wide, and something hard and unforgiving pushed at her puckered opening.

Shaking, she struggled to breathe, her toes curling as the large hard object was pushed into her.

Phoenix whistled. "Jesus, that's beautiful. It turned out great, Blade. With that thing that Hawke rigged up, she should be in a real mess soon."

Hawke pushed the object farther into her ass, and to her embarrassment, her pussy and ass clenched, her juices literally trickling down her thighs. "Just a little more. Don't worry. Blade made it wide at the end so it can't slip all the way into you. It's smooth and slick enough with the salve that it won't scratch you."

"It's too big." It felt so cool and hard inside her, nothing at all like their finger or Phoenix's cock had felt.

Blade patted her bottom. "You'll have this inside you every time you get spanked. Hmm, maybe I should start carving a bigger one."

Another chill went through her, her breath coming out in short pants as she struggled to adjust to the object Hawke continued to push into her. "No. I'll be good. I swear. I'll be good."

Blade laughed softly at that. "Well, maybe we're getting somewhere. We'll see how you are when we finish."

Hawke paused. "Hold her still. The widest part is going into her now, and I don't want to hurt her."

Phoenix bent to look into her eyes. "That won't hurt her. She's just not used to it. She took my cock in her ass just fine, didn't you, honey?"

The heat in her clit kept growing, the vulnerability of her position exciting her. The knowledge that the piece of wood carved for her would force her bottom wider, though, filled her with trepidation.

"Is it in? Oh, God. It burns."

Hawke paused. "Damn it. It's too big."

Blade stiffened. "No, it's not. Give it to me. Sarah, reach back and hold this pretty ass wide open."

Sarah's eyes went wide, wondering if he could actually be serious.

"Don't make me tell you again."

Alarmed at his tone, Sarah rushed to obey him, her face burning at the knowledge that all three of them watched her reach back and pull her ass cheeks wide.

"Good girl." Blade ran a hand over her back while pushing the object deeper. "It burns because it's stretching you. It won't hurt you. I'd never hurt you that way. You know that, don't you?"

Phoenix cursed. "I'd never have believed it if I hadn't seen it with my own eyes. Oh, just imagining all the things I can do to her."

"Just be careful. If you hurt her, I'll kick your ass." Hawke placed his hands over hers. "It's almost all the way in. Just a little more. That's it."

Sarah feared she might burst. "So full."

Blade slapped her ass again, releasing the carved wood and allowing her to feel the flat part of the end pushing against her opening. "You've been fuller. Now, put your hands back down so we can get to your spanking."

His hand came down on her ass again—harder than before. "Why are you being spanked?"

The heat stunned her.

She clenched on the object in her ass, making the inner walls burn as well. The heat quickly spread, engulfing her clit and pussy in a way that left her crying out and fighting his hold—her arousal almost more than she could bear.

Writhing on his lap for relief proved futile, his firm hold not allowing her to move much at all. "Please! Oh, God. It burns everywhere."

"Blade—" Hawke rushed to her side, kneeling to look into her eyes.

"I know what I'm doing, Hawke. Tug her nipples."

"No!" Sarah cried out as several more slaps landed on her bottom in rapid succession. "I can't stand it. Oh!" The tugs to her nipples nearly sent her over. "I'm gonna come. It's so strong. Please. Help me."

Hawke's gaze sharpened, his lips curving in a slow smile that made her insides flutter. "You really are something. How the hell am I gonna get any work done?"

Blade slapped her ass again, each slap shifting the object filling her ass. "Why are you being spanked?"

Her clit tingled in the way it did when she was getting ready to go over.

Knowing that he wouldn't give her the relief she needed until she answered him, she took several deep breaths and squeezed her eyes closed. "Because I d-disobeyed you. I never will again. I'll do whatever you s-say."

"Without argument, hesitation, or questions?"

"Yes!"

"We'll see." Sliding an arm under her, Blade lifted her to her feet, steadying her when she swayed. Flattening her hands against Hawke's chest, she focused on locking her knees, the shift of the plug inside her leaving her feeling weak and shaky.

It took several seconds before she realized that Blade was in the process of sliding a thick strip of leather around her waist, fastening it in the back. "What—oh, God!"

Hawke's warm hands covered her breasts, the slide of his callused hands over her nipples slowly driving her insane with pleasure. "Be still. Blade's not done with you yet. Spread your legs."

Looking up at him, she hesitated.

Hawke closed his fingers over her nipples, a dark brow going up.

Remembering her promise to do what they demanded without question, she spread her legs wider, biting her lip to hold back a groan when Blade thread a thinner strip of leather between her thighs, fastening it front and back on the belt. Kneeling in front of her, he parted her folds until the leather pressed against her clit.

Fisting her hands on Hawke's chest, she moaned. "It's pushing it deeper. Oh, God!" She moved experimentally, crying out at the sharp stab of pleasure.

Blade rose and stood back, apparently admiring his handiwork. "Yes. It'll keep you from taking the plug out while we're gone, and the beads sewn into the front will rub against your clit every time you move."

Hawke tugged at her nipples before releasing her. "Now, get dressed."

Moaning again when Phoenix closed in behind her and cupped her breasts, she leaned back against him and gaped at Hawke. "You're leaving? You can't leave me like this!"

Hawke shrugged. "We've got work to do with that stallion. We had to stop to take care of you. We'll be back for supper." Bending, he touched his lips to her nipple. "We'll go to the spring tonight. Get everything ready."

Shaking violently from the need still raging through her, she watched them walk away, realizing that she'd once again underestimated them.

Narrowing her eyes at the closed door, she started to remember all the things the women at the bordello had told her about driving men crazy with lust.

By the time she'd gotten dressed again, and gathered their things for the spring, need clawed at her.

Lifting her chin, she went to open the windows, watching them cross to the paddock again.

Still not believing they'd leave her in this condition, she rubbed her nipples where they ached, wishing she could rub the place between her thighs.

They'd taught her a lesson, all right—one she wouldn't soon forget.

She'd seen the looks in their eyes, the watchfulness.

The love.

Gasping again at the shift of the object inside her, she gritted her teeth and went to retrieve her sewing.

She knew she'd have to wait until they went to the spring for relief, but she was confident that by the time they left, she'd be sated and well satisfied.

She'd just have to figure out a way to give them the turmoil they gave her.

# Chapter Nineteen

Blade strode out the door and rounded the small cabin, his cock pounding so hard he found himself fighting not to come in his pants. Gritting his teeth, he looked over at Hawke. "Do you know how fucking hard that was? Christ, I've played with women for years and it never got to me like this. I wanted to tease her a little more, but I couldn't without coming in my pants."

He looked back toward the cabin, the idea of leaving his wife aroused and naked pissing him off.

Hawke's eyes narrowed to slits, his features like stone. "I've heard you talk about doing things like that to women before, but I've never seen it. She was so aroused that her thighs were soaked, and she couldn't even stay still. It was hard to walk away."

Phoenix grinned and adjusted his pants. "She's a passionate little thing."

Blade clenched his jaw. "Too passionate. I don't think we're going to have much luck in using that form of punishment against her."

Phoenix nodded, looking back toward the cabin. "Yeah, it's just as hard on us."

Blade wiped the sweat from his brow, willing his cock to settle. "I'm beginning to see why Eb, Jeremiah, and Maggie look so happy all the time."

"We got lucky." Hawke looked back toward the cabin. "She'll be mad as hell by the time we get back."

Blade laughed at the anticipation in his brother's eyes. "That she will. Being aroused for a few hours is not gonna put our bride in a good mood."

Phoenix threw his head back and laughed. "She'll be purring like a kitten by the time we finish with her."

\* \* \* \*

Sarah clenched her fists at her sides as she watched her husbands approach. "I see you finally broke that horse."

Blade grinned. "He's not entirely broken." Stopping in front of her, he touched his lips to hers. "Taking the spirit out of him isn't the point. Just teachin' him who's boss. Sound familiar?"

She'd spent the last several hours trying to figure out how to get the damned belt off, and when that failed, trying to figure out how to move without moving the beads against her clit or the hard, wooden object in her ass. Being aroused for so long left her cranky and irritable, and she'd just been waiting for them to come back so she could vent it. "Are you comparing me to a horse?"

Phoenix laughed at that while Hawke went to the porch to retrieve the saddle bag she'd packed. "A little. You're sure as cantankerous as he is." Taking her arm, he led her toward the stables.

Sarah stamped her foot, trying to yank her arm from his grip. "Cantankerous?" Frustrated that he held her with no apparent effort, she kicked at him. "After the way you three left me? I should have met you with the shotgun."

Hawke came up beside her, running a hand over her bottom. "Why didn't you?"

Phoenix all but dragged her into the stable, every movement sending another rush of heat to her slit.

Kicking at him again, she glared at Hawke. "Because I can't get this damned belt off. If I'd shot you, I would have had to ask someone else for help."

Throwing his head back, Phoenix laughed so hard he could hardly walk.

She kicked at him again, her boots having no apparent impact. "It's not funny."

Bending, he pressed his shoulder against her belly and lifted her over his shoulder, leaving her dangling upside down and staring at his back. "It's damned funny."

It seemed to take forever to ready the horses, but several minutes later, they were on their way to the spring.

Phoenix had positioned her on his lap, straddling the horse, his arm wrapped firmly around her. "I've been thinking about you ever since we left the cabin. My cock's been hard as a rock for hours."

Every step the horse took moved the beads against her clit and shifting the carved wood inside her. "I don't feel sorry for you. Oh, God. Phoenix, I can't stand it."

"Poor baby. Do you want me to take it off?"

"Yes! Please. Please." Lifting her, he turned her face down over her lap, his strength surprising her. The sharp reminder of just how gentle they'd been with her made her love them even more.

Lifting her skirt to her waist, he left her ass bare as he worked with one hand to undo the belt around her and the strip of leather between her legs. "Better?"

Sarah groaned as he pushed the heel of his hand against the object in her bottom, while pressing his fingers against her clit. "Oh, Phoenix!"

The sharp slap on her bottom cheek stunned her. "No coming until we're ready for you to come."

Hawke's soft chuckle made her aware of just how exposed she was. "That's a pretty sight." His hand pressed against her bottom with Phoenix's. "You know that I'll be the one taking this pretty bottom tonight, don't you? We're almost there."

Once at the spring, they tossed their clothes off and stripped her out of hers with a speed that left her dizzy.

She didn't even have the chance to admire their naked bodies before Phoenix carried her into the water, with Blade and Hawke trailing close behind them. Wrapping her arms around Phoenix's neck, she cuddled against him. "I thought Indians were savages until I met you."

Hawke smiled and loosened her braid. "We are. That's what the world thinks of us."

"I don't. I never did think you were anything but wonderful." Lifting her head, she took a deep breath and let it out slowly. "I love you. All three of you." She dropped her forehead against his chest, shivering with delight at the feel of Hawke's lips on her shoulder. "I think I fell in love with you the first time I met you—at least that's what Savannah says."

Blade took her hand in his, tightening his hold when she stiffened as Hawke pulled the carved wood filling her bottom free. "You asked Savannah?"

"Oh. Oh, my God."

Hawke moved in close, running his hands up and down her sides. "It's out, little one. So, you talked to Savannah about us?"

"Yes." Surrounded by her husbands, and with their hands gliding over her wet skin, Sarah shook harder, the combination of arousal and emotion bringing tears to her eyes. "I had to. I didn't know." Pressing her face against Phoenix, she whimpered. "I didn't know what love was. When I told her how I felt, she said it was love. Oh, God. I love you. I want to stay here with you forever."

Phoenix lifted her chin, staring down at her with eyes filled with wonder. "I love you, too, honey. So much that I couldn't live without you."

"Give her to me." Blade closed his hands on her waist and turned her toward him. He lowered himself to the upper ledge and lifted her out of the water, his eyes steady on hers as he lowered her onto his cock. "I love you, too. Probably too damned much."

Gripping his shoulders, she gasped at the fullness, awed by the love shining in his eyes. "Oh, Blade." She moved on him, aware that Phoenix watched them with a smile on his face as he hurriedly washed. "I can't believe this is happening. I can't believe that I'm really going to stay here with you forever."

Blade smiled and thrust into her. "I knew that you loved us, but I couldn't understand why you never said it." He slid his hands to her breasts, his eyes narrowing at her cry of pleasure. "I should have realized that you didn't even know what love is."

"Now I do." Cupping his jaw, she lifted her face for his kiss, thrilled when he bent his head to touch his lips to hers without hesitation.

Melting under his kiss, Sarah moved on him and reached for his braid. Loving the freedom to touch him this way, and the reassurance in his eyes that gave her the confidence to do it, she undid his braid and ran her fingers through his silky hair. "It makes it so much better."

His hands tightened on her waist, his hold firm but gentle as he moved her on his cock. "Makes what better, love? This? Sex?"

"Hmm mmm. It feels stronger. Closer." Wrapping her arms around his neck, she brushed her breasts against his chest, sucking in a breath when Hawke moved in behind her and slid his finger into her bottom. "I don't know how to explain it. It just feels so good."

Touching his lips to her shoulder, Hawke moved his finger inside her, the feeling of being impaled in both openings sending her senses reeling. "You feel good. We won't lose you, Sarah. No matter what it takes to keep you safe, we'll do it."

Blade pulled her against his chest, kissing her hair. "Even if it means spanking you again, no matter how mad you get."

Sarah smiled at his soft threat, not worried at all. "As long as you love me."

"That's a given, love." Blade's arms came around her, holding her body close to his. "I won't ever give you up."

"I knew when I first saw those sad blue eyes that I'd found what I never expected to have." Hawke pushed the head of his cock against her puckered opening. "You're mine. Ours. Easy, little one. Yes. Oh, hell, you're tight."

Blade groaned. "Even tighter with both of us inside her."

Sarah cried out, clinging to Blade. "Oh, God. It's going inside me." Her clit, already sensitive, tingled unbearably, but when she tried to move against Blade, he held firm.

With a groan, Blade held her closer. "Let Hawke get inside you and then we'll move."

Hawke held a hand to her back and pushed harder, his husky groan sending a thrill through her as he pushed the head of his cock through the tight ring of muscle and into her. "Tight. Hold her."

Hawke's gravelly tone made her smile, satisfying a need inside her to make her want her as much as she wanted him.

Without meaning to, she clenched on his cock as he slid deeper, the salve he'd used and her own hunger to have him inside her easing his way. Crying out again when Blade's hold loosened and he began to move, she clung to him, stunned at the sensation of having two cocks inside her.

Hawke withdrew slightly and thrust deeper. "Hmm. You feel so good, little one." His hands came around her to cup her breasts. "Mine."

"Ours." Phoenix stood on the lower ledge, fisting his cock. "I want to feel her mouth on me. I want her to take all three of us at the same time."

Blade groaned, pumping faster. "Yes. Take all of us, love. Open your mouth and take Phoenix inside."

Sarah smiled at the hunger in his eyes, a hunger that held a hint of hesitation as if he feared scaring her. "You're still worried about scaring me." Fisting her hands in his hair, she pressed her lips to his, thrilling when he immediately took control of their kiss.

The cocks moving inside her seemed to harden even more, their thrusts coming faster and deeper. With a cry, she lifted her head. "Yes. I want all of you so much."

Need made her violent, and she thrashed on Blade's lap, drawing a groan from Hawke.

She let their murmurs of hunger and encouragement wash over her as she watched Phoenix work his hand up and down his cock.

She looked up into his eyes to see that they'd narrowed to slits, the need in them evident.

Without hesitation, she leaned toward him and opened her mouth, thrilling at the flare of heat in his eyes.

A deep groan from Hawke seemed to trigger a reaction in all of them, the flames of heat licking at her. "Yes. Easy, Phoenix."

"Easy?" Phoenix groaned. "Every time I think it can't get any better, it does."

Sarah writhed against them, desperate for relief. Her hunger had her sucking Phoenix's cock hard, thrilled with the masculine taste of him.

Hawke's and Blade's cocks moved faster in and out of her pussy and ass, making it hard to concentrate on pleasing Phoenix.

She stopped trying, letting her hunger for him be her guide.

Blade cupped her jaw, becoming a part of what she did to Phoenix in a way that both stunned and excited her. "Suck him harder, Sarah. Use your tongue the way you did with me."

Phoenix groaned, his hands in her hair tightening even more when she did it. "Oh, hell."

"That mouth is incredible." Blade slid his hands lower to her hips, moving her faster. "Yes. So good."

Their movements created a delicious friction against her clit, adding to the sensations bombarding her.

She couldn't stop clenching on them, their hands moving over her body stoking the flames to a fever pitch.

Hawke groaned and wrapped an arm around her from behind, holding her for his thrusts. "I'll never stop wanting you. I love you so damned much." He thrust deep and groaned, his cock pulsing inside her. "You're never getting away from me."

Sarah barely heard him, the deep groan from Phoenix as he whipped his cock free startling her, her body tightening with every thrust. Dropping her head against Blade's shoulder, she tried to hold on to him, but the sizzling inside her took over.

Watching Phoenix fist his cock again and stroke himself to completion while the cocks inside her moved harder—faster—she let herself go, trusting that they would catch her.

The heat and pleasure exploded in a rush, stiffening her body and forcing a cry from her. "Oh, God!" Her body clamped down on both cocks, making them feel even thicker.

A strong of tingling pleasure held her in its powerful grip, leaving her shaking and crying out as the cocks inside her stilled and her husbands closed their hands on her.

Secure in their hold, she slumped, her eyes closing against the tears burning them. Feeling Phoenix drop to the seat next to her, she reached out a hand to him, smiling when he took it in his and lifted it to his lips.

"She all right?"

Hawke's lips touched her back, his hands moving up and down her sides. "She's perfect."

Blade leaned back, easing her head back, enticing her to open her eyes. With a smile, he studied her features. "Do you still think we could ever think anything about you is ugly? Don't you know how much you mean to us?"

Hawke eased from her bottom and wrapped his arm around her waist again, pulling her from Blade's cock. "She knows. Don't you, little one?"

Phoenix smiled and slid from the ledge to move closer. "And she knows that we respect her, and why we go through doors first."

Blade slid to the lower ledge, his cock now hidden beneath the surface of the water. "If you'd let her go first—"

Hawke pulled her closer, nuzzling her neck. "I don't even want to think about it." Nipping her earlobe, Hawke chuckled. "Hold your breath."

His words barely registered before she found herself under the water with him.

She came up sputtering and laughing, splashing water at him when he surfaced. "That was mean."

Hawke grinned. "I'm gonna get mean again." Gathering her against him, he took her under the water with him.

Phoenix joined in the fun while Blade watched from the ledge, washing himself and shaking his head at their antics.

Holding out a hand, Blade smiled. "Sarah, come here."

She went to him readily, easing over him and bracing her elbows on the ledge on either side of him. Pressing her lips to his sleek chest, she giggled when Phoenix pulled at her toes.

Lathering the scented soap she loved in his hands, Blade smiled down at her. "Good girl. No questions or hesitation." Threading his lathered fingers through her hair, he bent to touch his lips to her forehead. "That's what we need from you, love. The thought of you getting hurt is more than I can bear. We're not trying to be mean, but we need to keep you safe."

Sliding up to kneel in front of him, Sarah ran her hands over his shoulders, leaning forward to touch her lips to his, something that appeared to please him very much. "I know. I understand now."

His eyes flared, the heat in them unmistakable. "Good." His hands tightened in her hair, pulling her closer for another kiss. Lifting his head, he began to massage her scalp, working the lather into her hair.

Moaning at how good it felt, Sarah looked up at him through her lashes. "Of course, the next time you decide to spank me, I hope you don't leave me the way you did today." Shrugging, she fought not to smile. "How can I respect a man who doesn't finish what he started?"

Blade's eyes widened, then narrowed, his hands stilling in her hair as Phoenix and Hawke both chuckled from somewhere behind her. "You're getting awfully brave, little one."

Hawke eased to the ledge beside her, running a hand down her back. "Aren't you a little afraid that the savages you married will make you pay for that?"

Thinking back to how tenderly they'd cared for her, and seeing their love for her shining in their eyes, Sarah wrinkled her nose at them, unable to hold back a giggle. "I'm counting on it."

Leaping back into the water, she started to swim away, knowing they would catch her easily. After a split second of stunned silence, she heard them hit the water with a soft splash.

Phoenix's laughter filled the air as he caught her and gathered her against him. "You *are* brave." Hugging her to him, he turned her in his arms as Hawke and Blade approached, the playful gleam in their eyes promising retribution.

Phoenix's smile fell, his eyes darkening. "I love you so damned much. You scare the hell out of me sometimes."

Wrapping her arms around his neck, she slid against him, smiling again when his cock twitched. "And you scare me. But I love you, and you love me. I trust you—all three of you. I never thought I'd ever be this happy."

"Neither did I." Hawke's smile fell, his eyes glittering with emotion. "You're a miracle I never thought we'd find. I shudder to think about what would have happened if someone else had gone to the train station that day."

Sarah reached for him. "I would have come back here and found you."

Love for them welled up inside her, so strong it threatened to choke her. "I love you so much."

All playfulness fled as Hawke and Blade both closed in on her. Laying her head against Phoenix's chest, she let her eyes close, loving the feel of their hands on her.

She could barely remember her life in Waco now. She'd found her life here. With them.

She'd found the happiness and security she'd never hoped to find here.

And the love she'd never thought possible.

Savage only in protecting and loving her, her husbands surrounded her with their strength and love, showing her a world of desire she'd never imagined.

# Epilogue

Phoenix walked out of the stable, only to feel something soft hit him in the back of the head.

Whipping around, he put his hand to his head. Seeing no one, he looked down to see that he'd been hit with a clump of soft dirt.

Eb walked up to him on the other side. "Her aim's getting better. Maybe that's from all the pistol lessons you're giving her."

Phoenix grinned. "She's not so great at hiding, though. She giggles."

"Damn it!"

Phoenix looked over to see that Blade's back had a circle of dirt on it.

Blade looked around, his eyes sparkling with challenge as he started toward the side of the stable. "When I find her—"

Shaking his head, Eb chuckled. "You know, of course, that everyone on the ranch is going to be talking about this. Who would have ever thought one little woman could make such a change in the three of you? We'd all just about lost hope."

Hawke walked out of the stable just in time to hear Eb's words. Smiling faintly, he glanced at Phoenix. "She's behind the stable, laughing hysterically. Blade must have caught her."

Phoenix grinned. "She's in for it now."

Hawke shrugged. "That's why she did it." He met Eb's gaze. "She likes to play, and teasing us gives her the confidence she needs. She's getting stronger every day."

Eb nodded. "I heard she got a letter from her mother."

Hawke nodded. "And it depressed her for days. Even though her
mother's happy now, and married, Sarah doesn't like to be reminded
of that time in her life."

"Poor thing." Eb shook his head. "She's got spunk, though. No
one ever thought any woman would be brave enough to take you on.
She not only married the three of you, but she teases you in the way
no man here would ever dream of."

Phoenix laughed at that, thinking about the way the bosses were
with their own wife. "I think everyone here could say the same about
you. You and Jeremiah were bears until you brought Maggie here."

Eb's lips twitched. "Yeah, she gets away with a hell of a lot more
than she should. Hell, keeping these women safe out here is gonna be
a full time occupation."

Hearing Sarah's shriek of laughter, Phoenix turned in time to see
her running around the side of the stable, with Blade hot on her heels.
"Yeah, it will be, but having the women here brought life to this
place. Why the hell is he letting her get away? He could catch her
easily."

Hawke turned to watch them, smiling indulgently. "He wants to
drag it out. She runs fast in those moccasins, doesn't she?"

The pride in his voice made Phoenix smile again.

Sarah had changed their lives in ways that constantly surprised
him.

Blade would never have walked away from work to play before,
and if he knew his brother, he, and Sarah would disappear for hours.

They each cherished the time they each spent alone with her.

Phoenix shared a look with Hawke before his oldest brother shook
his head with a smile and strode back into the stable. "I thought my
brothers and I were close before, but having Sarah in our lives
changed even that."

Eb smiled and glanced toward Jeremiah, who stood at the fence.
"Yeah. I know. Dealing with a woman together has made Jeremiah

and I even closer." Slapping Phoenix on the back, Eb grinned again. "Wait until you have a baby together."

Phoenix nodded, his smile falling as he watched Blade and Sarah ride out toward the cave where he'd first taken her.

If they'd changed Sarah, she'd changed them even more.

* * * *

Sarah sighed and leaned against Blade, exhausted and elated after their time together. "You spanked me." The memory of it still had the ability to excite her despite the numerous orgasms since then.

"You deserved it."

"It was just a little clump of dirt."

Blade's hand slid down her side. "It was just a little spanking."

Looking up at him, she narrowed her eyes at him, fighting a smile at the happiness and male satisfaction shining in his eyes. "You look pleased with yourself."

"I am. I spanked my wife for daring to throw dirt at me, and made her come four times. Wore her out so much that she couldn't even dress herself."

"I was just resting."

"You were sound asleep, and didn't wake up until I used my mouth on that pretty clit. Orgasm number four."

Giggling at the memory, she slapped at him. "You're too cocky."

Blade's brow went up. "I didn't hear you complain when I was taking you."

"You're impossible!" She giggled again, her laughter becoming a moan when his hand covered her breast.

"Yet you seem to handle me just fine."

Reaching up, she kissed his jaw. "I like the way you handle me."

Bending, he touched his lips to hers, grinning as he lifted his head again. "I know."

Sarah couldn't help but laugh at him, turning again to watch their progress as they headed for home.

"I never imagined I could be this happy. Every day, I think I can't get any happier, but I know tomorrow, I'll be even happier."

Blade bent to nuzzle the sensitive spot just behind her ear. "Of course you will. You don't know what I have planned for you tomorrow."

Smiling, Sarah closed her eyes and turned her head to press it against his chest. "Whatever it is, I'm sure I'll love it. I love every day I spend with you."

She woke every day with a smile now, and fell asleep every night in the arms of the men she loved.

Blade kissed her hair, his arms tightening around her. "So do I, love. So do I."

They made every day an adventure, and surrounded her with the love and security she'd never take for granted.

As they approached the yard, both Phoenix and Hawke appeared, their smiles of indulgence and love warming her even more.

Smiling at each of them, she sighed, grateful every minute for the life she'd found with them.

Nothing could be any better.

# THE END

**WWW.LEAHBROOKE.NET**

# ABOUT THE AUTHOR

When Lana Dare (Leah Brooke) isn't writing, she's busy with her fur babies and plotting out new stories.

*For all titles by Lana Dare, please visit*
www.bookstrand.com/lana-dare

**Siren Publishing, Inc.**
**www.SirenPublishing.com**